Prayers for the Dying

Suzanne Jenkins

Copyright © 2012 Suzanne Jenkins
All rights reserved.

ISBN: 1-4681-4209-7
ISBN-13: 9781468142099

Nobody can hurt me without my permission.

Mohandas Gandhi

I

Ashton Hageman was sitting on the steps of the New York Public Library waiting for his lover to arrive. He had the Home Style section of the Sunday *Times* resting on his knees, but it was a prop. Certain that something important in his life was about to come to an end, the paper was a convenient screen to hide behind if too much thinking led to tears. *I deserve better than this*, he thought. Young and in love, Ashton had allowed himself to be at Jack's beck and call since they were boys, when Jack discovered his friend would do anything for him. Jack didn't set out to manipulate him; it just happened. And when he found that he had power over Ashton, he couldn't help himself. He would control Ashton until he died.

At precisely the time expected, Jack came into view in his larger-than-life way. Exquisitely dressed, Jack drew attention wherever he went. It was ridiculous really, him strolling down Fifth Avenue, a suit jacket thrown over a shoulder, but Jack pulled it off like he was playing a part in a 1940's Broadway play. Ash, his heart rate picking up exponentially, watched while people stood aside for the handsome and debonair Jack Smith. He sauntered down the street, his smile visible all the way to the steps of the library. The old-fashioned words used to describe a man dressed to perfection were appropriate. Natty, dapper, suave, and elegant; gorgeous Jack knew it about himself, and played it for all it was worth. He walked like a model on a runway with broad shoulders held still, one hand in his pocket, and the other holding on to that jacket. Women reacted as he got closer, becoming giddy and animated. Ashton had to smile as he watched the fuss in spite of what he knew was about to take place in his life. Jack finally made eye contact and turned to dash up the steps. He held out his hand and pulled Ashton to his feet. This was 1980 New York; gay men, especially one about to get married to a woman, did not publicly embrace Midtown.

"Were you waiting long?" Jack asked as the two men descended to the sidewalk. "Thanks for meeting on such short notice." Ashton wasn't as tall as Jack and he fought the urge to look up at him, tears too close to the surface for eye-to-eye contact.

"You've definitely got my curiosity going. And you're scaring me. What's wrong?" Ashton asked as they continued walking down Fifth.

"Do you want to get something to drink? I'm thirsty," Jack said. "Don't be scared. Our life isn't going to change that much." *There,* Ash thought, *he's admitted it.* "Let's get some lunch and we can talk, okay?" Jack looked sidelong at his companion. Ashton was clearly struggling to maintain control, breathing deeply, sighing out loud. Arms touching, Jack could feel the tension in Ashton's body as they walked along together. "Let's go to Faye's. We can have some privacy in there." Ashton nodded.

"How long do you have?" He looked up at Jack. "I mean, is this just lunch?"

Jack nodded. "Just lunch, but just for today, okay? I have to meet with my mother at two," Jack said, the intention clear. They were going to start planning Jack's wedding.

Biting his lip to keep an audible sob from escaping, he thought, *how had it come to this?* He thought Jack would have at least tried to live a dual life. If any choosing was to be done, it would be in Ash's favor. *Wouldn't it?* Not get married. Not abandon him. "Oh God, I don't know if I am going to survive," Ash admitted. In a rare public gesture, Jack put his arm around his shoulders, an innocent movement providing something intimate Ash needed. They got to the restaurant and Jack took his arm away, opening the door and holding it for him to walk through, not bothering to look around to see if they were observed going in. Faye's was one place in town where they could be together.

"You'll be fine," Jack responded shortly. "I'm not leaving the city, for Christ's sake." Ash didn't add, *You might as well be.* "What we have is not going to change that much, Ash," Jack said. He grabbed menus and led the way to their own table in back of the dark room. The booths were hard and uncomfortable, but the backs were high, giving them some privacy. They slid in across from each other.

"I won't be fine. And it will change. Really Jack, you are being a little naïve," Ashton said. "For one thing, you won't be able to sleep over anymore." He put his head down on his crossed arms and silently began crying. Jack grabbed his hand.

"Ash, try to pull it together," Jack pleaded. He hated seeing his friend so sad. But he had to get married. He wanted a wife and children, a home of his own, a family. He wanted a normal life. Jack took Ash's hand and kissed the fingertips, and then the palm. "I love you, but you knew it would be this way. Come on, Ashton," he said, losing patience. Jack hated drama in spite of being the author of much of it. "Man up!" He laughed a light chuckle, just loud enough for their benefit. But it didn't work.

"No, I don't want to," Ashton complained. "We've been in love since we were twelve. Why would I think it would ever come to this? Leaving me to get married to a woman. I think I might throw up."

"Oh, stop it," Jack said, picking up the menu. "If you want to spend our lunch together whining, go ahead. It is what it is. I want a normal life. Somehow, I just can't picture you pushing a baby carriage, or carrying a kid around on your back." He started reading the menu. They had been regulars at Faye's since high school, and it hadn't changed that much. "What do you want to eat?"

"Turkey on rye. Are you going to tell Miss Fabulous about me?" Ashton provoked.

Jack put the menu down and looked at his face carefully, like he was checking him out for an acne medication commercial, the sort of look Jack gave that withered Ashton's self-confidence. "No. And neither are you. She isn't what you think she is, Ashton. Pam is lovely, gracious, and kind. You will meet her soon, I promise. Even if you were cruel to her, she wouldn't get it anyway, so don't even try. She's made of different stuff than you or I," Jack explained. "Besides, I might have to kill you if you ever hurt her." Jack let go of his hand and picked up the menu again.

"Oh, I don't think I'll be the one hurting her," Ashton said. "Get me a Tab, too. I have to go the bathroom. He slid out of the booth. The bathroom was near the rear of the restaurant, and Ashton let a few sobs out, knocking before he let himself in. *I'm such an ass*, he thought. *I've wasted all of these years thinking Jack would make the decision that he wouldn't be able to live without me.* He looked in the mirror at his puffy eyes and swollen lips. *Great. Just the look to drop a man to his knees.* He washed his face and hands. *Enough*, he thought. He would make it an act of will to be pleasant and charming, just what Jack liked about him. And later, if he was lucky, he would take Jack to bed and do things to him that only a man could do.

Jack and Ashton had been best friends since second grade, since Ashton came to the mansion on a bet with other little friends to see if Jack really lived there. He'd struggled to open the iron gate leading to the front steps when the massive front door had opened and frail Jack, his eyes glassy and his face tear-stained, came dashing through. He didn't waste any time hiding his fear from Ashton.

"Hurry up! My dad's coming after me." Jack grabbed his hand, not caring or unaware that it might seem odd for two little boys to be running down the sidewalk, holding hands. But Jack was going to get out of there as fast as he could and Ashton had to come, too. They ran for blocks on Central Park West without looking back, and in a few minutes they were at the park. Ashton had to work at keeping up with Jack. They came to a rock formation and began to climb it, slipping on the way up, but finally getting to the top. They had a good view of Columbus from the top, and there was no sign of Harold Smith. It would be out of character of him to chase his son in daylight; although after sunset was another matter. Jack was safe for the time being.

"What'd you do?" Ashton asked. Jack was still sniffing, wiping his nose with the back of his hand.

"Nothing. I didn't do anything." Fresh sobbing, and then the little boy pulled himself together. *Stop sniveling,* as his father would say. Ashton saw what looked like blood and poop on the back of Jack's left leg. He smelled bad, too. It frightened Ashton enough not to say anything. *Maybe Jack's dad beat him until he cut him open,* he thought. "I *haf ta* go to the bathroom," Jack said. They slid down the rock formation and walked toward the public restrooms in the Ramble. Later, as an adult, Jack would make generous donations to the maintenance of the park restrooms, remembering the many times he took refuge there. "Wait here," he instructed Ashton. When he came out a few minutes later, he'd cleaned off his legs and washed his face and hands. Ashton was more fearful than curious.

"Do you want to go to my house?" Ashton asked. "It's on the other side of the park."

Jack nodded. Yes. He wasn't ready to go home yet and face his mother's questions and possibly to have to see his father. Once he escaped, he was safe. His father wouldn't attempt another attack if Jack's screams had alerted the staff. No one in the house had the courage to call the police. Ashton's gentle mother and cozy apartment would be the haven Jack needed. If Francine Hageman ever suspected Jack was being abused, she never intervened.

The two seven-year-old boys walked across Central Park to the Upper East Side. Until his brother Bill was born the next year, Ashton's house would be Jack's home away from home. But once Bill came along, Jack had to stick around to protect him.

Ashton had asked only once what was happening to Jack. "Does your dad beat you up?" Ashton, who'd never had so much as a pat on his behind, couldn't fathom his quiet father raising a hand to anything, let alone to the flesh of his son. Looking over at Ashton's closed bedroom door, Jack had whispered, "He rapes me." Ashton had no idea what that meant, but he thought it might have something to do with dirty words. Jack knew what it was because he'd heard his mother screaming one night—yodeling was more like it—and he'd run to their room and peeked through the key hole. Harold was doing basically the same thing to his mother that he did to his son.

"Stop raping me!" Bernice screamed, fighting her husband off. Jack went back to his room, frightened, sobbing, but from that moment on decided to fight his father. The only problem was that Harold's ardor increased with resistance and it took Jack another attack to realize that his parents were playing a game. Instead, he became adept at barricading his room, or yelling so the servants could hear which would further enrage his father. After Bill was born, Jack had the baby to worry about as well, so he offered himself up as the sacrificial lamb. When he left home after college, the only leverage he had to keep his brother safe was the threat of exposure. He'd tell whoever would listen if Harold didn't leave Billy alone.

2

Across town, Bernice Smith was trying her best to pull it together. Her beloved son, Jack, was due to arrive any minute, coming to the family mansion on Columbus Avenue from his Midtown apartment to begin planning the engagement party, rehearsal dinner, and wedding reception for his nuptials to Pam Fabian.

Bernice was a closet drunk. Only her devoted staff and family knew the truth, although it was suspected among a few acquaintances. Her future daughter-in-law thought she was what she appeared to be: a pillar of proper New York society. Jack would never betray her secret. She tried to present herself to her children as the motivated, dynamic mother they pretended her to be. Her dressing table mirror couldn't hide the pain of the previous night; not yet fifty years old, she looked seventy. Ice to the eyes helped some of the swelling; makeup would do the rest. She worked quickly and expertly, years of practice helping her to wipe away all traces of a weekend of binging and physical abuse.

There was a knock on her door; Mildred, her housekeeper, announcing the arrival of the wedding planner and Mr. Jack. Bernice got up delicately and, standing as straight as she could, walked to the door of her room. She turned around as she reached for the light switch; a slight smell of whisky lingering in the room just strong enough to give her away. Hoping Mildred didn't notice, she dug in her skirt pocket for another breath mint.

Voices coming from the den revealed where the meeting would be. Of course, Jack would want it there, where the action always took place in the house. A more appropriate room may have been the parlor; if Harold came home from his golf game, he wouldn't appreciate the intrusion into his sacred space. Bernice plastered a smile on her face as she entered.

"Hello!" she announced. Jack went to her and kissed her cheek. "Thank you so much for agreeing to meet with us on Sunday, Robert. This is my son, Jack," she said to the wedding planner. "The groom!" she added with a giggle.

Jack looked at her, concerned. He held his hand out and shook the other man's, and then looked around the room. "Where's Mrs. Fabian?" Jack asked. "Come to think of it, where's Pam?"

Bernice looked confused for just a second. "Why, I imagine they're home, silly boy. This is just a preliminary meeting, just a chance to meet Robert and see if we all want to work together." *Whew*! Bernice thought. *That was close.* She didn't like Pam; thought she was silly and ignorant, and her mother was worse—about as interesting as a turnip. But she had forgotten that they might insist on being consulted about the wedding plans.

"Oh! I rather thought we would be making real plans today. I booked you for two hours, Mrs. Smith," Robert said, thinking, *she* will *pay for it whether or not anything gets accomplished, that's for sure.*

Bernice thought fast, which was not easy so early in the afternoon. "Well, we can certainly plan the engagement party and get Pam's approval later, can we not?" She failed to see what the big deal was. "Besides, I think it may have been a wee bit presumptuous of you to assume you would come here and plan for two hours when we haven't seen your portfolio or references!" Bernice was sliding into her role as haughty matron. It had the right effect on Robert, but Jack was looking at her, horrified.

"Yes, of course, let me get my albums out for you to look at." The young man began to dig through several satchels and pulled out thick folders of photographs. Bernice pointed to the table.

"Sit down, sit down," she commanded. She had saved herself from a clumsy exposure yet again. That Robert Winegarten was the most sought-after wedding planner in Manhattan, booked two years in advance, had been forgotten. Bernice Stein Smith was in charge.

◈

The week before, beautiful Pamela Fabian, twenty-two and just out of college, was sitting at a local luncheon counter in Bensonhurst with her four sisters, sharing a huge order of French fries and listening to Sharon talk about school. Of the four girls, Pam, the oldest, was the prettiest. Four years after Pam, Sharon had come along. Born with a mild degree of spina bifida, after surgeries and rehabilitation she barely had a limp. Sharon was in her first year of college up in Hartford, but she missed her family and tried to get home every weekend.

Susan, a year younger than Sharon, was a senior in high school. She was the smartest of the four children, but the quietest and easily forgotten. Marie was the baby. She stood next to Pam with her head on her shoulder. Pam absentmindedly rubbed her younger sister's back while they talked. The three girls were close to Pam, but not so much to each other. She was the mother figure of the family, the nurturer and listener. Their mother, Nelda, held down the fort as the provider of meals and clean clothes, but because of her own issues, which included alcoholism and mental illness, she was unavailable to her daughters emotionally.

Jack Smith was going to ask Pam's dad for her hand in marriage that evening. He was coming into Brooklyn to be by her side when they broke the news to the family. Although the visit was supposedly for dinner, Pam's mother could smell an engagement announcement. It was God appearing in the flesh; Nelda Fabian was like a crazy person trying to get the house ready. While scurrying around cleaning, she took the time to put a sandwich down in front of her husband for lunch.

"We should have made arrangements to meet at a diner," she said, looking around the kitchen. "This place needed painting ten years ago."

"Oh, relax, will you? He's coming here to see Pam, not the house." Frank Fabian worked for the city of New York and knew all about the Smiths of Columbus Avenue. All he could think about was that if Pam left to marry, he would have one less mouth to feed. And one daughter marrying into a rich household might benefit the others. He bit into his sandwich; pork from last night's pork and sauerkraut.

"What are you making for dinner tonight?" His wife was Polish and he was Italian but they never ate macaroni. When Frank requested it, Nelda's response was that it was

Prayers for the Dying

too fattening and they had a house full of girls to keep thin and marriageable. Secretly, she hated Italian food. If he wanted it, he could go upstairs and let his mother cook it for him.

"Roast beef," she replied.

Perogies were the staple for Sunday dinner, but they were too smelly to serve someone from Columbus Avenue. Nelda was a classic snob. She was also a Jew-hater but she did not yet know Jack's heritage. Frank loved his wife and daughters but he knew his place in their Brooklyn household. His job was to bring in the money and they would spend it as fast as they could. Life went smoother if he kept his mouth shut. Money was tight with the girls in college, although his mother, bless her heart, paid living expenses for the household. Pam was finished and Sharon was in her first year. That one-year overlap was murder. Sharon had wanted to be a physical therapist since she was a youngster, which meant more college. Susan was right behind her and dental school was in her future if they could find the money. Hopefully, Marie would be satisfied working at Macy's or serving hot dogs at Devil Dogs because he didn't think he would live long enough to get her through college. Now, with Jack Smith in the picture, that might change.

"What time is he supposed to be here?" Frank asked, gazing longingly at his recliner.

But Nelda wasn't having it. "Don't even think about it," she snapped. "You've got to run the vacuum for me and get a shower." She looked up at the clock on the kitchen wall. "Better hurry up. Those girls will be back from the store soon and they have to get washed up, too." Raising four girls with one bathroom was easy as long as she kept them to a strict schedule. She wondered what was taking them so long. "If they stopped to eat anything, I swear to God I will whip all four of them." She swept the kitchen floor in a frenzy, beating the broom bristles against the wood.

Putting the last of his sandwich in his mouth, Frank got up from the table, resigned that the rest of his Sunday would be spent in domestication. Secretly, he was fine with it. And although he longed for the day when all four girls were independent, he was afraid of being alone with Nelda again. "I'm going out for a smoke and then I'll get started," he told Nelda, determined to waste as much time as he could before he got down to real work. He grabbed his cigarette pack and lighter and went out the back door, which led from the landing to the basement and outdoors. Nelda had made a place for him to smoke, providing an old coffee can filled with sand for the butts.

The houses on their street lined up evenly across the back and the men of the households sat outside on their fire-escape landings to smoke and catch up with the latest neighborhood gossip. Nelda counted on Frank to fill her in on the divorces, affairs, births, and deaths of Bensonhurst. Today, the talk centered on Jack Smith of Columbus Avenue.

"We got the stoop swept off just for yer' company today, Pizon. My wife drivin' me crazy. 'Get up off yer' lazy backside and do something about the trash!' she holler at me. Thanks a lot," Fredo complained from his stoop next door.

"Which of your girls is he comin' for?" Mario asked from the other side of the house. "It gotta be Pamela." The other men whistled or sighed in agreement.

"None of your business," Frank yelled. "You're all a bunch of perverts." Outside of the relief he could get financially, Frank didn't allow himself to dwell on the aftermath of what a marriage would mean to one of them. He wasn't raising them to be any man's sexual partner; the thought was disgusting, sickening, maddening.

Nelda told him he was being ridiculous. "You can't have it both ways, Frank. If you want another man to pay for your daughter, she has got to sleep with him."

"Yeah! Yeah! Yeah! Shut up! What are you trying to do to me! Jesus!" he yelled, holding his hands over his ears as she went on and on about what was wrong with him, did he think his children were above sex? "It's not something I want to think about, if it's alright with you." Having the neighbor men droning on about which of his girls were bait for the rich Smiths angered him because they had hit a nerve. He threw his cigarette down onto the grass and stormed back in the house, leaving the men to laugh at him. "He thinks his kid is going to stay a virgin forever! What a putz!"

Going to the kitchen sink to wash his hands, Frank stared out the window over the sink. He'd go upstairs and see his mother before he started vacuuming, further delaying the inevitable. Nelda walked in as he turned from the sink.

"I think I'll go up and see Mom first," he said. "Do you want me to take anything up to her?" His mother had moved to the third floor of the house when Susan was born nineteen years ago. The family had needed more room and the one-bedroom apartment on the third floor was too small for a family with three children. Being upstairs would give everyone more privacy. But Nelda didn't see it that way. She thought Genoa was fleeing from the children. Her help with them had made motherhood tolerable for Nelda.

"What kind of grandmother doesn't want to be around her grandchildren?" she'd challenged when Frank told her about the move. "I have never heard of such a thing." Her own mother lived in Hamtramck and wouldn't leave Michigan to visit them. Nelda didn't have the money to go there either, so the children had never met their maternal grandmother. Nelda had separate and severe standards for her in-laws that didn't apply to her own family.

"She does want to," he'd said. "She really wanted us to have more room is all."

But Nelda was used to it now, after all these years. She was fond of her mother-in-law, and grateful for the home she provided and all the help she'd given when the girls were younger. Nelda wouldn't have survived if it weren't for Frank's mother.

"Can you take her mail up?" Nelda asked. She turned her back to fish through a pile of papers and envelopes. "Ask her to have dinner with us too, okay? Pam said Jack will be here at six sharp."

Frank took the handful of mail from his wife. He climbed two flights of stairs to reach his mother; she rarely ventured down these days. The time may have come for her to revisit the lower floor of the house. Pam would be moving out soon; she could have her room. Frank knocked on the door.

"Mom, it's me!" He could hear her giggling to herself; his salutation always made her laugh. *Who else would it be?*

"Pam's boyfriend will be here for dinner. Can you come down at six?" He put her mail on a small table by the door and went into her sitting room where windows looked out on Bay Parkway. In front of the windows were two comfortable chairs on either side of a small, round pedestle table. He'd sat there over the years, having meals with his mother, listening to her tell stories of the family. Occasionally, one of the girls would accompany him. Pam liked visiting with her grandmother more than the others did because she could remember the days when her grandfather was alive and they lived on the first floor while Frank and Nelda lived upstairs with their growing family.

"Who's the boyfriend? Not the kid from Columbus Avenue?" Grandma Fabian asked, suddenly speaking with a Brooklyn accent. She shook her head no. "I don't like his mother; she's a lush, not that it matters much anymore." She thought of her own daughter-in-law.

Frank ignored the comment.

"I don't see Nelda warming up to her, either." Genoa Fabian liked her son's wife, but she didn't have any misconceptions about her. Nelda saw things a certain way and was unable to accept any other point of view. "Yes, I suppose I must come down. You know, it is getting more and more difficult to leave these three rooms," she told him.

"You should move into Pam's room when she leaves, Momma," Frank replied. "I don't like you so far up here, either." He thought about the years when his father was alive and the two families lived under one roof. His mother had picked up the slack until Pam was old enough to help out. When the children were small, Frank left the house each morning at dawn, worried about whether his wife would get through the day without any problems. Now, from the lower floors of the house, they could hear female voices shouting, laughter, doors slamming. His four daughters were home.

"Dad? Nonny? Can I come up?" It was Pam, Genoa's favorite grandchild. Genoa got up from her chair with the pep of a much younger woman and went to the door of her apartment. Hearing her granddaughter's voice had transformed her. Opening the door, she called down the stairs.

"*Siamo qui, Pamela, vieni su.* We're here, come up, *per favore*," she said, waiting while Pam ran up the stairs. Pam's radiance as she came through the apartment door brought a smile to her father and grandmother's faces. She always seemed to float into a room. Of all the girls, she looked most like a Fabian, with the blonde good looks of Genoa's Northern Italian heritage. Genoa had some German blood and she supposed that is where the light coloring came from. Pam had pale, almost alabaster skin; huge brown eyes; and long, black eyelashes. Her hair was golden, thick and wavy; the envy of the other three, who had dark, straight hair like Nelda's. Pam was Genoa's favorite, although she would deny it and the others ignored it. If it could be considered a flaw, Pam was shorter, barely five and a half feet, in a household of tall people. It made the rest of the family protective of her.

"Nonny, are you coming down tonight?" She hugged her grandmother, almost jumping up and down with excitment. "Dad, you know what's going to happen, don't you! Did Jack call you? Did he try to get in touch with you in any way?" Her eyes were sparkling, a smile almost as wide as her face betraying her attempt at composure.

She entered the sitting room, dragging her grandmother along by the hand. "He's going to ask you tonight, Dad, Jack is. He's going to ask you if we can get married." She swung around to look at her grandmother. "I feel like a fool, but I am so thrilled and have to hide it from the others because they'll tell him I am acting like this!" She started laughing, giggling almost, and Frank and Genoa laughed along with her. Frank knew when she said "the others," that is was really about Nelda. She'd find a way to expose Pam's excitement about her upcoming engagement. The only people on earth Pam felt safe with was her father and grandmother.

Genoa looked at her son, concerned. *The girl should be able to be herself in front of the young man, shouldn't she?* Frank, as though reading his mother's mind, frowned and shook his head no to his mother.

"He never got in touch, Pam. Did he tell you he was going to call me?" Frank asked.

"No, I just thought he might. Maybe he isn't going to ask me tonight." She had a doubtful expression on her face. "How embarrassing. I may have misunderstood him." To be with Jack meant putting aside her need for emotional security. He was on the continuum of Pam's unearned trust. He was more than domineering; he was both intimidating and secretive. She had to accept at face value that he wanted to be with her, that he loved her, that he thought she was special. For months she had observed him, had watched him watching her. Something about him spoke to that part of her that was confident, that said, *I am worth his adoration.* Pam had hidden strength and she didn't yet know what its origins were. But she wanted Jack. She wanted what he was capable of giving her, which was more than financial security, the envy of other women, and a family. A marriage to him meant freedom from her roots. He made it clear from the beginning that he wanted someone to have his children and make him a home while he built his financial empire.

"Tell me now that you don't want a life with me and we can end it. I won't waste your time and you won't waste mine," he said. Pausing, and then putting his arm around her—they were sitting on his bed in his Midtown apartment—he went on. "Well, what do you think? Babies with me? The ride of your life? Or an ordinary existence. Plain. Blah. Boring. I guarantee you will never be bored with me." Pam turned her head away from his eyes; she didn't want him to see her smiling, almost smirking. *He had such a goddamned big ego!* She thought for just a second. What had been her one desire from the time she could recall memory? A home and a family completely different from the one she was born into.

"Yes, I want children. Two of them, a boy and a girl." She stopped because possibly that was going too far. She'd been the recipient of his derision in the past over things she'd said. She held her breath. *What other kind of children were there?* she could hear him ask. But the ridicule didn't come. She felt his body shaking; was he laughing at her? She slowly turned her head to look at him and he was crying, unabashedly sobbing, with tears rolling down his cheeks.

She had never, ever seen a man cry before. Paralyzed, she didn't move at first, not sure what to do for him. She took his hand and held it until he was able to calm down.

"Well, I'm a very lucky man if you really mean it," he said. "I just imagined my kids. We can have two if you want. A boy and a girl." He smiled at her, tightening his arm around her shoulder, not making fun of her as she had feared but agreeing with her. He saw their children in his mind's eye. Two children who looked like them melded. In a split second he visualized a home they would make together with a sober, involved wife and mother and happy, well-adjusted children. "We should tell your parents. I don't want to wait."

He'd never said anything to her about getting engaged or married. She'd assumed it was what he meant. Now, the night was upon them and she didn't have a clue what he was going to do once he got to her house. He was aware of their modest circumstances and it didn't seem to bother him at all. Pam hated to admit to herself that she was ashamed of the way they lived, the shabby furniture and cheap knickknacks, the pervasive food odors. Her grandparents and parents put her through college; she should be grateful, not embarrassed.

"Genoa, is Pam with you?" Nelda yelled up the staircase.

"I'm here, Mom," Pam yelled back.

"Can you get your shower up there? Ask your grandmother." It was a constant shuffling of needs, trying to get four girls ready for an evening. "Ask Daddy to come down, will you please?" So their afternoon was interrupted; Frank had to vacuum and get his own shower before the important visitor showed up.

Miraculously, everyone was ready by six p.m. Genoa made it down the stairs in one piece, the house was neat, and dinner was ready when Jack Smith, son of Bernice and Harold Smith, arrived at the Bensonhurst home of his girlfriend, Miss Pamela Fabian. Pam met him at the door and was surprised when he swept her into his arms for a hug in front of her entire family. He appeared slightly red around the eyes, too. She hoped it was happiness and not regret that was making him cry. Without waiting to see if everyone was present, not really knowing who should be there anyway, he dove right in. He looked over at Frank first.

"With your permission, sir?" Then, getting down on one knee, he proposed to her. Nelda and Pam gasping, Genoa doing her best not to snicker, and the younger girls sighing in harmony, Jack pulled a ring box out of his side pocket and opened it, facing Pam. Frank almost fainted at the size of diamond.

"Pam, will you marry me?" he asked, not wasting any time.

As she had taught herself from the onset of their romance, she took it at face value. He didn't say anything about loving her, about his feelings for her. Just "will you marry me?" Without hesitation, she answered yes.

He stood up, fighting back tears, and scooped her up in his arms again. The family clapped and cheered. It was a happy time! They were going to have a wedding.

"When's the big day?" Nelda asked. She was sensible enough to know that she and Frank would not be responsible for the financial end of the wedding. If they were, the reception would be held in their Bensonhurst backyard. Jack looked down at Pam, hesitant to answer because Bernice had picked the date without conferring with the bride. Her reaction could determine whether the engagement would move forward.

"June 15," he replied.

Pam's face broke into a smile. "I'm going to be a June bride!" she said, trying not to jump up and down. She kept her enthusiasm in check as she had practiced since she was a small child until it became second nature, the result being that no one ever really knew what she was thinking, except perhaps, her father. If it crossed her mind that she wasn't consulted about the date of her own wedding, she hid it well. Nelda was taken aback by the date, taking a surreptitious glance at her daughter's abdomen. *What was the hurry?* With her hands behind her back, she counted the months. Not even slightly ashamed of her thoughts, as soon as they were done eating, Nelda got up from the table and started to clear the plates.

"Mom, we'll do the clearing. Stay here so we can talk about the wedding plans," Sharon said. Genoa was appalled. Nelda was not interested in the least and it showed. But Jack and Pam didn't notice her behavior and went on talking about the wedding. Frank was interested and asked questions, prompting his daughter to think about who her attendants would be, her sisters; where they would honeymoon, Hawaii, of course; and where they would live.

"We haven't talked about that yet," Pam answered, but she looked at Jack. *He had everything else figured out. Did he know yet where they would live as husband and wife?*

Jack didn't hesitate. "The Upper West Side. Not Columbus Avenue, further west. He looked at Pam, gauging her reaction. Once again, he was on target. He had chosen his new partner wisely. Pam was smiling happily at him, nodding her head yes to everything he said.

The Upper West Side? If he wanted to live there, what reason could she have not to want to join him? It was like a dream. After living in Brooklyn all of her life, hiding her enthusiasm for life from her pessimistic mother, making it to Manhattan was a dream come true. She would realize later that living there had its drawbacks.

Marie left her chair next to her Nelda and moved over to where Pam sat. They assumed their usual posture, Marie standing alongside a sitting Pam. Marie would have to consciously remind herself as an adult that it was inappropriate to cling to her sister. But as a child, it was her birthright. The only reason she sat next to her mother during the meal was so that Nelda could clamp a hand over her daughter's mouth if she started to say anything that might embarrass the family. But tonight she was quiet and well-behaved. She thought Jack was the most handsome man she had ever seen. She kept her mouth shut because she didn't want to miss out on the plans. Would she be included? A little trickle of fear brewed in her chest; what would become of her if Pam got married and moved out? She would ask Pam as soon as Nelda was out of earshot and everyone else was occupied. In the meantime, she stuck like glue to her sister's side and Jack didn't seem to mind a bit.

3

A week later, as Jack left the restaurant to head uptown to his mother's, Ashton Hageman lingered over his coffee. He'd pulled himself together and morphed back into the dependable lover who never made demands and had no needs. Jack seemed happy with the recovery, literally patting him on the head as he got up to leave.

"You'll see. Everything will work out. And you'll love Pam. Call me tonight." And then the humiliating pat. Ashton asked the waitress for a cup of coffee. He wasn't going to waste any time rationalizing why it would be okay to continue a relationship with Jack, and why it would be devastating to his well-being to do so. He was hopelessly in love. It would be easier to leave things as they were and try to adapt. Breaking up with Jack wasn't an option. He would rather die.

Jack had paid the check on his way out, so when he finished his coffee, Ash threw a tip down and left quickly through the back door. He wasn't in the mood to run into friends and as the afternoon progressed, there was a greater chance that he would see someone he recognized from the close circle who knew Jack and Ashton as a couple.

It was a beautiful autumn afternoon. The leaves on the few trees along the sidewalk had changed and were beginning to fall, and chrysanthemums and pumpkins were everywhere. When he reached his neighborhood, he stopped at a corner store and sorted through a box of pumpkins displayed outdoors on the pavement, the closest he would get to a farmer's market on the Upper East Side. He found a small, perfectly round one that had a little dried stem on top. It would be his one gesture to the season. Walking up Fifth Avenue, he was happy that he'd chosen this area to live in, rather than Midtown where Jack lived, or Downtown, which had the reputation of being more liberal than his neighborhood. He was isolated up here. His neighbors were older and wealthy. The women in his building doted on him, no one questioning why he was alone on weekend nights, or about the handsome guy who came by but never stayed long.

Arriving at his building, he remembered how lucky he'd felt to have found his apartment. At the time, he wasn't even looking for a place to buy. He was out of college and wanted to stay uptown because it was where he grew up, his parents still close by. He arrived at Seventy-Second Street and walked the few hundred feet to his front door, the entrance to a prewar building that had been restored and renovated to classic beauty.

He got on the elevator, relieved to be alone, and the moment the doors slid shut he began to cry again. Grateful that the hallway to his apartment was empty, he quickly made his way to the apartment door. Unlocking it, he stumbled over the threshold, but not before seeing the view out his window. It was a straight shot from the door though the living room to a bank of floor-to-ceiling windows. He could see the tops of the trees along Seventy-Second; a few golden and orange leaves still hanging on, and the blue sky and sunlight between the buildings across the street. He put the pumpkin down on the floor and went right to the windows. They were surrounded by ornate moldings. The beauty of the windows brought unexplainable happiness to him. Possibly that was why he had failed so miserably at human relationships; the superficial beauty of a selfish man brought him the only joy he experienced. Leaning against the windows with his head resting on his forearm, Ashton breathed deeply; one, two, three breaths. The stress of the encounter with Jack lingered, but his resolve to deal with it, to shun the hopelessness of being alone and in love strengthened. He could see the East River and Roosevelt Island. Jack said their life together would not change much. Their friends would protect them from exposure; it wasn't uncommon to have to hide relationships. The embarrassment of being in love with a married man was yet to be experienced. Nobody in their group gave it a thought when Jack was seen with women. But to marry Pam and still be dating Ash; well, he'd have to see how that played out, what his tolerance was.

He went to his bedroom and took his clothes off, getting into sweatpants and a T-shirt. Periodically, as he went around his apartment neatening up, he would start to weep. He'd stop what he was doing, sit down with his head in his hands, and sob away. After a minute or two, he'd calm down enough to start puttering again. He repeated the sequence all afternoon, straightening up his kitchen pantry, organizing cabinets, dusting shelves between bouts of heartbroken sobbing.

Around five, his doorbell rang. He walked to the front door and pressed the intercom. "Hello?" He spoke softly into the speaker. *Who would bother me on a Sunday afternoon?*

"Hello? You are kidding me, right? Buzz me in, goofball!"

It was Jack! Reduced to his grade-school vocabulary, but Jack, there at Ash's apartment door, in the flesh. Not at Pam's house in Brooklyn, where he should be, but on Seventy-Second Street and First Avenue. Ash pressed the unlock button and ran into the bathroom to wash his face and brush his teeth, splashing cold water on his eyes, hoping that the telltale redness wouldn't put his lover off. Jack must have had to wait for an elevator because it took him a few minutes to get upstairs. Then, the pounding on the door.

"I can't believe I don't have a key," Jack yelled. Ashton ran out into the hallway and threw the door open. He flew into Jack's arms and they began to kiss in the open doorway. Jack slowly moved into the apartment, never separating his mouth from that of his lover. He shut the door and moved toward Ashton's bedroom. Jack picked him up so Ash could wrap his legs around Jack's waist. Ash could feel Jack's erection through his suit pants and Ash's sweatpants. He tightened his legs around Jack's waist, pressing himself against it. Jack moaned, the vibrations of his voice, his mouth next to Ash's ear, went down to his chest, into his heart, and Ash began to cry.

"I love you, Jack! I love you." They kissed again as Jack walked backward and lowered the two of them onto the bed. He took his right hand off of Ash's back and undid his belt and fly while he moved Ash around to his left side on the bed.

"I love you, too, Ashton. Oh God, I love you, too," Jack whispered, his lips against the skin of Ash's neck. "Take care of me first tonight, okay? Take care of me, Ash."

Jack lay back on the bed and Ashton, still sobbing with a broken heart, knew the futility of their relationship, but didn't care. He would take whatever crumbs Jack threw his way and give himself completely in return.

4

From Bay Avenue, Bensonhurst, any onlooker standing on the sidewalk could look up into the lighted bedroom window belonging to Pam Fabian. She was smiling, whistling a little tune, and twirling around her room, packing for her honeymoon. The style of the era was broad shoulders with extreme padding, narrow-hipped jumpsuits and pants, big hair, and colorful makeup. But Pam was wearing a classic, sleeveless shirtwaist dress with a wide belt and a full skirt that emphasized her tiny waist. She had on her signature shoe: comfortable ballet slippers. Her blonde hair was pulled into a ponytail with a black velvet ribbon tied around it. Her wedding to Jack Smith was in three days. She had never been so excited in all of her life; the idea that someone as uninteresting and dull as she thought herself to be could be engaged and about to be married to Jack had an aura of unreality about it. Although they hadn't seen each other since the previous weekend, they spoke on the phone constantly. Jack had a phone in his car, a luxury and a rarity in those days. Pam was the first person he wanted to speak to in the morning and often, the last one at night.

If he was aware that his mother was not thrilled with his selection of bride, he didn't acknowledge it. He was as *in love* with Pam as he was able to be with anyone. Those last few days of bachelorhood before his wedding to Pam were packed with dangerous, aberrant behavior, reckless in its risk of exposure. He didn't want her to know about his other life, but he needed to pack as much in as possible before they left for two weeks in Hawaii. Knowing that the chances were slim that he would be able to stay on the straight and narrow while he was in a hotel with her, he had already researched the area for activities that the more "adventuresome" tourist might enjoy and had discovered there was a lively and progressive escort service there. Thinking about the possibilities was more exciting than the actual wedding and honeymoon. He pushed those thoughts out of his mind, though—an action that was the only attempt at self-control Jack would make. A realist, he was also a positive thinker. It was one of his theories that if you allowed yourself to question your motives, negativity would set in. He accepted who he was as a person, having rationalized that as long as he didn't hurt anyone, what he did in his free time was inconsequential. What Pam didn't know, couldn't hurt her. Jack had deluded himself into thinking that he could live a life of deceit and never suffer a repercussion.

Since college, he'd rented a studio apartment in an area of town where he was free to come and go without being observed. His neighbors lived in the building for the same reason he did: it was discreet. No one in the building wanted relationships with neighbors. No one cared if he brought different women there every night, or every hour. Once Pam and Jack were married, they would move into the three-bedroom apartment he bought off Broadway in the Upper West Side. Pam had rarely visited his shabby apartment. Once he had the keys to their new place uptown, however, he took her there, both to get her input and to spend some time alone with her. They weren't sexually involved with each other, but she wouldn't have stayed the night anyway because she wouldn't be disrespectful to her parents. Remarkably, her virginity was extremely important to Jack. He couldn't stand the thought of Pam being touched by anyone else. He was going to put her up on a pedestal, where she would be safe and sound while he continued with his depraved and dangerous lifestyle. In contrast, Pam was eager to have sex and made it clear to Jack that although they hadn't done it yet, she could barely wait.

"All I know is that I want you!" she told him when they were in a passionate embrace and Jack was struggling not to succumb to desire. "Is sex important to you?"

She had not dated much, preferring to be alone rather than spending one minute with someone who bored her to tears. But after the few dates she had accepted, there was always a struggle at the front door while saying goodnight. Her dates expected her to get intimate. Jack was the first man she'd ever felt anything physical for, any excitement or sexual desire. He was the first man she had introduced to her parents; the only one whose desire for her she had ever questioned.

"Pam, I want you, too," he exclaimed. He was practically lying on top of her, kissing her, and she was returning his passion. But every time she allowed herself to really feel him, to let go in a frenzy of sexual feeling, he would pull away from her. "Sex is *very* important to me. But we should wait for our wedding night. It will be a once-in-a-lifetime experience," Jack said, amazed as the words came out of his mouth. *Where the hell did that come from?* he wondered. He waited for her to ask if he had been with very many women, but she never did. She never questioned him about his past, or his life outside of where it meshed with hers. She didn't seem to care. The trust she had for him, if that was what it was, was unnerving. But it didn't make him want to change. He was unable to do so. So while he was with her, in her presence, he would become a different man, respectful, moral, controlled, and virtuous.

The night before the wedding, Nelda and Frank Fabian hosted the rehearsal dinner at the Smith's mansion. They were grateful to Bernice and Harold for their generosity. The offer to host the event was made when Nelda expressed concern over the number of people she would have to fit into her tiny, Brooklyn backyard. Pam and Jack had six attendants each, a flower girl, and a ring bearer, and with the attendants' partners, the parents of the ring bearer, family, and out-of-town friends, the number of guests would be well over fifty.

"I would be delighted to offer our house," Bernice told her. "My kitchen and staff will be at your disposal. I would think for the number of people we have to include, we should hire some temporary serving staff. Also, what do you think of a caterer? What were you going to do about food if we had the affair at your home?" Bernice knew that the Fabians were in no position to hire a caterer, even for a small gathering. But for Jack's sake, she would be sensitive to their status and not overbearing, as she was sometimes accused of being.

"We'll start cooking and freezing now," Nelda answered honestly. "It's the way we do it in our family."

Bernice thought for a moment. "I like that idea. Would you be comfortable if I helped?"

Jack, who was listening to the conversation, almost fainted. He had never eaten Bernice's cooking. "Mother, I'm sure Mrs. Fabian has it under control. Let's let her be in charge, okay?"

Bernice saw his concern and backpedaled. "Maybe you're right," she said. "But that's a lot of cooking. How can we help? I have an idea!" she exclaimed. "Why don't you allow us to hire caterers for the main course and you do the desserts?"

Jack resisted the urge to hug his mother in front of everyone. For all her faults, she had some good qualities. He wouldn't have to worry about his future in-laws going broke cooking for their friends.

The night of the early June dinner was warm enough to use the walled garden for the party. The gardeners had transformed the space into a fairyland with twinkling white lights in the trees and candle luminarias winding along the pathway. White linen-covered tables were placed around the garden and a buffet table and bar were set up just inside the double French doors leading into the den. Bernice, looking radiant in a pale gold silk worsted suit, her hair perfectly coiffed in her signature French twist, took the mandatory stroll through the public areas of the house with her housekeeper, Mildred, and the leader of the temporary hired staff. The wedding planner hadn't shown up yet. She looked with approval at most of what she saw, but took exception to the centerpieces on the tables.

"These vases look a little sparse. Can you find something to fill them out more?" Then she turned to the area where the band would play. "I'm not sure about this. Where will people dance? We should have thought to place a false floor out here." There was an area of slate about twelve feet square that would have to do. "I guess this is as good as it gets. However, I'll have a word with Robert Winegarten before the day is through." She needed a drink, but was going to wait until the evening was well underway. As she was heading back into the house, Harold walked out. He wasn't to be ignored; six foot six at the least and two hundred and fifty pounds, he had a commanding presence just due to his size and giant, balding head. Bernice went to him with open arms and a smile, and he greeted her in the same way. Observers would think that it was a happy, loving marriage. As they were embracing, Jack came up to them with a big smile on his face, too.

"Just the two people I wanted to see!" he exclaimed, a little too heartily to be sincere. "Hi Dad, how'd it go today?" Jack was in the same type of business as his father was—real estate demographics—and although he had left the family firm to start his own company, he did so with Harold's blessing. Secretly, Harold was glad not to have to share a portion of profits with Jack. His son, William, would be graduating from college and then he would come into the company as a partner. There would be enough business for the two of them to continue to live comfortably, lavishly.

"Very good! Very good, thank you. We picked up another client today, thanks to you," Harold boomed, reaching out to shake his son's hand. "How'd that come about, anyway?" He wondered how it could be that his son was able to send business his way when there seemed to be so little of it anymore. Jack's company was growing and it was overly generous of him to refer a client to Harold, whose company who did essentially the same thing as Jack's did.

"I don't have the time for it right now. They have a deadline that I know I can't meet because of the wedding," Jack explained. "It won't be the last work they have, either."

"Well, son, thank you. It won't be forgotten, believe me," Harold said. To the onlooker, the exchange was of a proud father and his grateful son. But the three of them standing together in a circle, mother, father, and son, knew that it was fictional drama for the benefit of those in the vicinity. It was the way they always communicated when other people were around. Once the others were out of earshot, any dialogue between them would end. Jack was respectful to his father out of consideration for his mother. He wasn't sure what was driving him to stay in a relationship with his family, except possibly for pride. He liked being a member of the Smiths of Columbus Avenue. He wasn't able to admit to the society of Manhattan that the smoke screen he had developed for his survival was just that: a cover up. Jack had arranged his life so the horror of his childhood was a faint memory. If there was any pain left, it was buried so deep in his sexual escapades that it had become part of his fantasy life. Not knowing what normal was, he'd yielded to perversity for so long that it was *normal* to him. He would have to learn whether he could have a relationship of love and respect with a woman. But he knew he was excited about being with

Pam and building a life with her. He didn't allow himself to fantasize about her, about what she might be like in bed, because he didn't want to taint the experience with any habits he had.

The family would walk to the church together in a few hours. It made him slightly sick to his stomach thinking about what they were getting ready to do. He loved the church they were getting married in. It was an old Gothic Episcopal church, candlelit and fragrant with incense. His mother was Jewish, but she wasn't religious. She'd deferred to her son when it came time to choose a place for the wedding. When he was a child, he often ran to the church to hide in its sanctuary.

As they entered the building together that evening, he was suddenly overwhelmed with gratitude for how his life was turning out. He was educated and working on his Master's while having so much work he could turn down new business, had a gorgeous fiancée, and an enviable future. He wondered why he deserved all of it when he'd been a less than deserving child. What was it about that small boy that would make his father abuse him? Had he done penance and that was why he was being lavished with such grace now? The questions haunted him, but for just a moment. As he walked down the aisle of the church toward the altar, he saw Pam coming in from the nave with her parents and sisters. The sight of her filled his heart with joy and tears filled his eyes in spite of his efforts to not get emotional. His mother noticed and went to him right away, offering her support to him.

"You'll be okay, son. You'll be okay," she said. Harold pretended not to see it and busied himself with his Day-

Timer. *What was the goddammed boy crying about?* He lived in constant fear that Jack would make good on his threat to expose Harold to the community. But he needn't have worried because the night, the entire weekend, would go off without a hitch. Bernice played the role of Lady Bountiful, with Jack and Bill showering her with adoration. All of the wealth that was flashed around was thanks to Harold the generous, Harold the doting father. Nelda, Frank, and Genoa sat on the sidelines, not sure if what they were witnessing was genuine or fake. "The mother's a lush," Genoa whispered to her son, winking at his surprised face.

Although the parents might be putting it on a little thick, Pam hoped Jack was genuine. She was learning that he was emotional, and not afraid to show it like most men. It must run in the family, Pam decided, because Harold practically yodeled when she walked down the aisle. Nelda was appalled, elbowing her husband in the side. Bernice didn't seem to notice. Only those closest to her, her sons and husband, saw that her eyes were the slightest bit bright that morning. She had succumbed to a shot or two of scotch before she left her bedroom.

Jack's efforts to introduce Pam to the friends she had not yet met turned out to be a waste of time, diminishing any fear Jack had of exposure, because it would all be a blur the next day. Neither Jack nor Pam understood that the wedding was going to go by in flurry of activity. After all of Bernice's plans and the mountains of cash spent, they wouldn't remember a thing except for how wonderful they looked to each other. When Pam spotted Jack up at the altar, his tuxedo impeccable, brother Bill and friends—whose names escaped her—lined up behind him, she gasped and then giggled. Her father looked down at her and squeezed his daughter's arm.

"What'd you see?" he whispered.

"Isn't Jack ravishing?" she whispered back. Onlookers smiled at the beautiful bride and her exhausted-looking but handsome father, the two having a final shared moment.

"If you like that obvious good-looking type!" Frank replied.

Pam laughed out loud. Later, Jack would ask her what was so funny as she was walking down the aisle and he was pleased when she told him.

"You are so darn handsome. How do I rate?" she asked him.

"Have you looked in the mirror lately?" he whispered in her ear.

Pam, he discovered, was insatiable. And that suited him just fine. She was ready and willing to try every sexual position he could think of, or act out anything that he could come up with. She posed, stripped, danced in the nude, jumped on the bed, even did a summersault that almost caused Jack to faint. He was mesmerized watching her orgasm, which she accomplished the very first time he went down on her. He'd never bothered to satisfy other women, but she was so beautiful and so *into it*, that making her happy became more important than his own satisfaction. It didn't occur to him that it could be love that he was experiencing. Except for a few forays into the seamier places of Poipo Beach after Pam was asleep, their honeymoon became what it was supposed to be; a time for a new bride and groom to get to know each other intimately and completely. Years later, Pam would marvel that it could have been such a farce.

5

Ashton did finally get to meet Pam formally, but it didn't seem to register with her. He watched her during the rehearsal dinner and again throughout the wedding and reception, and by the end of the weekend of festivities, he decided she was deeper than she let on. She floated around, first at the rehearsal dinner, wearing a slender, navy blue silk sheath that came to her knees and black patent leather flats, while the other women, looking like hideous clowns to him, wore broad-shouldered jackets with tight, ankle-length pants, or palazzo pants and jackets with huge shoulder pads.

Pam kept it simple, wearing classics, even down to her wedding dress. The style of the decade was high-necked, long-sleeved, and lacey. She wore a soft white silk-satin, tea-length gown with a full skirt, highlighting her trim calves and ankles. The bodice was sleeveless, which showed her buff arms; the neckline was scooped and the waist tight. Her feet were shod in white silk-covered shoes. No lace or beading or frills or bows adorned her. It was elegant and it was so Pam. She left her hair down, thick curls that tumbled over her shoulders, and on her head she wore her grandmother's diamond hair-comb instead of a veil or hat. Ashton watched as Jack and the other men in the wedding party stared at her with unabashed admiration. Ashton was just jealous—so jealous he couldn't look at her without sobbing out loud once he came to his conclusions about her. He was sure that Pam had an agenda. And he wanted to be her so badly. He wanted whatever it was about her that drew Jack in. She couldn't stay in character forever, so he would wait until the true Pam emerged.

Of course, eventually Ashton had to give up because Jack was right about Pam. She was incapable of negativity. Or, as Ashton decided, Pam was so controlled that she didn't express it when it was present. Other friends thought of Pam as Jack's beard, but Ashton knew better. Jack really did love her. At the rehearsal dinner, Jack led Pam over to him and asked him to dance with her while he took care of some "important business," which was Jack's code for going to masturbate. *He can't get through his rehearsal dinner without jacking off,* Ashton thought, disgusted. Pam fluidly moved into Ashton arms. She followed him with no trouble, and Ashton wasn't always used to being in the lead.

"Have you and Jack known each other for a long time?" Pam asked, looking into his eyes. "I haven't met many of his friends yet." She talked directly to him, willing him to relax, to pay attention. Ashton was caught off guard; she seemed to be searching his face for something. He could smell her. Her breath was soft, warm, perfumed. Ashton closed his eyes as they danced, trying to avoid looking at her, tears near the surface again, and the tension between them palpable. Heat spread through his body, settling in his groin. He was afraid his hand would burn an imprint into Pam's satin-covered back. He felt her thinness, too, her rib cage right under his hand. Her dress covered her body, but he could sense her breasts right under the fabric, rising and lowering with each breath she took; all he had to do was hold her slightly closer and he'd feel them against his chest. Sweat formed on his upper lip. *Where the hell was Jack?* She was a woman, the enemy.

He knew Jack had allowed this one encounter in a safe place. It was meant to appease him. But it backfired. Ashton suddenly wanted to be Pam's friend, to exchange phone numbers, and when the honeymoon was over, invite her to shop with him, to have lunch and play cards. He wanted to help her decorate their apartment on the West Side. When the children came, he'd babysit for them, be Uncle Ash. But none of it would happen. Jack wouldn't allow it and Ashton was too jealous of her to suggest it.

At Jack's funeral, she would be reminded that she'd danced with Ash at the rehearsal dinner, but she would claim to have no memory of it or of him. That unnerved him. It unnerved him because she had been in his thoughts continuously all of those years. The first thing Ashton thought of when he got up in the morning was Jack. And after the wedding, Jack and Pam. He often thought of Pam as she was in her wedding gown. Pam dressed in silk satin and *peau de soie*-covered shoes, Pam standing at a white kitchen stove, frying bacon. Or Pam on the treadmill, as Jack had often described her, in that same wedding dress. He encouraged Jack to speak of his wife and once Jack trusted that Ashton wouldn't use it against him, he relaxed and began to share the minutiae of married life with Pam.

Jack was in love with Pam. He worried about her, wanted the best for her, kept her from harm. He wanted to grow old with her, and saw their future together raising a family. But Jack was incapable of fidelity. He tried after the honeymoon. Pam's enthusiastic devotion to him and ardent passion forced him to look at what extramarital affairs would do to their relationship. He was insatiable, but he was human. Performance-enhancing drugs weren't on the market yet. He would have to find out what his tolerance was. Soon, he and Pam worked out a sort of routine that would take them to the end of their marriage and of which she would be unaware. He used business obligations as his excuse for being gone until the wee hours of the morning. On the weekends, he was hers and hers alone. Or, more accurately, hers and Marie's. Because it wasn't very long before Marie was staying with them from Friday after school until late Sunday or early Monday morning.

Jack was feeling his way, discovering how much he could get away with without hurting his wife or arousing her suspicion. And as it turned out, he could get away with a lot.

6

Pam Smith sat at the kitchen counter, looking out the big window facing the sea. She and Jack raised their children in this house on the Atlantic side of Long Island, a short commute and worlds away from Jack's life in Manhattan. A light, late fall snow was coming down, blanketing the sand and beautifully, the waves. Soon, if the deluge continued, there would be a ridge of white ice along the tidal line. Earlier that morning, Pam donned a long, goose-down filled coat, a woolen hat and mittens, and insulated Wellingtons, and braved the weather to walk along the beach. Only a young man and his two dogs shared the vast expanse of snow-covered sand with her, and although they nodded in each other's direction, neither said hello even though they'd seen each other there daily for years. The cold wind and spitting snow hit her face, cutting short the trip. She was hoping that it would help her clear her head.

Now back in the house, the pile of papers on the counter next to her cup of coffee taunted her. Covered with names, hundreds of women's names, the papers demanded Pam's attention, but she didn't want to give it. Weeks before, they seemed more important than they did now. At that time, she thought she owed the women whose names appeared on the pages some consideration. She felt responsible for them. After all, if what she thought they were was true—a list of her AIDS-infected, late husband's sexual conquests—they could all be infected as well, spreading their DNA around as Jack had. Thumbing through the papers, one name jumped off the page: Frieda Romney. She had to be Peter's sister-in-law. Peter was Jack's former business partner. The impact of that realization—that Jack could have infected her—and then the thought of Peter finding out, if he didn't already know, unnerved Pam. She decided to call Peter about business and somehow bring up Frieda's name.

"They're divorced, unfortunately," Peter told her. "She moved back to Argentina. I liked Frieda, too. But my brother is a jerk. He is incapable of fidelity. Last summer they reconciled for a short time, but it didn't take. He took off to parts unknown. Why do you ask? I didn't know you knew Frieda." Pam forced herself to speak calmly, her heart racing, nausea building.

"I don't really," she said. "We were invited to the wedding but Marie went in my place. Jack told me you wore a top hat. Is that true?" Pam said, trying to change the subject. When they hung up, all she could think of was AIDS-exposed Frieda having sex with her wanderlust husband. Who knew how many new cases of AIDS would be attributed to Frieda? She'd be spreading it all over South America, while her ex-husband was *where?* It made Pam ill.

Slowly and without her approval, something was happening to her. Pam, the gentlewoman; Pam, the understanding one. She was getting angry. She was pissed off that her sister, Marie, had betrayed her, sleeping with Jack. She was angry because something about her character allowed his mistresses to seek an audience with her at the house on the beach. She was now afraid to open the door when there was a knock; so many women had just shown up. It had happened often enough in the past months that she didn't bother looking out of the window to see who was there. She didn't want to know, and further, didn't care. If someone was bold enough to come to her door unannounced, she deserved to be ignored. The first five or six times she let them in, served them cake and coffee, walked on the beach with them if necessary. She heard stories about her husband that made her sick to her stomach, tales of his affairs, of his relationships with other women's children. One young woman brought Jack's two-year-old son to the beach house. Pam fell into a deep depression after that encounter, and it changed her. She realized at the time that the very trait that would propel a woman into sleeping with a married man would also drive her to seek out his widow, and possibly to demand something of her.

Maryanne had done it. She was a pathetic older woman with a special-needs child who showed up on Pam's doorstep a few months after Jack died, asking for money. Maryanne and her daughter were an enigma to Pam. Meeting her forced Pam to rethink every single aspect of her life with Jack. She had to contemplate her children's relationship with their father. He had chosen Maryanne's child over his own, going out of his way day after day to see her rather than taking the time to see his son and daughter. *What was that all about?* Pam thought. She no longer made excuses for Jack after meeting Maryanne. Her opinion of him sank to a new all-time low and managed to stay there in spite of the inner dialogue that she formerly listened to, one she utilized to cover over his many shortcomings; that he was a good father and provider. Pam, baffled by what she learned about her husband, struggled with forgiveness for him. She knew intellectually that the only way she would get over the many surprises Jack had in store for her after his death was to forgive him, but she couldn't. Well, she did over and over again, but then she would find herself in such a state of disbelief over his conduct that she would be forced to start back at square one.

The list of names lingered for weeks after Marie gave them to Pam, unearthed from a long forgotten file of Jack's. At first, Pam thought she would have the strength to call each person and warn her to be tested for AIDS. But it didn't take long for that idea to be revealed for what it was: an altruistic notion, an abomination. *Not only is it not my responsibility to inform Jack's partners, but it might open me up to some kind of danger if one of the contacts gets angry enough.* Now she was left with the list, not sure if she should destroy it or hand it over to the health department. She had already been in contact with the health department regarding Jack's sexual contacts; the public health officials had agreed to keep her informed without revealing identities, and they had. Having the knowledge, hearing the number of women he had been with, was brutal. It was enough to make her bitter for her remaining lifetime if she allowed it. She reached over and pulled the pile of paper in front of her. In a moment of clarity, she decided to call Betty James from the health department and tell her about the list. *Let them do something about it.*

The ringing phone startled Pam out of her revelry. She went into the hallway to get it, checking the caller

ID. It was Marie. She had avoided talking to her sister all week and was resigned that if she didn't answer soon, Marie might find it in herself to leave the comfort of her boyfriend Steve's apartment and travel to the beach to investigate. "Jesus, Pam, it's about time!" she said. "Why haven't you called me back? I left four messages this week."

"I need some time alone right now," Pam replied. She didn't feel as though she owed Marie an explanation for her silence, but decided to offer it to get her sister off her back. "I'm not happy about the way things turned out between us." It was just enough information to either force Marie to probe further at her own risk, or back off and get out while she was ahead. After five seconds of silence, Marie chose the risky route.

"What are you talking about Pam? We haven't even seen each other in a month."

Either sly or stupid, Marie was walking a tight line here. Pam, exasperated, decided to let her have it with both barrels. "You know what I am talking about, Marie! It's nothing new! Why'd you sleep with Jack? Why'd you let it happen? As soon as you came of age it became your responsibility to end it if you cared about me. We were supposedly so close, yet you betrayed me all of our life!" Her voice shrill and shaking, Pam was headed to new territory. She had always walked away from conflict in the past.

"Why now?" Marie countered. "Why right before Thanksgiving? You've had six months to bring this up. Why now?" Repeating herself, Marie felt sick. Having a confrontation about Jack was the last thing she ever wanted to do with Pam. Marie knew she was wrong; with Jack dead, she alone was to blame. Getting defensive was a losing battle. She had to give up. "There is no way we will ever resolve it. I was wrong. I'm sorry. What more do you want from me?" Marie lay back on her bed and closed her eyes. *Why'd I make this call?*

Strength was building in Pam, giving her what she needed to be confrontational. Something had shifted in her thinking. Having Marie in her life, thinking about Marie interacting with the children during the holiday, suddenly had become unbearable. "I don't want you to come here anymore. You are not welcome," Pam replied. "I'm glad you called because we can have it out. You are correct, Marie. There's no point in dragging it out now. If I had been smarter, or less tolerant, I would have shut you out of my life the day you told Sandra and me that you'd been Jack's lover. You sat right here in my house, on my veranda, and blurted that out in front of a stranger. You didn't have any respect for me when you were screwing my husband in the bedroom next to where our children slept. And you didn't have any respect for me the weekend after he died. I'm not willing to take the risk that you won't expose more of your garbage to my children. I don't want them to know you have AIDS. That you got it from Jack."

Marie cut in here. She knew that if she wasn't able to talk her sister out of it, the bond they'd had all of their lives was about to be terminated. Or the bond Marie had felt, as it seemed Pam hadn't benefited much from their relationship after all. "Pam, please!" she said in a trembling voice. "I promise I won't say a word to the kids about it! I swear to you, I'll do anything you ask of me! You're right, I was awful, selfish. I didn't think of the consequences!"

Against her will, she began to cry. She got out of bed and went to the door to shut and lock it; she didn't want her boyfriend to come in and he was respectful enough not to come in if the door was closed. She started to pace, tears streaming down her face, her nose running. "The shock of everything must be coming to you all of a sudden. Let's try to work something out."

Marie, the peacemaker? Marie, the sensible one? Something had definitely shifted. But the more she spoke, the harder Pam felt. She could see things clearly for the first time. What had been done to her was done opportunistically. Jack and Marie had walked all over her because Pam was a trusting, loving soul who only saw the good in people. Not anymore.

"No, I think we're finished. I don't care what you say to Mother. Tell her you have AIDS and that Jack gave it to you. But if you do so, she won't be welcome here either. Neither of you are invited to Thanksgiving; I want to be here with my children, alone. I'm hanging up now." And she ended the call without saying good-bye.

The phone began to ring again. Pam checked the caller ID and saw that it was Marie. She let it ring, shutting off the answering machine before it could pick up. She was finished with her sister. The effect was unexpected. She was suddenly light-hearted. The burden of having Marie, the emotionally damaged, anorexic, depressed Marie, out of her life for one evening was freeing. Pam didn't owe her sister anything. She had been thrust into the position of Marie's caretaker when they were young children at home, and it had continued all of their lives. That Marie was abused by Jack was horrible and Pam had punished herself over it, taking responsibility for sticking her head in the clouds because there must have been a sign—some evidence—that she'd ignored. But she was finished with doing penance. Her two children, Brent and Lisa, would be home from college for the first time since Labor Day and she wanted the experience to be beneficial for them. It would be difficult enough that the subject of Pam's AIDS diagnosis would be discussed and possibly its source uncovered. Imagining the conversation with her kids made her physically ill.

She poured herself another cup of coffee and took it into the den, determined to unwind and move beyond the family drama. With a click of the remote, Pam started the gas fireplace. She curled up in her chair and looked out over the sea, the snow fall diminishing, the waves churning as they crashed on the beach. No amount of turmoil would ruin the beauty of this view; that is until the phone rang again. Wanting to let it go on ringing, she was worried that it might be one of her kids, so she went to answer it. But it was a welcome call from Dave, her new friend. Dave was the owner of her favorite grocery store, Organic Bonanza.

"Another crazy Saturday here! Do you need anything? No point in going out in this if you don't have to. There have been three fender-benders in the parking lot already this morning," Dave said.

"Are you serious?" she replied, happy not to have to go out. "I have a list." She read off a few things that were essential, not wanting to take advantage of his generosity. When they first started to see each other socially, Pam thought he was the store manager. But she wondered about his financial status since he lived in her neighborhood, a place inhabited exclusively by the wealthy and privileged. It turned out that he and his brother owned the store, which was hardly a big money machine, but it made enough so they could live comfortable lives at the beach. Dave came home for lunch every day to see his dogs, a trip that took him by Pam's house. Their relationship was slowly evolving into one that she had hoped for; they shared some interests. He was single, divorced early with no children, gainfully employed, and had no vices that she could discover, yet. After they had been seeing each other for about a month, she told him about her AIDS diagnosis, sticking to the facts only, in case he bolted like Andy, the cop, had.

Pam and Dave were walking on a deserted beach in early October, talking about how their lives had crossed just when it was possible for them to be together. He came to her rescue when employees at his store were rude to her. His graciousness had bowled her over, so she let her guard down. There was an instant connection. That day on the beach was chilly and overcast, fog rolling inland from far out to sea. The smell of brine was thick in the air; Pam loved the weather and the smell. She absentmindedly reached for his hand as they walked. For just a second, she forgot where she was.

"I was so happy for the presence of badly behaved employees that day," he said, looking down at her. "It was the first time we'd ever had a real conversation in the store." He was smiling at her. When he felt her hand in his, it startled him for a moment. She was always proper, if not slightly distant; avoiding any contact with him and scurrying off if she suspected that he might be about to embrace her, or worse, kiss her.

"I have AIDS," she blurted out, stopping in her tracks, the sudden cessation of movement surprising him, their hands tugging. He was facing her, his back to the ocean. He could feel the salt spray on the back of his neck. For just a second, her words made no sense. She was looking at him with sadness, but it didn't register.

Although only seconds passed, his silence was frightening her. *Not another one.* Perhaps he wanted to make sure he understood what she meant by it, but wasn't it clear? She had AIDS.

"You have AIDS?" He repeated her words, suddenly concerned. What did it mean for her? Death? *Oh, no.* It didn't make any difference to him that she had it. It didn't affect the way he felt about her or thought he might in the future. What to say? He took a step toward her and grabbed her by the shoulder, pulling her to him. He buried his face in the top of her head. He wrapped his arms around her body and held her firmly. And then he felt her shaking. *Was she crying?* "It doesn't make any difference to me as long as you are well," he told her. "I'm worried about you. Are you okay?" He whispered these words into her ear. "I really like you, Pam. If anything were to happen to you now, I couldn't bear it." He didn't wonder how she came to have AIDS, yet. The thought that her own husband could have given it to her was so horrible that when a tip of the idea penetrated his brain, he pushed it out. But it wasn't important at that moment. With his arm around her shoulders and her arm around him, they turned to walk toward the house again in silence.

They walked up the wooden path to the house, through the veranda to the sliding doors. Pam pushed them open. They took off their coats and shoes, and without missing a beat, Dave took her back into his arms. He wanted to make love to her right then, it seemed urgent to do it so he could show her that nothing mattered to him but being with her. But Dave wasn't a ladies' man and would stumble getting his point across if he wasn't careful. He decided the best way was to simply tell her that he wanted her.

He bent down to kiss her, but she backed up. "Did you hear what I said?" she asked. "You could be in danger."

He shook his head no. "I have read a little about AIDS. I won't make you kiss me, but I know that isn't how it's spread. I want you, Pam. This news doesn't change that fact."

Pam turned her back and walked into the kitchen to put the coffee pot on, hoping that Dave wouldn't be offended, but she was frightened to have this discussion and did not know how else to deal with it. She had ignored the signs that he wanted to take their relationship to another level; or had she? Maybe the admission of her illness was an overt attempt to dissuade him from any further advances. Whatever it was, it didn't work and now she had to face that fact of her own sexuality. Was she going to stifle it until it died again, as it had when she met Sandra last May?

When she saw Sandra Benson in the hospital corridor, leaving Jack's deathbed before Pam entered the room, she knew in her heart that the young woman had been Jack's mistress. It was the beginning of a downward slide in which even the remotest possibility of ever again loving another man slipped away from her. For the past six months, the idea of being intimate again occasionally would pop up but she squelched it immediately, refusing to examine the possibility. She felt she was too damaged emotionally to love a man, and having sexual intercourse was out of the question now that she knew she had AIDS. But for a brief moment when she was with Detective Andrews—Andy, the cop—she had imagined being in love again, having the kind of relationship with a man that would be honest and real. When he learned of her diagnosis, he ran, never to surface again. It was embarrassing and hurtful. Now here was Dave, not caring that she was infected, saying he wanted her. *What am I supposed to do with this information?*

Pam could feel Dave following her into the kitchen. Both relieved and frightened, it meant that he wasn't put off by her actions. He was going to force her to confront her own fears. While she puttered with the coffee pot, Dave slid onto a bar stool at the counter so he could watch her.

"I know you must be scared," he said. "It must be terrifying. But I truly don't care. That you could be sick and in danger; that scares me to death. I don't care that you are infectious. I mean, for lack of a better word."

Pam turned around with the pot in her hand. "I *know* what you mean, okay? And I am grateful. But that doesn't change the fact that I never imagined I would have sex again. It seems too dangerous to pursue. What's the point?" She turned her back again, but Dave started laughing, a deep, hearty laugh.

"Boy, you really know how to hurt a guy!"

Pam could feel the heat spread through her neck and face. "I'm sorry! I also have foot-in-mouth disease. I should have warned you," Pam explained. "Thank you for being so wonderful about everything. I am more than a little surprised that you didn't run from me."

Dave was smiling at her. He didn't want to treat her confession too lightly; it was serious, life-threatening, even. But it didn't mean anything to him outside of how it affected her well-being. "Well, it is upsetting because I want you to be safe, but it doesn't affect how I feel about you at all. As far as I'm concerned, nothing has changed between us. Except I made a pass at you and you turned me down!" Pam giggled, still red-faced at her faux pas, but relieved that he wasn't angry with her.

Their relationship stayed comfortable after that day, although they still hadn't gone to bed. Pam just wasn't ready for it; she didn't know if she ever would be. *Sex outside of a committed relationship? What was the point?* She had meant it when she said it to Dave. If the day came when she was ready for sex, they would talk about it. But for now, it wasn't going to happen. What was surprising was that Dave agreed. He thought that letting Pam know he wanted her in spite of having AIDS was important, and in retrospect, she was grateful. But they didn't need to do it yet. He was of an age; you couldn't see a TV program without the ads about low testosterone. So his low libido may have been a blessing in disguise. If he had been a younger man, her reluctance to sleep with him might have been a problem.

Dave spent some of his time thinking of ways to make Pam happy. Unfortunately, he had to work a lot, but when he wasn't at his store, he tried to make sure her needs were met. If she wanted to go somewhere, they went. Dave loved to dance and when he discovered that Pam did as well, he took her to a local dive bar and they danced with the house band until midnight every Saturday night. Pam admitted that she hadn't had so much fun since high school. The owner of the bar told Dave under his breath that the simple act of having Pam walk into his establishment had increased business dramatically after word got around that the beach house crowd was welcomed.

7

After Pam hung up on her, Marie was stunned. Pam had never, ever spoken to her as she had during that phone call. *Was it inevitable? Was I deluding myself that life could go on as before?* She got up from bed, slightly nauseous. Having a fight with Pam was the last thing she thought would happen today. She'd hoped to go to the beach later that afternoon. She had imagined being away from Steve for a weekend, lazing around her room at the beach, eating delicious food. Now she wondered if she even had a room there. *Had Pam been planning this? Just waiting for the right moment to tell me off?* She ran to her bathroom to throw up; rarely spontaneous, barfing was something she made herself do by sticking her fingers down her throat. It would appear that she was more upset by Pam's treatment of her than she thought possible. After she brushed her teeth and tidied herself up, she left the bedroom and went out into the living room to find Steve Marks reading the paper. He looked up at her, not liking what he saw. She was even paler and skinnier than she usually was.

"Do you want some breakfast before you head east?" he asked. She pulled her robe around her knees and sat on the couch.

"I'm not going," she replied. She leaned her head on her hand, looking at him. "Pam said I wasn't welcome at the beach anymore." Steve put his paper down. *Now what the hell was this all about?*

"What happened?" he asked, almost afraid to hear about it. Marie looked embarrassed.

"She finally came to her senses, I guess," she said. "I could tell something was wrong when she didn't call me back all week. That something had changed. It was due, you know? I had it coming. I was hoping she would stay in her 'Pam Mode' and let me get away with it. With everything. The worst if it is she doesn't want me to see the kids when they come home for Thanksgiving. She doesn't even want my mom to come for the day." Marie was miserable.

Steve looked out the window. *More drama. Hell.* "Can I call her for you?" he asked, eager to do anything he could to make things right for Marie.

She laughed out loud. "No offense, dear, but I doubt a call from you would improve the situation. No, I think I am getting my 'just desserts,' as my mother used to say. I have it coming to me. Now the only question is what the hell are we going to do for Thanksgiving?" Marie asked painfully. "I have never spent it anywhere but the beach from the day they bought the place."

"I'll cook! Or we can go out. Don't worry about Thanksgiving," Steve said. He got up from his chair and went to Marie, sitting down on the sofa next to her. "I think what we need to do now is get you fed and dressed, and shovel our sidewalk before someone slips and breaks their neck out there. He put his arm around her and squeezed. "Come on, you'll feel better if you keep moving." There was no way he was going to let her take to her bed. She had done it in the past, not moving for the entire weekend, nor eating, for that matter.

"Not shovel! I don't do physical work," she whined. "I'll stay in here while you do it."

But Steve wasn't standing for it; he pulled her off the couch. "Come on, I'll fix you something to eat and then we'll do it! You aren't staying in today." Marie allowed herself to be led to the kitchen. Maybe he was right; maybe if she kept busy, the sadness she felt because of her sister's rightful anger wouldn't take hold, wouldn't smother her as it was trying to do. She wanted to lie in bed and remember days at the beach when Jack was alive. How they would play all day—tennis or golf, or running on the beach—and return to the house, sneaking into her bedroom for sex while Pam was shopping or napping and then spend a mealtime eating the delicious food she had prepared for them. She'd wasted an entire weekend doing it in the past, but Steve wouldn't allow it now.

"If you're going to live with me, you're not moping around here," he'd say. "Get moving and do something worthwhile." She'd pout for a while, but then she did as he told her and felt better for it.

~

Sandra Benson woke up Saturday morning to the smell of coffee and cinnamon. *Tom must be baking something again.* She'd been living with him in his Brooklyn condo since September and so far, it was working. He drove into work every day, and she went with him, avoiding having to take the train. They drove home together, too, unless work required one of them to stay later in the day and she was forced to take the train.

Her job was evolving into a huge problem for them. She didn't want to be a business owner. Her partner, Peter Romney, was expecting more and more from her and she was finding that what she wanted was just a job, not a career. She wanted to be home for dinner every night, to be free to spend the weekends playing with her boyfriend. It was a problem because of its origins, too. Her late lover, Jack Smith, had willed the business to her, more out of his concern that it would be too much trouble for his wife to deal with rather than for the benefits it would offer Sandra. Half of the profits went to Pam and Sandra collected a substantial draw. Resentment was growing daily between Sandra and Peter, and now Tom was starting to pressure her about the time she was putting in at the office. It was a losing situation. She made the decision that she would follow through on a proposal she had made to Pam after the will was read and Pam discovered that Jack had left the business to Sandra. She was going to offer the business to Pam and her son Brent, first. She would arrange for them to pay Sandra a small stipend; she knew its value would be more, but she only wanted enough to live on until something else materialized for her. Peter would have a fit when he found out. But she would offer it to him only if Pam declined, and then it would be have to be at its full price. *Thanks, Jack.*

Her plan was to call Pam that Saturday and make her offer. Slowly, their relationship was fizzling out. It was okay; Sandra knew it to be for the best. If she could get rid of the business, the final link to Pam would be broken and therefore the final threat for Tom eliminated. Sandra knew that the "Jack issue" between Tom and her may not ever go away, but she had to find out. She wanted to give their relationship every chance possible. She reluctantly got out of bed. It was cold and snowy outside and warm and toasty in the apartment. The steam-heat radiators were whistling away. She never wanted to leave.

Tom had heard her getting up and had her coffee poured. He leaned in to peck her on the cheek when she came into the kitchen.

"Good morning! How'd you sleep?" he asked, handing her a cup.

"I slept great, thank you. How about you?" She smiled her Cheshire grin; they'd had wonderful sex in the middle of the night. Sandra had never lived with anyone and she and Jack rarely had spent the night together, so middle-of-the-night sex was something new. She woke up with Tom's arms around her and his lips on her neck. The next thing she knew, he was wedging his knee in between hers, prompting her to spread wide so he could climb on top. It was quick and wonderful. She fell into a deep sleep immediately afterward. Tom laughed his light laugh, almost high and girlish. She loved it.

"I slept like a log, thanks to you." Tom raised his coffee cup in salute. "Now this is what being in love is all about!"

She shook her head yes, laughing at him.

"What's on the schedule for you today?" Tom asked. They never made plans to do anything together on Saturdays. It had just evolved that way. They would go about their separate ways, taking care of business, catching up from the week, and if there was time or energy, they might do something together in the afternoon or early evening. Tom often went to his mother's on Saturday afternoon, giving Sandra time to be alone and do whatever it was women needed to do.

"I'm going to call Pam as soon as I have my coffee," she said. "You know, about the business deal." Earlier, she'd told him her plan and although he was worried that she might regret letting that much money get away, he knew that it was best to keep his opinions to himself. He didn't realize that she was doing this mainly to eliminate the unhappiness Jack's business was causing Tom.

"Oh boy, that's a tough one," he countered. "What do you think she'll say?"

Sandra just frowned. "I have no idea. Her life won't change one way or the other." The more they talked about it, the more certain she was that getting rid of Lane, Smith and Romney was the wisest thing she could do after only six months. She was sure that Jack had left it to her to protect Pam from his greedy brother. Once again she thought, *Thanks a lot, Jack.*

8

Jack was true to his word. He did make time for Ashton after he and Pam returned to Manhattan from the honeymoon in Hawaii. Years later, Ashton would wonder if it wasn't during the famous honeymoon that Jack picked up HIV. It was easier to blame the Hawaiians even though Jack's behavior was suspect in New York long before he got married.

Jack and Pam were gone ten days. Jack said it was torture being away from the city for that long. The only way he survived it was by continuously fucking his wife.

"I hope she doesn't expect that attention now that the 'honeymoon' is over," he said. "I almost killed myself."

Ashton rolled on the bed laughing hysterically as he listened to Jack's exaggerated tales of their daily lovemaking marathons, and then late at night after Pam fell asleep, the wild sex with Hawaiian "she-males." He said he'd had his fill of that strangeness and didn't intend to seek it out on the mainland. But Ash was never sure. He knew that once Jack had a taste of something different, it would be very difficult for him to not try it again and again.

"She-male is a derogatory term to transsexuals," Ashton told him. "You can use it talking to me, or to your hookers in Maui, but don't try it in town. You'll end up with a knife in your back." Jack tried to limit his involvement with illegal prostitutes because he was afraid of getting caught by the police. Ashton struggled with his feelings about his strong, omnipotent lover being afraid of anything, especially the law.

"Most I know are too passive from estrogen injections to knife anyone, especially me!" Jack exclaimed with his usual arrogance. "They love me. Come with me downtown sometime. I don't have to pay for it."

"You just lied to me!" Ash exclaimed. "I thought you said you weren't going to do it here." But Jack just giggled and gave him his sheepish, "you caught me" look.

Jack discovered that he also liked a little violence with his sex. Ashton wasn't a willing partner, but he knew of a group in their circle who had the same proclivity and they were thrilled to have Jack join them. Ashton would marvel again and again how Jack could satisfy his need for the exotic while being married to Miss Fabulous. He would stay out late, night after night, using the excuse of business, which was sometimes true. With all of his extracurricular activities, he needed a huge income. Jack was known as a maniac in his sector of the real estate market, so the work came steadily. He had so much at stake, and was able to juggle everything smoothly for years, right up to the end.

After old man Lane died, Peter and Jack left his name on the marquee. Mr. Lane left his share of the business to them, his only relative an ancient sister living in Florida. The men faithfully sent her generous checks and took care of her living expenses until her death. Jack had karma coming from every direction: goodness and generosity from his over-the-top gift giving and depravity and cheating from his trysts and liaisons. His friends couldn't rationalize why someone who was a satyriasis would jeopardize another's life by getting married. It was so selfish, so cruel, that no amount of excuse-making could explain it. As time passed, it became obvious that Jack was mentally ill. How he managed to support his lavish lifestyle, have a lovely, devoted wife and two beautiful children yet continue on a road to destruction baffled even his most immoral friends.

Luckily for manic Jack, he required minimal sleep. He'd be out until one or two during the week and up at seven, day after day. In the beginning, Ashton saw him almost every day. Jack would meet him for coffee in the morning, or stop by his apartment for sex at night. Jack avoided the nighttime club scene after his wedding, and friends bemoaned that the club circuit wasn't the same without him.

Ashton was rabidly jealous of Pam. He wanted to be her, or be her best friend. It was the most difficult thing he had ever done, not getting in touch with Pam. Jack would have been furious and Ash had seen the result of disobedience to Jack. As a form of punishment Jack would disappear for days. If Pam minded Jack's late hours, or complained, Jack never confided it to anyone. Ashton was the only friend to whom Jack spoke of Pam. And according to Jack, everything was great. He said that during the first months of marriage, Pam seemed slightly confused when the realization finally sunk in that Jack wasn't going to be hanging around much, but she never addressed it. Ashton wondered if she preferred the time alone. Pam was finished with college and didn't have to work, didn't have any desire to have a career. Her only hobby was exercising, so Jack got her a membership to the New York Athletic Club.

"You have to be dressed appropriately when you walk through the building to get to the gym, okay? No sweatshirts or spandex," Jack said, handing the membership card over to her.

"Well, that's a little odd!" she replied. Pam had never heard of a gym with a dress code.

"You'll see when you get inside the building," he said. "It's not your average gym."

She loved it from the first visit, however strange she found the dress code. It was a beautiful building and the people walking through it looked like any business people in the city. Pam's obsession with fitness began when she started working out at that gym. She'd always been conscientious about her body, but something about regimented, purposeful exercise appealed to her. She became a regular fixture there, even during her pregnancies.

After the first year of marriage when Pam didn't get pregnant, they went to a fertility specialist who told Jack privately to lay off masturbating if he wanted to impregnate his wife. What few sperm he had were immature and it was obvious that he was going to town on a fairly continuous basis. Of course, Jack didn't tell him it was not just self-abuse. He followed orders and Pam got pregnant within the month. Jack told Ashton she positively glowed.

"For someone who doesn't have a word to say for herself, she is really basking in the limelight of this pregnancy, like she invented it." Jack was proud of her, too. She made her own maternity clothes; sleek sheaths with room for her prominent belly and nothing baggy or blousy. It was during her pregnancies that Jack displayed the rare attentiveness that Pam would enjoy for a brief time. They went out to eat together in the neighborhood, took after-dinner walks, spent time playing games on the weekends. After the babies came, Marie spent even more time with the young couple, and Jack spent more time at home. He started to feel slightly suffocated though, and that was when the idea to move the family to the island came about. Ashton was upset.

"I'll never see you!" he complained. He and Jack were lying in bed on a Wednesday afternoon. "It's bad enough the short time I see you now." He was nestled in Jack's side, his arm across Jack's chest.

"Stop complaining, will you please? I come here to relax." Jack reached over Ashton to get the sports page. "Besides, I'm staying in the city during the week. We'll see each other more after the move." He moved just enough so Ashton would get the hint and take his arm away.

"You are? What's Miss Fabulous have to say about that? I mean, is she willing to be away from you all week?" Ashton asked.

"She didn't say anything. Trust me, Pam has her own agenda. We barely see each other at all now," he stated. "The weekends are family time. During the week, well, let's just say that during the week, I work," Jack said with sarcasm and a laugh.

"I don't want to hear about that, either! You're sure as hell not here during the week!" Ashton got up, picking his pants up off the floor. He knew he was on dangerous ground but couldn't help himself. Jack put the paper down on his bare chest and looked at his lover.

"Now see, Pam would never say that to me. She might try harder to please me, but she wouldn't whine and complain. You're beginning to get on my nerves, Ashton. I might have to take a break from this relationship." But he was smiling. Ashton jumped back into bed, tearing the paper away from Jack.

"Just say it! Tell me you love me! Tell me you love me more than you love her!" He had straddled Jack and was playfully bouncing up and down against Jack's hips. Jack started laughing, but he was getting aroused again.

"I love you! Now knock it off! I have to get back to work." He lifted Ashton off of him and got up from the bed. "I love you as much as I love Pam. Are you happy?"

Ashton shrugged his shoulders. It was good enough, for now. "Do you want coffee before you go?" he asked, sure that Miss Fabulous would have had a four-course meal prepared for Jack. But no, Jack was late. He pulled on his clothes without showering, and Ashton wondered who would get his sloppy seconds today. Surely not Pam. Ashton walked him to the door of the apartment and they kissed good-bye, Jack promising to call later. Ash stood at the door with his eye to the peephole, watching Jack go to the stairway door, bypassing the elevator. Feeling empty and depressed, he went back to the bedroom and stood next to the bed for a good minute. The urge to get back in and sleep for the rest of the day was strong, but he had an appointment before dinner. He reached down and with unaccustomed violence, yanked the sheets off the bed. He suddenly wanted no sign of Jack Smith in his apartment. He grabbed the pillows and shook their cases off, throwing them across the room into the chair by his desk. Striping off dirty sheets felt empowering. He made up the bed in fresh linens and took the sullied sheets to the hallway where the washer and dryer were closeted. Stuffing them into the washer, he shook at least twice the recommended detergent over them. Jack's DNA would be eradicated, too. Feeling better, he got into the shower and washed the remaining evidence of their lovemaking down the drain. The feeling of decisiveness would last into the night, but by the next morning, he'd be crying again, missing Jack, begging him to come over one last time.

9

In Babylon, light snow continued falling throughout the day without much accumulation. Dave dropped off bottled water at Pam's in case the power went out, along with the few groceries on her list. He promised to return in time for the evening news. It had become a tradition for them to spend a few hours together during dinner each night, watching the news and eating dinner on TV trays, just like an old married couple. Pam remembered feeling content doing similar things with Jack until she found out the truth about him. She was up front with Dave.

"Are you sure this is what you want to do? Sitting in front of the TV, eating dinner like old folks?" she asked. "I'd hate to find out that you are bored silly. I mean, would you rather go out?" She was pouring fresh coffee for him while he ate. He looked up at her, concerned.

"What's this all about?" he asked in return. "I like our routine. It is what I do when I'm home alone, except the dogs are begging for food while I try to eat. I should be asking you if you are okay with it." They hadn't talked about Jack yet, so he was in the dark about the origin of Pam's misgivings. Realizing what he said may have been insulting to her, Dave continued, "Maybe asking you to do what I do with my dogs when I am home isn't fair to you, either."

Pam started laughing. "Trust me, this is exactly what I like; being in my own home, cooking for someone I care about, sitting here at the window overlooking the water. In my opinion, it doesn't get any better than this. But if you get bored with this arrangement, you have to tell me, okay? Don't make me guess after it's too late, and you are ready to move on." She hoped he wouldn't press for details, and was relieved when he didn't. But she decided to share a little more with him. "My husband and I did this very thing on the weekends that he was home and I thought he enjoyed it. Since his death, I discovered he led a different life when we were apart. I don't want to repeat the same mistakes I made with him," she said, careful to leave out, "when I am with you." She finished pouring the coffee and sat down to eat. Dave brought prepared food from the store frequently, but Pam was beginning to enjoy cooking again, almost as much as she did when her children were home and Jack was alive. Dave was a grateful dinner guest after having to cook for himself for most of his life.

"This is a delicious salad," he told her. "I rarely eat raw vegetables because they always taste dirty to me."

"Do you wash them?" she asked innocently.

Dave was discovering that there was a naivety about Pam that was both appealing and made her ripe for teasing. "Are you supposed to wash them?" he asked.

Pam burst out laughing. "Okay, okay. Knock it off. How is that vegetables taste bad to a man who owns an organic store? It doesn't make any sense!" But she was happy that he was comfortable enough to tease her. Jack did it all the time, but his teasing was tinged with sarcasm, and sometimes it stung.

They finished dinner and had coffee and dessert, and before he left for the night, Dave helped Pam clean up the dishes. He had to spend some time with his dogs and get to bed early; his day often began before five in the morning when he would meet his brother at the store to open for the day.

"Thank you for a lovely evening," he said to her, bending down to kiss her cheek. "Another great meal. Saturday night we have Downtown Pub to go to. We better rest up for it."

She was suddenly so content that without thinking, she wound her arms around his shoulders and reached up, eyes closed, and starting kissing him passionately. He kissed her back, tongue and all. His hand moved down and squeezed her rear end, giving Pam a thrill she hadn't thought she would feel again. She pulled away from the kiss and started laughing again.

"I'm highly insulted," Dave exclaimed. "Here I give you the best ass pinch I have and you laugh at me." But he continued holding her and rubbing her back. She rested her head on his chest, his chin on top of her head. She would remember this moment as the beginning of their intimate relationship.

"I'm sorry. I just didn't think about what it would be like to have someone do that to me at my age. I wondered how we move on to the next phase of relationship, and I guess that's how! I didn't think it would be that easy." She had forgotten already that she had started it with the kiss, and he didn't remind her; the moment was too nice. Dave held her tightly and then they stepped away at the same time. It seemed like letting things play out on their own was working for them.

"You probably better leave if you plan on getting any sleep tonight," she said, surprising him with her flirtatiousness.

"Ah, forget sleep! I can sleep another time!" Dave said. But he let her guide him to the door.

"No, we better slow down," she said. "That was nice; let's not get carried away here!" He bent down to kiss her again and she reached up to meet him; it was a real kiss on the lips and not the cheek peck they were used to giving each other. The ice had been broken.

✥

The next morning, Pam went into the kitchen to start the dishwasher when the phone rang. She walked back out to the hallway to get the phone, but checked the caller ID first. It was Marie's boyfriend, Steve Marks. *What did he want? Nothing good would come out of any call this guy makes.* She considered letting the machine pick up, but gave in and answered it.

"What's up, Steve?" she said curtly, no hello or chance for small talk. He seemed confused but pulled himself together; Pam remembered that he was over sixty and backed off, regretful that she was being mean.

"I have someone here who wants to talk to you. Is it okay if I put Marie on?" He hesitated, and Pam remembered that she had told Marie not to call her anymore. Feeling unlike herself suddenly, with anger at the surface, Pam had to catch her breath before she could continue. *What was going on?* "Yes, of course, put her on," she said, the conversation having an air of unreality about it. She could hear Steve talking softly to Marie and then Marie came on.

"Pam? Pam? Are you there?" Marie sounded weak, and for a moment Pam was frightened, and then concerned.

"I'm here, Marie, what's going on?"

"I'm in the hospital, and I just got some news that I wanted to tell you about first," Marie said.

Pam's heart quickened, her hands started shaking, and she willed her voice not to betray her worry. "What's going on?" she repeated. "Are you okay?"

"I am now. I fainted this morning and Steve got worried so he called the squad to come and take me to the hospital." She stopped for a moment and Pam could hear her begin to cry. "Pam, I'm pregnant! Remember I told you about the week that Steve and I had unprotected sex? It just took those few times!" She began to unabashedly sob now. Pam could hear Steve comforting her in the background, telling her she would be okay and that the baby would be fine. Pam couldn't bear it. She had to be there for her sister and her first baby! Nothing she had done should prevent Pam from helping her out as Marie had helped Pam out when her two children were small. In that second, she forgave Marie once again.

"Oh, honey! I'm so happy for you! This is just wonderful news. Are you okay? I mean, why did you faint? How far along are you?" Pam asked, wishing she was there with her sister. Pam could hear Marie blowing her nose, and then she spoke again.

"Thank you Pam, thank you so much. I need you so badly right now. I am so worried about the baby! How can I only know about it for this short amount of time and already love it?" She blew her nose again.

"How far along are you?" she asked again. "There's no reason to be worried. Everything will be fine!" Pam was off in her own world, thinking about the baby things that she would buy, the love she would lavish on this new little life. And then Marie came back and destroyed it for her.

"No, everything will not be fine! I have AIDS, remember? And I am sick. Sicker than I thought. I'm just three months along. I haven't had a period in so long, who knew I could even get pregnant." But Pam was back at *I have AIDS. Oh, my God. Oh, my God.* Pam had forgotten. She had completely forgotten about everything for about twenty seconds. Heat flooded through her body and bile rose in her throat. She didn't know what to say, wanting to validate her sister's fear, but not wanting to be negative. Someone had to be positive about her health.

"What can I do for you right now?" Pam asked once she had caught her breath, deciding that immediate needs were better met than anything long range.

"Can I come there?" Marie asked without hesitation. "I obviously can't work anymore and I miss my room at the beach."

Pam felt a quick mix of emotions; terror that Marie would die, a thrill that her sister would be there, soon with a new baby, but resigned that her privacy with Dave would be usurped.

"I know you aren't thrilled with Steve," Marie continued. "But he's so regretful about everything that happened, I hope you will forgive him, too. He has been so wonderful to me. This is his first baby. Imagine! A forty-five-year-old mother and a sixty-something father." Marie started to cry again. "Oh, Pam, I am so sorry about everything. I am scared that karma is going to come and pay me back now."

Pam decided she was going to play the positive role. "I'm not going to listen to any negative talk from you, sister! We have to think positively!" She wondered why Marie was sick, if she had something opportunistic from the AIDS or if it was just her poor nutritional status that was at fault. But she didn't want to start the conversation about it now. "When are you getting out of there?" she asked.

"Soon, I hope. They took my IV out and I'm waiting for the doctor to come in and discharge me. There's nothing they can do about the other stuff on a weekend and I don't want to lie around here waiting for Monday to come. So what do you think? Can I come to the beach?" Marie asked.

Pam had forgotten to answer her, but of course, the answer would be yes. They would work out the details later. Marie said she would call Pam back as soon as they were told what time she would be discharged. Pam hung up the phone, a combination of disbelief and excitement filling her brain. She thought of her mother. *Oh hell.* But then she decided that it was Marie's decision when to tell her. As long as Nelda lived in town at the Smith mansion where she stayed with Bernice, she wouldn't need to know much. It would be better this way. But Pam was determined to let Marie lead the way.

If Marie's here for Thanksgiving, she thought, *the children might find out she has AIDS*. She sat down at the counter, the excitement about the new baby overshadowed by what was yet to be revealed. As difficult as it seemed at that moment, she realized that honesty and truth would be the best thing in the end, no matter how awkward. Hopefully, her kids wouldn't get angry and storm out of the house. They had taken the news of her own diagnosis so well that she almost thought they might either be in shock or denial.

A cup of coffee and a long contemplation at the window in the den was called for. The snow had stopped, but the wind and the waves were brutal. It would be a rough day out at sea. As she gazed out at the panorama, Pam wondered how her family had gotten to this place. Jack was gone, so much pain and deceit exposed, and now, finally, this happy event. A baby, not conceived under the best of circumstances, but wanted by his parents. It was a symbol of something good to come. It might mean an end to the awfulness of the past six months. The baby meant hope. Then she came back to AIDS. That lingering horror, something catastrophic lurking right under the surface, AIDS was something the entire family was forced to acknowledge. The last vestige of Jack. She knew she still had issues to deal with because of Jack. That she could allow herself access to an intimate relationship so soon after his death was enough of an indication that he was worth getting over quickly. But it didn't negate the damage that had been done to her spirit. She was still angry at him, and at his mistresses who had been bold enough to show their faces at the beach. *Where did they get off?* Marie was right there with the rest of them, but she had to be forgiven, mostly because she had asked for forgiveness. None of the others had, if Pam remembered correctly. *Had they? Did it make any difference? Couldn't she just keep going forward without spending time worrying about the others?* She was going to have to think about this for a while. For now the baby would be the focus, as Sandra's had been when Jack's death and absence were overwhelming. Pam smiled to herself thinking about how asinine she had been to make an icon out of Jack's unborn baby, and how rapidly things had changed once the baby died. She raised her eyes to the ceiling. *Please don't let that happen to Marie's baby, God.* Marie had said she was three months pregnant. That would make her due in the spring. They had six months to plan for its arrival, six months to hide her pregnancy from Nelda. It was panacea for Pam's pain and anger.

※

Marie's doctor came in and told her that although he was letting her go home, she needed to see a neurologist on Monday. They made an appointment for her and the doctor gave her a piece of paper with the name of the doctor, his address, and the time she needed to be there. He looked at Steve to emphasize the importance of keeping the appointment.

"Mr. Marks, its imperative that Marie see Dr. Garpow," and then to both Marie and Steve, he dropped the bomb. "Marie, your CD4 count is below one hundred. You are vulnerable to so many infections right now that we are concerned for you being exposed to the general public. It also puts your baby at risk." He paused for a second, giving

Marie enough time to ask why she needed to see a neurologist. The doctor coughed, clearly uncomfortable. "Your eyes didn't respond to light as they should and that is a sign of a possible neurological problem. Please, keep your appointment on Monday." He shook their hands and quickly left the room. Marie and Steve didn't say anything for a few moments. The nurse came in with Marie's discharge papers.

"You can go whenever you are ready, Marie." She pulled a small bag out of her pocket, and out of the bag, pulled a mask, handing it to Marie. "Dear, you should wear this when you are out in public. The doctor told you how low your lymphocyte count is, correct? You need to protect yourself. Hand washing is very important. No raw fish or salad bars. If you have a cat, don't go near the cat box. If you have any questions, just ask, okay? I'll get answers for you." She showed Marie how to put the mask on, making sure it covered her nose and mouth. "Stay in if you can."

"I'm leaving the city now and going to Babylon," Marie told her. "Right on the ocean."

"That's a great place! The wind will blow all the germs away." She said good-bye and left the room.

Marie got ready to leave the hospital. She placed her hands over her belly and said a silent prayer. *Please God, protect our baby. Don't let it suffer on my account! I'll do anything it takes to allow the baby to live.* Steve was watching her out of the corner of his eye, worried about his new family but powerless to protect them. He'd get her to her sister's house that afternoon, but besides taking her to her doctor appointments and supporting her as best he could, there was nothing else he could do. He suddenly thought of the dive bar he had followed her to the second day after they met, and wished he was there alone now, drinking himself into a stupor.

10

Ashton had worked out a rigid schedule for himself that Jack knew nothing about. He got up very early every morning and spent an hour working out. Then he cleaned his apartment, showered and dressed, and by nine got down to work. He made his calls, set up appointments for the afternoon, did any design planning he needed to do, and tied things up by one. At one sharp, if he hadn't heard from Jack, he'd begin his vigil at the window. Unless he heard otherwise, Jack would pop in sometime between one and one thirty and stay until two. Rarely, he would take the afternoon off so the two of them could go out and do something fun. Since the wedding, Jack wouldn't go out in public with Ash unless it was on the Upper East Side. Anything south of Seventy-Second Street was too risky. If he didn't arrive by one thirty, he probably wasn't coming and Ashton would get ready to go to his appointments. Jack would call during the afternoon, so it wasn't a total waste. After five or ten years, Ashton was used to it, not minding any longer when there was a change in the schedule and Jack couldn't make it. He never got used to not seeing Jack on the weekends, but in contrast, it was a relief that he didn't have to wait around for him. Ash had a social life of sorts and even went out on the occasional date, but of course, no one could measure up. Jack had ruined everyone else for him.

Before resignation set in, early in Jack's marriage on the weekends before he moved his family to the beach, Ashton would sometimes go to the west side of town and hide out in one of the local coffee shops, hoping to catch a glimpse of Jack. Occasionally, it would pay off. Once, he saw Jack and the beautiful Pam and her kid sister walking three abreast, pushing a stroller with a hitchhiker seat for the older child to sit in; a boy. The striking couple and their lovely children took Ashton's breath away and he started to cry. He spied a few more times and seeing the happy family, decided he'd had enough. No more torture. *If the bastard doesn't want me I'll make myself go find someone who does.* He waited until Jack's next midday visit that week. When he opened the door for Jack, it was with swollen red eyes and tears of anger. It was clear Ashton was upset.

"What did I do now?" Jack asked as he walked into the apartment. He was concerned, but took a passive stance. Ashton was never afraid to tell Jack what was bothering him.

"I can't go on like this," Ashton said angrily. "You're using me, Jack! If we were going to keep having a life together, experiencing things, planning, I could do it. I could wait for you day after day. But this booty call thing sucks!" He sat at the dining table and resumed crying, hiccupping sobs. Jack was appalled, but he withheld comment. His wife had never, ever made a scene like Ashton was doing. Obviously, he had come to the end of his rope. Jack wished he had called and cancelled, instead.

"Okay, I understand. Of course, you're right. But I can't offer you anything else." He turned to walk back to the door and Ashton didn't get up to see him out. He didn't want to get shrill, to start crying and yelling, but it wasn't working to will himself to let Jack have the last word. Almost against his will, Ashton leapt up out of the chair.

"You said our life together wouldn't change that much! Those were your exact words! You promised me that we would still be together. Now you've added more people into the mix. It might work if it were just Pam and I, but there's Maryanne, too," he said, mentioning Jack's latest mistress, a women older than he was with a mentally retarded daughter. "What the hell is that all about, anyway?" He had to stop to blow his nose, he was sputtering and blowing snot all over with the yelling, and Jack was looking at him with pity, almost disgust.

"Ashton, don't go there. They have nothing to do with you and me." His hand was on the doorknob. Jack knew that if he turned the handle and walked out at that moment, that it would validate what Ashton had said. He was using him. But he was using everyone in his life. It's what Jack did. He had a huge hole in his chest and he got what he needed to fill it up from what different people had to offer him. Although Ashton was sucking the life out of him, he needed him, too. He gathered up a little extra tolerance, and stepping away from the door, took his hand off the knob and tried to rearrange his facial expression into one that showed some compassion.

"I'm sorry. Please forgive me for upsetting you. I'll try to be more attentive, okay? Will that help?" He took a deep breath. It was often easier than he imagined to give in and let people hear what they needed from him. It didn't cost him much but a little control. He would let

Ashton think he was having his way, but in reality, Jack would continue doing exactly what he wanted. Evidently, he had failed in some way with Ashton. That his friend was under the impression that he could get away with this behavior and still have a relationship with Jack proved that Jack needed to gain some respect from him. When Ashton didn't answer Jack, he turned to the door again. "Give me a call when you pull yourself together," he said with a hint of sarcasm in his voice. He opened the door and walked out. He'd stay away for a few days, maybe a week, and Ashton would either call begging for forgiveness, or if Jack really needed to see him, he'd call first and pretend nothing had happened.

Jack's life was starting to get complicated and he wasn't going to allow any drama to infuse it. But the day was only half over and he still needed to get fucked. Then he remembered his old friend, Dale. She was better than nothing.

Dale lived five blocks west of Ashton's apartment. Where Ashton looked at river views, Dale saw parkland from each of her windows. Twenty years older than Jack, she'd taught Jack mathematics at New York University. She was a mentor of sorts, someone who would advise him regarding the next semester's class requirements. She'd also helped Jack formulate exactly what it was that he wanted to do to make a living. He'd chosen demographics; his father's business, too. A competitor was looking for a partner and Peter and Jack came together to approach old man Lane about joining the firm. Harold thought it was great because then the competition would be family.

Dale was in love with Jack. She fell for him while he was a student and then after he graduated, she allowed herself to begin a fantasy life in which they would get married and spend the rest of their lives together, reading by the wood fire in the coziness of her two-bedroom co-op. But the reality was that she never knew when he would show up. Now that he wasn't at NYU anymore, she didn't see him every day and there was no chance for spontaneity. He'd married someone else and was starting a family. She was lonely for him, longing to be able to pick up the phone and invite him for coffee or a movie. But they didn't have that sort of relationship. She didn't even know his number.

After Jack left Ashton's unfulfilled, he sprinted to Dale's apartment, hoping she was home. The brass intercom listed the names of the eleven tenants who lived at 1700 Park Avenue. He ran his finger down the list until it stopped at E.A.D; Elizabeth Abigail Dale. Pressing the buzzer, he heard the bell ringing off in the distance. "Yes?" A quiet voice from the speaker.

"It's Jack, Dale. Buzz me in," Jack said, grabbing the door handle. The lock clicked and when he pushed, the door opened to him. He ran up two flights of stairs to her door. She was waiting with a big smile for him; Dale with her straight bangs and simple hairstyle, no makeup but lipstick, and at any time of day, a Chanel suit. Jack had come to her house unannounced at all hours and she was always dressed like she was getting ready to go to tea. Her perfect white teeth and clear eyes belying her age; how old was Dale? Her face was unlined. The only evidence that she had aged at all in the fifteen years that he knew her was from a few extra strands of silver in her hair. She held the door open for him and he walked in, familiar with the space, and went to a wingback chair by the fireplace. He took his jacket off and loosened his tie. She stood in front of him with her hands folded at the level of her flat belly, nervous because she knew what was required of her. He unbuttoned his neck button and pulled his tie out further.

"What are you waiting for?" he asked her.

Dale's face turned red, but she took two steps toward him and began to unbutton her jacket. She removed it gracefully, keeping her eyes on his nose, and placed the jacket on the floor. She'd found over the years that if she looked him in the eye she would either giggle nervously or lose courage. She reached to her side and unzipped her skirt, letting it fall to the floor and stepping out of it. Pulling the silk shell she wore under her jacket out of the elastic waist band of her slip, she grasped the edge and slowly pulled it up over her head. Jack liked her to stand in her bra and slip for a few moments. Her body was completely unlike Pam's buff physique. Dale was a maiden lady, with thin arms and virginal breasts, the nipples beginning to atrophy as what little estrogen she had left was slowly depleted. She had no body fat to store estrogen, and it was silly to replace hormones when she wasn't "sexually active." Except for this.

Once Jack had his fill of the slip, he'd nod at her and she'd slip it off, stepping out of it one high-heeled shoe after the other. She handed him the slip and he put it to his nose where it would stay until she was finished. Now in just bra and full, old-lady panties with an old-fashioned garter belt, she turned her back to him when he motioned for her to do so and began the next, most exciting part of her performance. She did as he directed, and when she was facing the front windows of her apartment, she reached up under the garter belt for the band of her underpants and began to pull them down. She bent over at the waist and pulled them down over her knees, stepping out of them.

"Stay bent over," he said, and a little thrill went to her chest. "Spread yourself apart." She did as he asked, and then heard him drop to his knees behind her and go right to her with his mouth. He pushed her to the couch so that she lay across the seat, and then she heard his zipper and felt him push up against her. *If only all my old lady girlfriends could see me now,* she thought. She had her hands in front of her face and the thrill she got each time she heard him moan and grunt and push her deeper into the down-filled sofa cushions, well, it was better than anything, except maybe the orgasm. She could do it for herself, but it would never, ever feel as good as when he did it for her.

II

Sandra finished having breakfast with Tom and when she left for his mother's, decided she would make the call to Pam. It had been several weeks since they had spoken, and longer since she had seen Pam. Pam answered on the first ring.

"I'm thinking of selling my half of the business," Sandra said right after they exchanged pleasantries. "You get first right of refusal, according to Jack's will, so I'm bothering you on a Saturday morning. With Peter hanging around, I'm never sure if my calls are private in that office."

"Wow, already?" Pam asked, surprised that Sandra would come to this decision so soon. "I guess I can see how that place might drive a person away."

"It is pretty hairy there," Sandra said, not sure if she should confess the real reason, and then decided that being honest was the best policy; it wasn't the company that was forcing the decision on her. "But that's not why I'm selling out. It's a great company, well run, thanks to Peter now, but it's my personal life. I'm afraid Tom must feel threatened by it. He won't admit it, but I'm smart enough to see that my owning a multimillion dollar company that was left to me might be intimidating." She left out *by my former lover.*

But Pam wasn't stupid. She knew right away what Sandra was getting at and although she didn't voice it, Pam thought that it was small-minded of Tom to expect Sandra to conduct her life so that he wasn't threatened. Their days of having opinions about each other's lives were over, and Pam was glad of it. But she wasn't going to give Sandra an answer today about the business.

"You must have thought long and hard about it. I'm sure it wasn't an easy decision to come to. Send me your proposal, okay? I will take it to the attorney and talk to Brent and Lisa about it. Jack was pretty specific about what was to happen if you didn't want the business. I don't remember exactly what was stipulated, but it should make an exchange fairly easy," Pam said. She remembered exactly what the will said, and it would make any transactions work in her favor. The problem was that she didn't know if she wanted the company, and if she didn't, Sandra would have a devil of a time unloading it unless Peter wanted it, because half the profits would always go to Pam. The generous draw would have to be enough to entice any potential buyers. Pam was confident Peter would want it if Brent didn't.

"I'll talk to the company attorney on Monday," Sandra answered, thinking, *it will be a relief to be out from under that burden. But would Tom still have a problem if I continued to work there?* Unless she was allowed to stay on as an employee, she would need to find another job if she sold Lane, Smith and Romney. Another problem was that, although she had only been collecting the draw since June, she'd gotten used to no longer having money concerns. Going back to a researcher's salary worried her. Tom's police detective salary certainly wouldn't support them both. Maybe she should play the money card as a way to get him to work on his feelings of inferiority and pride, which she was sure were at the root of the problems they were having. "I wish things had been different between us, Pam," Sandra admitted sadly. "I guess there is just too much baggage for us to get past."

"For us, and for Tom," Pam reminded her. "If I can forget, you'd think he could." It was uncharacteristic of Pam to brandish self-righteousness, but she had had it with Tom and Sandra. Because of his pride, Tom would pout until a woman he'd known only for a few months to change her life dramatically so that he felt more loved and secure. It made Pam angry, but she had said enough. "Anyway, enjoy your weekend! Are you going to do anything fun?" Pam didn't really care, but she didn't want their conversation to end on a sour note.

"Not really," Sandra answered, still pondering Pam's veiled insult about Tom's character. Should she call her on it? A strong feeling of loyalty toward Tom was growing, and she wanted to address it with Pam now, before its importance diminished. "But before we hang up, I'm feeling uncomfortable about your comment about Tom. Do you think I am making a mistake trying to eliminate the things that are troubling him?" She was trying to weigh her words so they weren't overtly challenging.

"It's not my business and I am sorry I let that comment slip," Pam said.

"Well, it is your business in many ways; I wish you would elaborate, please Pam." Sandra was feeling more and more uncertain about her decision now; would Tom ever be satisfied? She had stopped talking to Pam and Marie, no longer went to the beach, miscarried Jack's baby, and now was thinking of selling his business, too. What if her relationship with Tom ended? Then she wouldn't even have a job. It would appear she was getting rid of every last connection to Jack. What guarantee would there be that he would feel secure when the business was gone? "You know what, Pam? Never mind. Thank you, though. I really mean it. I just saw things clearly, thanks to you. Please don't stop being honest with me, okay? I need that in my life." She didn't say anymore and Pam didn't question her. They said good-bye and hung up the phones.

Pam felt strangely empty after the call. She could only trust Sandra to be honest with her after all they had been through. If she was okay with Pam's character evaluation of Tom, then Pam had to believe it to be so. She walked into her bedroom to put her workout clothes on. Snow or no snow, she was headed to the gym. Then she would go to the store and see Dave for a moment or two. Hopefully, Marion and Jean, the deli clerks, would be there. Since Pam had filed a lawsuit against Jean's sister, the ER nurse who told Jean about Pam's AIDS diagnosis, she loved being the pot-stirrer and made a point of cheerfully greeting the deli clerks on the frequent occasions she went into Organic Bonanza. Their discomfort in her presence was palpable, but Pam was enjoying it. Until they complained to their attorney or Pam's lawyer told her to knock it off, she was going to continue taunting the clerks. Unfortunately, she didn't have a case that would hold up in a court of law because although the clerks had been rude to her, they never came out and said why to her face. Jean's sister had been reprimanded, but she didn't lose her job. Dave wanted to fire the clerks, but he needed more documentation of their behavior to customers and he was watching them like a hawk.

At the gym, Pam spent twenty minutes with a trainer going through the weight machines, and then got on the treadmill. As she was turning the speed up she felt a tap on her arm. It was Linda Potts, the woman with whom Pam had seen Andy at the hardware store after his hasty exit from her life. Pam turned the treadmill off.

"Sorry to interrupt your run, but can we talk?" Linda said.

Pam was thinking, *hell no*. But good manners forced her to step off the machine and be polite.

"I know you saw Andy and I together and I wanted to tell you that I felt awful and he did, too," Linda said.

Pam had a fake smile on her face. "Linda, don't give it another thought. Andy and I are friends, just friends. You have nothing to feel awful about and neither does he." She turned to get back on the treadmill when Linda reached out for her arm again. Pam looked down at her hand but kept smiling. *What now?*

"I do feel awful, though. He told me about you having AIDS. He said that's why you two broke up." She was whispering now, playing the confidant. "I won't tell a soul. But I have to ask you, did you sleep with him? Because there is no way in hell I am going to if you slept with him with AIDS."

A burning sensation starting directly under her sternum made Pam feel that possibly she was having a heart attack; that maybe if she concentrated on breathing shallowly the pain would go away. She was uncertain what her next move should be. Should she get back on the treadmill and start running? Run until she collapsed, or should she just scream? She knew she was capable of it. She had not felt a response this physical to any but the worst of Jack's betrayals. But then she had an epiphany. Almost without thinking, Pam began a charade. With a brief pause, Pam smiled and grabbed Linda's forearm like a long lost friend.

"Oh, Linda. He's just angry with me because he couldn't get it up!"

Linda Potts stood at the side of the treadmill with her mouth hanging open while the gracious Pam Smith talked away. "We were trying to do it and his penis just wouldn't cooperate. It was as limp as a pair of socks. I tried everything, trust me. But it was hopeless. Now he's embarrassed and you can understand why. It must be so hard for a cop to go around thinking he could sleep with a high society woman like myself and then not be able to do it." As she talked, Pam's heart rate climbed into a dangerous zone, but she was getting into the role. Lying about Andy Andrews was as satisfying as taunting those ignorant deli clerks. She held onto Linda's arm like a vulture. "Poor Andy. He practically stalked me less than two weeks after my poor husband died. Did he tell you that? I tried several times to get away from him, asking him to leave me alone. But he kept showing up." Pam kept the silly smile plastered on her face. "Now you go on and let me get my workout in. Tell Andy that Pam says hi!" She let go of the woman's arm and turned to get on the treadmill. She didn't look back at Linda, but turned the treadmill speed up to six miles per hour and started running like the wind.

    Linda Potts backed away, stunned and silent. She turned and left the gym without saying good-bye. Pam decided she'd better call her attorney when she was done at the gym and let him know what she had done. Chances were, she had broken some law. The letdown she felt after the high of stepping completely out of her comfort zone wasn't pleasant. Maybe her old way of sticking her head in the clouds was easier after all.

    Pam forced herself to finish her workout. She'd decided to bypass the store; she wasn't in any condition to see Dave and taunting the deli clerks had lost its allure. What had she done to Andy Andrews to make him hate her so much that he would tell Linda Potts her personal business? While she drove home, Pam thought about Andy and Linda. Linda Potts was a barfly. She must have been one of the women Andy referred to when he told Pam early in their relationship that the divorcees in town were always bothering him. Pam could feel her own snobbery seeping in, remembering how, shortly after Linda's divorce about twelve years earlier, she had asked Pam to babysit for her daughters, who were classmates of Brent's. Then, she didn't show up until five hours after the designated time to pick up her children. Pam didn't mind them being at the beach at all, but Linda's delay had caused her unnecessary worry. When Linda finally arrived, she had a friend with her and her breath was fetid with alcohol. Pam was appalled. Linda did not offer an explanation or even a thank you for taking care of the kids. The entire Linda/Andy thing would baffle Pam for the rest of the day.

She got home and decided to shovel the sidewalks in front the house before she got out of her gym clothes. A police car slowly cruised toward the house and she almost fainted, but it wasn't Andy.

As it turned out, because Andy Andrews was still working on a case involving Pam's brother-in-law Bill, who'd been arrested for breaking into her house and attempting to harm Nelda, knowledge of Pam's AIDS diagnosis was privileged information and he would be reprimanded for divulging it to Linda Potts. Andy wouldn't be confronting Pam about her lies, after all.

12

Ashton's resolve not to speak to Jack lasted for three hours. By the afternoon that day, he was in turmoil over having passed up a chance to spend time with Jack, sending him off without so much as a good-bye. He called Jack's office but Jack wasn't available. Jack had a mobile phone in his car, but he wasn't picking up. Ashton waited until the evening and called the house, preparing to hang up if Pam answered. He and Jack had a signal: ring twice and hang up. But Ash knew that Jack might be angry enough over his behavior that he'd ignore it. The phone rang and rang, but no one picked up. Pacing around his apartment, he decided to go out and see if he could find Jack.

    He got a cab and went downtown. He searched three clubs and finally found Jack, leaning against the bar talking to a beautiful blonde woman. Jack didn't change his expression when Ashton came into his field of vision, but made his displeasure known with a movement in his jaw that was only discernible to Ashton. Walking to the back of the room, Ashton saw a group of men he knew and joined their conversation, keeping his eye on Jack. After about twenty minutes, Jack left with the woman. Ashton felt the sob rising in his throat.

"Looks like Jackie boy has a date for tonight," a man named Paul whispered to Ashton. "Take me home with you tonight, Ash. You know we are good together."

Ashton looked at him, at his slender body and his perfect, girlish features. He was completely different than Jack, and he was correct, they had been together before and it was good. Would spending the night with him be worth it? Using another human being? And then he closed his eyes and imagined going home, taking the subway uptown alone. He saw his dark apartment, and the big, empty bed. Another lonely day would start at dawn, probably without hearing from Jack. When he opened his eyes again, Paul was still there, smiling sweetly at Ashton, hopeful and eager.

"Okay, yes. Come home with me." Ashton got up, throwing money down to pay for his one drink and turned to leave, the man following him out of the bar. They walked side by side in silence to the train. Ashton didn't think of Jack once for the rest of the night.

13

Sandra sat at the window in Tom's apartment, looking between the buildings at lower Manhattan. Her cup of tea had grown cold. She felt empty. At one time, she could count on a chat with Pam to warm her and fill her with a feeling of peace and security. Pam had a way of making whatever it was seem not so threatening, but not this time. Sandra was afraid that if she succumbed to Tom's insecurity and got rid of Jack's business, she would regret it for the rest of her life. Pam's subtle criticism of Tom opened Sandra's eyes. As she slid off the stool to get more tea, the realization that she was moving too fast came to her. What was the hurry? If Tom didn't like her working at Lane, he'd have to wait. It was sort of thing one shouldn't rush into. She thought about what she had been through in just five short months: Jack's death, finding out she was pregnant and then infected with HIV, meeting Tom when Jack's brother was stalking her, the loss of baby Ellin, and then moving in with Tom. Maybe changing jobs would be too much.

Sandra put the tea pot on, leaning up against the counter and looking around his apartment. A decision would have to be made soon about her place; her rent was too high to justify keeping it if she wasn't going to live there. Surprisingly, she liked it in Brooklyn. Williamsburg was a great neighborhood, less congested than the Upper

West Side. She liked the grocery store and the laundry around the corner. It was closer to work, too. The empty feeling wasn't coming from the decision to live with Tom. It was because she was still grieving.

Although Tom was a sweetheart, he'd already said something to her that made her think his tolerance for her grief was limited. They were snuggled on the couch one night watching TV and an ad came on for diapers. It wasn't a particularly dramatic piece, although the music was slightly melancholy. Without warning, Sandra had teared up. She'd tried to reach for a tissue without him seeing the tears, but he'd caught on. "Oh no, you're not going to cry every time a baby comes on the television, are you?" He was immediately regretful, and she could see it in his eyes, but rather than leaving it alone, he got defensive even though she said nothing to him. "I mean, I know it's only been a few weeks, but you need to get on with it, Sandra. You can't go on feeling sad whenever you see a diaper commercial."

She hadn't responded because she knew it might lead to an argument. They hadn't had one yet, mainly because she kept her mouth shut instead of calling him on it when he made an insensitive remark. But how long could she do that? *Should* she do that? It boiled down to the old conversation she'd had with herself about Tom. He wasn't smart enough for her; he was too conventional, too bourgeois. He'd been there for her when she lost the baby and showed so much compassion that she'd fallen into the trap of allowing him to rescue her, providing a place for her to run to when the isolation and memories of her own apartment filled her with anxiety.

The teapot started to hiss, and as she poured the boiling water over a tea bag, she realized that she still wasn't in a position to make any decisions. She'd already made one about moving in with Tom and making another to move out wouldn't be smart. She was with him out of fear—fear of being alone, fear that no one else would love her because she was HIV-positive—and although she thought she loved him, her hyper-critical view of him was making her doubt that, as well. *What should I do? Pam is the only one I trust enough to ask.* The ludicrousness of her predicament hit her and she laughed out loud. The only person on earth that she could think of who would give her the answers she sought was one of the weakest people she had ever met. And then she stopped. *That was awful! Pam isn't weak!*

Sandra recalled a phrase she'd heard Pam use: *We have just the lives we want.* When Sandra first heard it, she thought that was ridiculous. She didn't purposely set out to be with a married man, one who would give her HIV, impregnate her, and then die. It was all chance. Karma. But then, as Sandra began to think about what it really meant, she began to see that there was some truth to it. She wanted an easy life without too many encumbrances, and being involved with a wealthy, married man guaranteed she'd attain some of those goals. She was self-centered and prideful. Jack fit her to a T. How did she know he would die? If she had it to do over again, she probably would have done the exact same thing. The knowledge that she would purposely set out to hurt someone as she had hurt Pam shamed her. Had she learned nothing? She took a sip of tea and heard the key in the door. Tom was home from visiting his mother. Another plus—he was good to his mom. But then, so was Jack.

14

Saturday morning, Bernice Smith woke up thinking clearly for the first time in ages. Getting out of bed was easier than it had been for months, and she got into the shower under her own steam. Hearing water running, her maid came up to the bedroom to investigate and was surprised to see her employer accomplishing her morning toilet much the way she used to when she was feeling better, before the shock of losing her sons, one to death and one to jail, had aged her overnight. Mildred straightened up the bed covers and went back down the stairs to the kitchen to get coffee for Bernice.

"Guess who is up on her own and taking a shower this morning?" Mildred asked the cook, Bea. "I wonder how long it will last this time?" She was referring to the periods of self-reliance, which were coming further and further apart and lasting for shorter amounts of time. When Bernice was feeling well, it was almost pleasant to be there. But when she was out of sorts, the entire household would be in an uproar. Nelda was the only person who could cajole the old lady into getting dressed or eating.

"I'm afraid she is a candidate for assisted living. It's ridiculous to keep this big house for two little old ladies, one of whom no longer knows where she is more than half the time," Bea said. "I'm getting tired, myself. Don't know how much longer I want to do this. What about you?" she asked, directing her question to Mildred.

"You know I've had it," she answered, fixing the coffee tray. On good mornings like this, the two ladies in residence would have coffee together in Bernice's bedroom. Mildred placed the coffee pot Bea had prepared on the tray, along with a plate of fruit salad and toast points, like baby food. The days of lavish pastry for breakfast were long gone.

"I'm thinking we better get in touch with Miss Pam. The old lady is having a good day; this might be the time to bring up the assisted-living topic rather when she doesn't know where the heck she is. Why wait until the spring, like she said before? Time to do it is when she is still in her right mind, so she can have some input into the decisions." Mildred lifted the tray, groaning under its weight. "My days are definitely numbered here," she said.

Bernice was sitting at her dressing table when Mildred returned with coffee. She was carefully applying her makeup, hands shaking.

"Good morning, Millie. Don't quote me, but I think my days here are numbered," she said, mirroring her maid's thoughts. "I was standing in the shower thinking about how ridiculous it is that we are spending all this money for two old ladies to live like queens. Would you get my daughter-in-law on the phone for me? I think it's time to do something about this old mausoleum." She turned to look at the maid. "I mean the house, not me." Mildred smiled at her employer, thinking, *the planets must be lined up perfectly.* Mildred brought Bernice a cup of coffee and went to the phone to dial Pam's number. When Pam saw the mansion number on caller ID, she thought, *Oh no, what else is going to happen today?* Good news rarely came from that house anymore.

It was Mildred. "Mrs. Smith asked me to get you on the phone this morning, Miss Pam. Would you hold the line please?"

Pam heard murmuring in the background and then her mother-in-law's voice. "Pam, I think it's time for us to get together to plan for the sale of the mansion. I was looking around here this morning and it is either renovate soon or get out now." Bernice paused, looking around her lovely bedroom, but seeing clearly that the priceless wallpaper was beginning to peal, and in the bathroom, the plumbing was starting to show its age. "The old place deserves to be taken care of properly and I can't ask you to spend the money."

"Shall I come into the city so we can talk?" Pam asked, wanting to give her mother-in-law all control. Although she hated having to drive into the city on a Saturday in the snow, she wasn't sure how long the lucidity would last. By this afternoon, she might be a lunatic again.

"Why not come for lunch?" Bernice said.

Oh great, Bea's going to love this, Mildred thought. Pam agreed and Bernice said good-bye. There was a knock on the door. It was Nelda, coming for morning coffee.

"Did I hear my daughter's name mentioned?" she asked. Bernice told her the plan to talk to Pam about selling.

Nelda didn't agree. "If it ain't broken, don't fix it," she retorted. Allowing her daughter any more control over her life would happen over her dead body. "Everything is working out so nicely. Why upset the apple cart now, of all times? Right before the holiday?" Nelda had been looking forward to a festive Christmas in New York City. Being dragged away to one of her daughters' suburban houses with their monstrous kids was the last thing on earth she wanted to do.

"I know, I know," Bernice said. "But look at this place. It's starting to fall apart. We can't ask Pam to lay out the kind of money it would take to bring everything up to date. After all, Nelda, she is your daughter! I would think you'd have more consideration for her."

Mildred turned her head to snicker. The haughty matron defending Pam? She must be coming down with something. She tiptoed out of the room so as not to draw attention to herself.

"My daughter is loaded. How much will it cost her to put us in assisted living? That's what she'll do, you know. She hinted at it a few weeks ago. 'You two would love it at the Eagle's Nest. You would be right next to all that shopping on Fifth Avenue.' I'd rather die than move to that high-rise nightmare." Nelda picked at the plate of fruit Mildred had set out for her. "Speaking of dying, I'd die for a pile of eggs this morning. Hurry up, will you? Let's go to breakfast."

Bernice got up from her dressing table and walked over to the coffee tray. "You really are uncouth," she said to Nelda with a smirk. "I was just starting to believe you weren't so bad and then you say something like that. Dying for a pile of eggs would defeat the purpose. Besides, Pam will be here for lunch."

"Oh no! Why'd you go do a thing like that? She is the last person I want to see today. I thought we would have our Saturday to ourselves, like we always do," Nelda complained. Bernice was struggling with the clasp of her watch and walked over to Nelda for help. The two women spent minutes trying to buckle the clasp while they bickered. "I want to go out for breakfast like we always do on Saturday." Nelda got the buckled closed, but she was pouting. Her daughter was coming to spoil her day. She looked up at Bernice, who had applied her makeup perfectly and had every hair in place.

"You look just like the old Bernice!" Nelda exclaimed. "I better go double check my own appearance. You will put me to shame."

Nelda's praise pleased Bernice, but within minutes, she would forget the compliments and decline into her usual miserable, demented state. The two women descended the grand staircase, chatting about how they would spend the weekend, when the first sign of Bernice's decline reared its ugly head. Nelda later said she could see the transformation in Bernice's eyes before she opened her mouth.

"Why are you still here?" Bernice whined, looking at Nelda with confusion. Bernice motioned to Mildred to join them. "Mildred, why is she here? I don't want to be bothered today! I demand that someone tell me what's going on in my own house."

Mildred got to Pam before she left; no point in coming to the city today because Mrs. Smith had lost her moment of lucidity. The final decision to sell the house would be Pam's, after all, and she'd do it knowing the fabulous mansion of Columbus Avenue, home of a Smith since 1855, would be torn to the ground and high-density housing put up in its place.

15

Marie lay on her back in the MRI machine with her hands crossed over her belly. The machine was making the most God-awful clanging and banging; there was piped in music, but who could hear it? A disconnected voice periodically asked her if she was okay. *Just a few more minutes and they would be done.* After she'd spent the weekend in Babylon, Steve came to get her Sunday night to keep the appointment with the revered Dr. Garpow. Marie was disarmed when she met the doctor. She had expected another disheveled bald man. Instead, she was so distracted by his handsome appearance and friendly demeanor that she forgot everything he said to her the minute it was out of his mouth. Fortunately, Steve had taken over, and except for one embarrassing moment when a nurse referred to Marie as his daughter, he listened carefully to every single word the doctor said. And none of it was good.

When the MRI was completed, the doctor performed a spinal tap; a procedure in which Marie laid on her side while a very slender needle was threaded into her spinal column. A small amount of cerebral spinal fluid was obtained for testing. It didn't hurt especially, she said afterward.

"The hardest part was lying perfectly still, curled up in the fetal position. I really need a glass of wine," she said. Steve kept quiet.

"You can get dressed," the nurse said. "Dr. Garpow will come out to see you in a moment."

After she left the room, Marie looked at Steve with a grimace. "I don't feel good about this. Someone is going to say something to me about eating, or not drinking, or placing blame on me, I know it." He put out his hand, palm down, pumping the air in classic Steve Speak. Marie wanted to slug him.

"Just shut up for a minute, will you? You're making yourself crazy," he said. She was making *him* crazy. He felt the same vibe; something bad was going to be revealed and he was going to be the one responsible for taking care of her. And it wasn't just going to be about eating and drinking. He'd felt it for days; unless it was simply stress that making her so totally out of control.

He'd caught the look Pam gave him at the door the previous day, eyebrows raised and head to the side, she was trying to convey something to him. Before Marie woke up Monday, Steve was on the phone with Pam.

"What's going on?" he asked. "She was mumbling something about you making her eat carrots all weekend."

Pam snickered. "She was worse than a five-year-old about the food thing. I finally gave up. She did eat, but only junk. I even tried her favorite, fried chicken and potato salad, but she didn't want that unless it came from a drive-through. I kept smelling cigarette smoke, too."

Steve was embarrassed but didn't confess to Pam that it was probably his fault.

"Well, thank you for taking over this weekend. She needed the rest," Steve said. "Is there anything else you noticed?"

"Yes, I thought she acted like she was about ready to fall asleep all the time, but that could be the pregnancy, too." Pam didn't know what to make of her sister; she had changed dramatically from someone who had been able to take care of herself, hold down a full-time job and live alone, to needing almost continuous reminders to eat, bathe, and even to go to the bathroom. Marie was crossing her legs while standing up talking in the kitchen, the way a six-year-old who had to go to the toilet would. Pam didn't mention that Marie also looked like a meth addict.

"She seems like a child to me," Pam confessed. "But it could stem from her simply wanting me to wait on her like I used to." Pam didn't tell him about Marie's nightmare on Friday night. Pam woke up to a blood-curdling scream from the children's wing. She ran to Marie and tried waking her up, soothing her, and repeating that she would be okay, and then in a strange, childish voice, Marie had started crying to her about how sorry she was about everything.

"Oh Pam, I miss Jack so much, I miss the way our family used to be. I'm sorry Pam, so sorry," she cried. Pam held her, patting her back as she did when they were youngsters, and finally Marie calmed down and closed her eyes for sleep. Pam tucked her in and left the room. The next day, Marie didn't seem to remember it had happened. Pam helped her get into her sweatpants and hooded sweatshirt, alarmed at her sister's skeletal frame.

Marie wanted to sit out on the beach, close to the house, to wait for Steve, who was coming from the city to take her back home. It was warm in the sun, but Pam wrapped her in a blanket, an extra layer against the wind off the water. The bright blue sky and the sounds of the wind and water hitting the sand, along with the calling of gulls, stirred a deep, visceral emotion. Marie let the tears fall once Pam was out of range. Marie and Jack had loved each other, or at least he'd pretended that he loved her, and the fun they had, the sheer rush of joy she had whenever they were together was never going to happen for her again. The knowledge that she wouldn't find it even with her baby made her sad. The wanton, forbidden edge that her relationship with him had would make every single thing pale in comparison. It was selfish and immature, but it was what she felt for him. Steve certainly would never be able to compete with Jack. *Am I still here?* Marie thought. *Am I such an ass that I'm crying over a ghost? Stop wasting your life and be grateful.* She struggled to get out of the chair and started walking down the beach. Somehow, she would get some strength back so she could return to work. Maybe her angst stemmed from inactivity.

Without warning, a premonition came over her; a vision of someone who she thought might be Pam, lying in bed with the family surrounding her. At the head of the bed, a priest with a rosary in his hand bent over and made the sign of the cross on a head. It was sudden and powerful, bringing Marie to a standstill. She looked over her shoulder at the house and determined that she was far enough from it to light up a cigarette and not incur her sister's wrath. The first drag almost knocked her to her knees. She stood with her back to the line of homes and faced out to sea; a position she'd taken many, many times over the years, often with Jack. She couldn't shake the feeling of doom. Marie hoping peace would return to her but the tranquil view did not deliver this time as it had so many times in the past. She remembered feeling abandoned by Jack when he would finally extricate himself from her to go and spend a few hours with his wife. She never let him go peacefully.

"Stay here, or I'll tell," was her common mantra. They often got into physical fights when Marie made demands that Jack didn't want to fulfill. He would hold his hand over her mouth, threatening to suffocate her if she didn't shut up. Another favorite involved Jack turning the tables on Marie, telling her that he would confess to Pam their longtime relationship and Pam would forbid her to ever set foot in the beach house again.

"You wouldn't dare!" Marie would scream. But Jack was convincing. He controlled their affair right up to the end. Week after week he made excuses not to see her, claiming it was on behalf of her sister, when all along he was seeing Sandra. Marie hiccupped a sob; if she had only known, she would have done something about it. The memory of seeing them on the street together, as she had the day he died, would permeate every moment of the rest of her life. There was no getting around it. He might still be alive if she had acted.

She heard her name being called and turned toward the house to look; it was Steve. Poor Steve, he looked so out of place at the beach. Steve belonged in a saloon, or at the track. She flicked her cigarette behind her, but he'd smell it on her, so it was no use hiding it. They walked toward each other.

"Are you ready to go back to civilization?" he asked, reaching out for her. They embraced and he bent down to kiss her, not mentioning her smoke breath. He had more pressing things to nag about her about now, like eating, or more importantly, going back to work. They would never survive on his pay alone.

"I guess so. I was just wondering if I would ever feel normal," she said, realizing that wasn't exactly what she was thinking, but it was close enough to distract him from asking anything too probing.

"Tomorrow, let's ask the famous Dr. Garpow," he suggested.

<hr />

Marie sat on the edge of the exam table and Steve was in a chair while they waited almost an hour for the doctor to come back. They played Sudoku and tic-tac-toe, made-up word games, and Scrabble on their phones. When Dr. Garpow walked through the door, Steve felt his discomfort.

"I'm sorry to tell you, Marie, but you have a brain infection. It won't be easy to treat. What I'd like you to do is to allow us to treat you at home; a visiting nurse will come and administer IV antibiotics and other drugs. You're too vulnerable to be in the hospital. There are too many resistant bugs and I don't want you exposed," he explained. Steve was numb. What did that mean? But he remained silent, hoping Marie would ask the difficult questions. He was afraid she would blame him if the answers were negative.

"What about the baby?" she asked, pale and shaking.

"The baby should be okay if you are okay. But it means several things, Marie. You have to take your antiretroviral drugs. You have to eat," he said. "Alcohol is out, totally. If you want to give your baby a chance, you must do as I tell you or there is really no point at all in either of us wasting our time." He went on to describe how the brain is infected with the AIDS virus itself, and the toxins given off by the virus begin to destroy brain tissue. Since Marie didn't know exactly when she became infected, it was uncertain how long she'd had the infection. If she wasn't treated, it could have devastating consequences. Steve knew Dr. Garpow was holding back. If they wanted more information, they could Google it when they got home; Dr. Garpow actually suggested it. When he left the room, Marie slid off the table and reached for her coat and purse. "Well, he didn't really tell us a fucking thing, did he?"

Steve knew she was scared; what she wanted to hear was that she'd be fine. "Does it mean I made myself sick by not taking the drugs?"

"No, for God's sake, that isn't what it means. You just found out you had the goddamned virus, remember? Get your sweater on and let's get out of here," Steve said, trying to keep it together for her sake. He thought of all the times she seemed irrational and now wondered if it wasn't AIDS eating her brain. He put his arm around her shoulder and pushed her out of the door in front of him. "Let's get something to eat before we go home. I saw a burger joint around the corner."

"I'm not hungry. I want to go home," Marie whined.

"What did the doctor just say? You have to eat or it will hurt the baby." He knew he was pushing, that he might even upset her saying it, but he didn't care. She had to eat or risk her health further. It didn't sound like she would be going back to work, either. He would talk to Pam about selling her apartment and then research getting her on disability. She'd worked for the past twenty-five years; there had to be something available for Marie. She'd earned it.

The smell of frying onions greeted them when they turned the corner. "Oh, that does smell good. Okay, I'll have something," she said.

"After we eat, I'll get you home and then I have to go to work," he said. "Will you be okay?" He decided to involve her family in every aspect of Marie's life from now on; he wasn't shouldering this responsibility alone, no matter what. He'd call Pam as soon as he had Marie situated.

After lunch, they returned to Steve's apartment and once Marie was settled in what was now *her* recliner with a bottle of water and TV remote, he left for work. Calling Pam on the way to the subway, he told her without holding back. He needed her help; Marie was very ill and unable to work. He explained his plan for getting her on disability if he could, but his biggest worry was leaving her alone all day.

But Pam heard only that Marie's brain was infected with AIDS, a progressive condition that was going to get worse if she didn't toe the line, and that the baby would be in danger if Marie didn't begin to comply. *Her brain was infected with AIDS. It was rotting in her skull.*

"Her mother is just five miles uptown. She needs to come down here and help out her daughter," Steve said.

Pam was sitting at the kitchen counter with her head in her hands. Steve was right; Nelda had gotten away with murder in regards to Marie and now she was going to have to step up to the plate and lend a hand. "Okay Steve, I'll call my mother. Thank you again for taking care of Marie today. Good-bye." She hung up without waiting for his reply. She started to cry. Marie could die. Having thought she'd dealt with the guilt over Marie already, it reared its head again. Marie had AIDS because she'd slept with Jack. And Jack had been able to abuse her as a teenager because Pam looked the other way. She owed her sister something. As much as she wanted to turn her back, the right thing to do was to help out in some way. But she couldn't take care of Marie herself. Having her at the beach for just two days, being aware that Marie needed help with activities of daily living, made Pam feel like she had a conjoined twin who needed to be bathed and dressed, fed and toileted. She couldn't do it permanently.

Pam moved to the sliders leading out to the veranda, and although it was cold and dreary, winter on its way, she grabbed a coat and went outside to sit. Her life wasn't complicated enough already. Now a pregnant, ill Marie had to be dealt with. Marie's confession last summer that she had conceived Jack's babies twice, once while she was in college and once shortly before he started dating Sandra, came to mind. He forced her to have abortions both times. *How was it that someone could relinquish her identity to the extent that she could be talked into such a sad and permanent thing when she didn't want it?* Pam closed her eyes for a moment, the surf hitting the sand with enough force that she could feel the freezing salt spray on her face, mingling with the tears that she allowed to fall. She had turned her back, ignoring signs, just like her mother had done. When an anorexic Marie was hospitalized for six months, her mother said someone, a therapist or a social worker, had suggested that their father may have abused Marie. When they came to the conclusion it was untrue, did anyone ever think that the next man in her life, someone she spent every waking minute with on the weekends, may have been at fault? The anorexia reached a serious state when she was sixteen; she admitted last summer that Jack started abusing her when she was fifteen. It took a year for the tragic consequences to unfold. She'd said Nelda took care of her when she had the second abortion. Did their mother know why she needed care? It was another example of someone's remarkable ability to stick her head in the sand.

Pam snickered out loud when she thought of poor, loser Steve. He'd really walked into a hornets' nest. *I bet he's kicking himself now for having stalked Marie.* He'd been transferred to her office and pursued her in spite of her begging him to leave her alone. *It serves him right.*

Before the call, the week had stretched out before Pam, empty yet full of possibility. Now, she'd have to go into the city to deal with whatever was happening with Marie and at Columbus Avenue. She couldn't go on allowing Nelda and Bernice to live in that moldering old place. She decided the wisest thing to do was to contact Peter Romney, Jack's former business partner, and ask him to help her market the property to a commercial developer. It would cause hard feelings in the community if they sold it to be divided, but Pam didn't care. It wasn't up to her to preserve the neighborhood. Once she had made the decision to sell, she couldn't get it done quickly enough. Peter would help her list Marie's apartment, too.

Pam was getting too cold to stay out any longer. She went back into the house, intermittently crying. Worry over her sister had to be the cause of the apprehension she couldn't shake. As she pulled the glass sliders closed, she noticed the waves. The wild surf was beating the sand away from the tide line, eroding the beach. In autumns past it was a sign that a destructive winter was coming. Pam would get a local handyman to erect snow fencing across the front of their beach area to help keep the snow from blowing against the house. She would make the call today. She felt an urgency to tie up loose ends; get the house ready for winter, call the lawyer about her will, make sure her children would be okay if she were to die. She was also waiting to get some kind of proposal from Sandra about the business. In a few days the children, Brent and Lisa, would be home for Thanksgiving. It was a mystery how that would play out. Would they pressure her into more information about the source of the AIDS she'd acquired, or would they choose to ignore the entire situation? So far, they'd inquired after her well-being and said nothing more. She would have to approach them about their interest in their father's business; hopefully, that crucial issue would take them through the holiday. Slowly introducing Dave to her dilemmas gave her some relief, and he often had some helpful ideas.

"I don't have kids, but my brother and I inherited the store when we were about your kids' ages. I'd present them with the idea of taking over from Sandra," he suggested. "Young people are fearless. Who's the other guy? Your husband's partner? He should love that," Dave chuckled.

Pam wasn't sure what to think. "Neither of my kids has ever worked. I guess that isn't such a good thing, but at the time it seemed right. They were always too busy. I certainly don't want it," she said, referring to the business. Pam thought of her selfish, protected life. Work? She'd probably starve first. "Let's not get ahead of ourselves. Besides, it's making me nervous talking about it."

Dave looked at her with concern, noting a pattern that had emerged over the weeks they'd been seeing each other. Pam didn't like confronting anything that might cause dissension. He could see her getting nervous as they talked, wringing her hands, and barely able to sit still, jumping up to pour more coffee or straighten up imaginary clutter. She was making a gallant attempt to overcome it by forcing herself to talk, but the physical signs were still there. He thought, but didn't say out loud, that if those pampered kids of hers didn't want the business, he would take it. He had worked at the family store from the time he could talk. Wasn't it odd that Jack Smith hadn't involved his own children in the business? He didn't feel like it was a topic he could bring up to her, and it was a done deal now, with the man dead and gone. Each of the revelations Pam made regarding her life shed new light on the elusive Jack Smith. In all the years that Pam had shopped at his store, Jack had never accompanied her. Dave was curious about him, but Pam was tight with information, almost loyal in her refusal to get into details too deeply. It was obvious that her husband was a jerk. *She got AIDS from him, wasn't that enough?* Dave left her house that day knowing little more about the issue, and was willing to let it be for now.

Pam wandered around the house, being proactive by making lists and setting up appointments, trying to squelch her apprehension. Steve's calling her about the apartment had set the gears moving. Why in God's name did she need so many properties? The rent she received from Jack's apartment on Madison and Bill and Anne's house in the Village, was substantial; the latter was rented to a grad student. She didn't have to do anything about either place for now. But the housing thing kept popping up, first with the mansion and now with Marie's apartment. If she sold it, that would mean Marie had better stay in a relationship with Steve because she would have no place else to go. From the looks of things, she wouldn't be living alone ever again.

That settled it. Pam called Peter Romney and gave him power of attorney to sell the two properties.

16

Ashton made do with the young man he'd picked up at the bar until Jack missed him enough to come around again. Paul was a great kid. He came back to Ashton's apartment every night after work. A low-level accountant in a big firm uptown, he lived in New Jersey, an hour's commute away. Ashton's place was only a few blocks from his job. He loved Ashton's swanky place with its view of Roosevelt Island and its proximity to restaurants and shopping. And Ashton seemed happy to have him there, relinquishing the cooking and cleaning to Paul. The sex was sweet and sane. They played house for almost a week, and then on Friday, out of the blue, Jack showed up at lunchtime. Ashton was getting ready to leave for an appointment when the he heard a knock on the door. He'd given Paul a key, so it wouldn't be him. His heart skipped a beat as he went to the door and looked through the peephole. There he was, Adonis; perfectly groomed, sticking his tongue out, and crossing his eyes.

"So you don't call me anymore?" he asked as he walked past Ashton.

Ashton closed the door and placed the chain, just in case Paul decided to show up for lunch, too. Jack was loosening his tie as he sat down in one of the uncomfortable armchairs positioned by the window. Ashton noticed that Jack had lost weight. Probably from a week of debauchery.

"You leave me hanging all week? Boy, that's not a very nice way to treat someone who you are supposed to love." As usual, Jack fidgeted while he talked, running his hands through his hair, pulling on his earlobe, lining up his tie with the buttons on his shirt.

The antics usually drove Ashton crazy, but this afternoon he could only watch, leaning up against the wall with his arms folded across his chest. "Why didn't you call *me*?" Ashton asked. "Too busy with Blondie?"

Jack looked confused for a second, and then recognition crossed his face.

"Oh. Right. I had almost forgotten. You were stalking me. You know better. Pam needed me midweek; both kids are sick. A virus or something. She needed to run out for food and her mother couldn't get over," Jack explained.

Ashton did know better. Jack often got lonely for his family and would go to Babylon on Wednesday after work and spend the night, returning to the city with the rest of the commuters the next morning. He wondered why Jack couldn't admit it. Years later, he finally would. "I missed my wife, so I went home last night," he'd say. Ashton was glad that Jack had that much normalcy.

"So, did you miss me?" Jack asked.

Ashton saw the subtle change in Jack's face. He was ready to get down to business. "No actually, I didn't. Paul Friend was here all week," Ashton confessed. He looked to see if Jack would react, and all he did was smile.

"How was it?" Jack was an ardent voyeur. He knew Ashton wouldn't tell him details, no matter how much he begged. "Are we a better team?" he asked.

Ashton shook his head no and laughed. "I'm not telling you, so don't pry. Besides, you were only in Babylon Wednesday," Ashton challenged. "What'd you do the rest of the week? The question is did *you* miss *me?*"

Jack got up and walked toward him, smiling. "Why don't I show you?" He reached for Ashton's fly and unzipped with one hand, pushing him into a chair with the other. It was while they were in this posture, Ashton moaning with pleasure and about ready to ejaculate, when the door opened and banged against the chain.

"Hey! What's going on? Open up!" Paul yelled. The men separated and Jack went into the bathroom, leaving Ashton to pull himself together, bitching, and get the door.

"Just a minute," Ashton yelled. He was trying to keep himself from laughing out loud. He went to the door and pushed it closed so he could take the chain off. "I didn't expect you."

"That's obvious. I had some extra time so I thought I'd come home. Why'd you have the chain up?" Paul asked. No sooner were the words out of his mouth than Jack Smith sauntered out of the bathroom, looking like the cat that swallowed the canary. Ashton was mortified. It was clear that some hanky-panky had been going on.

"Oh. Well, shit," Paul said and then to Jack, "I should have known. Don't you have a wife and some kids who need you?"

Ignoring him, Jack said, "I'll leave you two alone now. I'm heading out." And to Ashton, "Call you later?" He reached over to kiss him, whispering, "You gave *him* a key?" Smiling, he left the apartment.

Paul was shaking with anger. "Does he come here every afternoon?"

"It's none of your business, Paul. You were very rude," Ashton admonished. "This is my apartment and I didn't expect you today. You should have called."

But Paul looked at him with surprise. "You are kidding, right? We have been together for a week! What was it to you? Play time? Didn't it mean anything?" Paul's voice was getting shrill, and he started sputtering and crying. "I thought we had something special! You said you loved me!"

Ashton was worried he would start screaming, so he tried to be gentle with him. "Would you like some water? Here, have a seat," Ashton said, leading him over to the chair he'd just vacated. The smell of sex lingered in the air and Ashton was hoping it would go unnoticed. He left to go to the kitchen and when he came back, Paul was standing by the door with his overnight bag in his hand, disgust on his face. *He must have recognized the odor. Oops.*

"I'm leaving. Go fuck yourself, Ashton." With that, he turned and left the apartment.

Ashton went after him to the elevator. "My key, please," he said. Paul reached into his pocket, got the key, and threw it at him.

"Suck my dick!" he yelled. Ashton picked the key up off the floor and rushed toward his apartment door. Fortunately, the elevator came quickly and was empty. Ashton watched from the safety of his apartment through the peephole as Paul got on the elevator, crying his heart out. Ashton felt badly because Paul was a really nice guy and they were good together, but not as good as Jack. No one would ever measure up to Jack. Paul would be the last man Ashton picked up and brought home for a while. He'd have one-night stands and finally, stopped even that much interaction. It just wasn't worth the risk of angering Jack.

17

Sandra spent the rest of the weekend aiming to see the good in Tom. They had fun on Sunday; Tom took her to his father John's cottage on the water in Bayside. His stepmother, Gwen, was a charming woman, twenty years John's senior. She and Sandra hit it off from the start. The two couples went to a flea market and then lunch; it would be the first of many outings together. Gwen was interested in Sandra, curious about the woman who had corralled her particular stepson when so many others had tried and failed. Sandra had expected an interrogation but Gwen gave an exposé.

"I don't know what you did, but I can see Tom is head over heels. Well, that's not true, I can see by *looking* at you why he would be attracted. He's almost fanatical about women, did you know that? John told me that he's never had a serious girlfriend because no one could ever measure up to his expectations," Gwen said, shaking her head. "How can that be in this day and age of permissiveness?"

Sandra blanched; what would Gwen think if she knew the truth about their introduction and the subsequent experiences the couple already shared? She felt sick. Here, she'd judged him for being provincial when he was forward enough in this thinking to embrace her in all of her perversity. *Why would a guy who was "almost fanatical" even give me a second look?*

"Well, I'm glad he would give me a second look," Sandra said. Unless Tom thought it was necessary, her HIV-positive status wouldn't be revealed at this family gathering. "He's really a wonderful guy!" Embarrassed at how weak it sounded, Sandra hoped the fact that she was living with him already was enough indication of her feelings for Tom.

"Have you met the rest of the family yet?" Gwen asked. When Sandra shook her head no, Gwen gave her a little smirk. "Well, you didn't hear it from me, but *don't* let them know you met John and me. The girls can't stand me and have cut John out of their lives. It's sad, actually."

"Tom didn't think they would mind me, or at least the idea of me. He said they weren't possessive," Sandra said.

Gwen seemed surprised. "I don't want to worry you because there is nothing you could do to change their opinions anyway. Just be yourself. Of course, they will be jealous of you because you are beautiful. Unfortunately, both girls look like their mother—a sort of gnomelike creature," Gwen confided in a whisper.

Sandra was taken aback but tried not to be judgmental. Evidently, Tom looked like his dad. "It must have been difficult coming into the family," Sandra replied, hoping she sounded compassionate enough.

"Did Tom tell you the story?" Gwen asked, seeming hopeful that Sandra would say no.

"Just that his parents are divorced, and he thinks you're wonderful," Sandra told her. The little prompting gave Gwen the opening she needed to launch into full disclosure.

"They were married for twenty-five years before he found the courage to leave. Did you know John's an alcoholic?" she asked, but didn't wait for Sandra's response, which would have been no. "They'd stayed together for the kids' sake, and when Tommy, who's the youngest, turned twenty-one, John left. The girls love to tell everyone I broke the marriage up, but it's a lie. We didn't even meet until the next year. He's a retired NYC cop, did you know that? I don't think I would have survived with him if he was still working. He walked a beat for all those years, riding the subway. Tommy's lucky he made detective so young, just in time to save his knees. Anyway, John was assigned to the park during a summer fitness expo and I was teaching a class for Crunch. The rest is history. He likes telling people that he had to chase me, but that's not true. I fell in love with him the first time we talked. I have a thing about uniforms...and he said he had a thing for athletes!" she exclaimed, laughing. "I saw admiration in his eyes. Later, I discovered that he tried all those years to involve his wife in things they could share and she wouldn't have any of it. We golf, hike, bicycle, you name it. You do any sports? You're in such good shape, you must work out, at least," Gwen said.

Sandra shook her head, trying to hide the horror she felt at the prospect of spending time on the golf course or in hiking boots with Tom's family. Tom had never said a thing to her about doing any of those activities. Walking to the park was the extent of their physical activity. Maybe socializing with the gnomes would be easier.

"Well, don't worry. I can see by your expression you aren't interested!" Gwen said, laughing again.

"I have an extensive wardrobe of spandex that I wear to clean house in. That's the extent of my exercise routine. Tom and I walk a lot, though, if that counts," Sandra answered, thinking that since she lost the baby, she'd taken to walking long distances when the sadness became too much for her. She put those thoughts away.

"I have an obsessive personality about it," Gwen admitted. Sandra thought of Pam and her daily, sometimes twice daily trips to the gym. "It grounds me. If I start to worry about something, there's nothing like a good run to clear the mind."

Sandra wondered if any of those "worries" would be shared, and was relieved when the men caught up with them. Tom was holding a bag with something that looked like a sword sticking out of the top.

"My son is pack rat, Sandra," John warned.

"Where does he keep it?" she asked.

"In my mother's basement," Tom answered. "Weapons. Hundreds of them."

Sandra thought, *Ugh, guns. I hate violence and I end up with a cop who collects instruments of murder.*

"Well, whatever makes you happy. I guess. I sort of collect books," Sandra said, thinking how dull it sounded. *I really am a dud.*

"She runs a successful demographic company! Don't let her fool you with putting herself down," Tom exclaimed, coming around to put his arm across her shoulder in a possessive stance. They started laughing.

"Well, whatever," Sandra said, embarrassed. Tom was certainly sending her mixed messages. Either he was proud of her or threatened by her. Which was it? She could see that perhaps she was being hasty; they were both young and immature. Maybe she'd better speak to him tonight, rather than guessing what she should do to make him feel more secure. The simplicity of it surprised her. *Am I stupid? Would I second-guess him and make another big mistake?*

The couples parted; John Adams hugging Sandra and telling her how happy he was that his son found someone so nice, and Gwen chiming in with the promise to call her later. Was Gwen going to be her new best friend? Sandra was confirming the wisdom of having no family. She hadn't talked to her own sister in over six months. There were moments when she definitely felt the absence of an intimate friend. But the criticism she knew would have been forthcoming if Sylvia knew the truth and how her life was evolving would be unbearable.

The car was quiet on the trip back to Williamsburg. Tom looked over at Sandra; her head back against the headrest, her eyes closed. Her eyelids were translucent, cheek, jaw, and collar bones prominent. He felt a rush of tenderness and concern for her. Reaching over to place his hand over hers, he thought of some of the things that had bothered him lately and how ridiculous and unimportant they were. He couldn't seem to shake the jealousy he felt toward a dead man. Some guy who was twice as old and a leech. He didn't have any control over Sandra's memories, but why would he doubt her commitment to him when Jack was dead? He had to do some soul-searching; he sensed she was holding back some feeling from him because of his reaction to her job, which was consistently unsupportive. She no longer shared her day-to-day experiences with him. Shamed, he was determined to overcome the resistance he felt when confronted with her job. He'd even surprised himself today when he praised her in front of his father. He *was* proud of her. Even though her business was acquired in a sort of clandestine way, Jack wouldn't have left it to her if he thought she couldn't be trusted to make a success of it; it would continue to support his family and he wouldn't risk that, would he? Tom decided he would be honest with Sandra and try to make amends. If she wanted to remain there as a partner, he would support her in it.

When the car came to a stop in front of his apartment Sandra opened her eyes.

"Wow, that was intense! I hope I didn't snore," she said stretching her arms above her head. "How long was I sleeping?"

"Not long, about twenty minutes. Listen, can we talk for a second? I want to say this while it's fresh in my mind," Tom said. Sandra nodded her head, curious. "I feel bad about the way I have acted, about being jealous of your job and giving you a hard time about Pam. I'm sorry that I was sharp with you the other night about being sad about the baby. That was really fucked-up of me. I won't make any excuses for myself. Forgive me?"

Sandra looked at his eyes, at the way he was looking at her with compassion and regret combined, and was happy that she was taking her time with this relationship. They were both so young; what did either one of them know about being committed? About compromise and tolerance? Not much. She'd be as patient with him as she had to be. If what Gwen said was true, and Tom was a fanatic about the woman he would be with, she should be honored. She decided to tell him.

"I'm honored that you want me," she said. "I'm honored that you allow me to share your life. I wish things could have been different, that we had known each other a few months sooner, and that none of the bad stuff had happened. But since it did and you still will have me, I am honored. I want to make you happy." She leaned over and met him in the middle; they held each other and kissed. Finally Sandra fell back against the seat laughing. "Well, one of the best things about us is your kiss! Oh my God! I love it."

Tom was embarrassed, but he smiled at her. "Let's go inside," he said, grinning a devious grin. "There are other good things about us and I want to have some of it now."

18

Jeff Babcock lived down the beach from Pam and Jack Smith for fifteen years, but it wasn't until Jack died and Jeff briefly dated Marie Fabian that he and Pam became good friends. He was more than a confidant of hers; she assumed that role for him, as well. Days before Thanksgiving, he was crossing the sand in the worst wind storm Long Island had had in over ten years to make sure his friend was okay. Her phone had gone unanswered for the past three hours. He went around to the front of the house and through her garage as was their agreement, and when she didn't answer the door, he let himself in through the mudroom. He called her name three times and then listened for a full minute. Fearful that she had taken ill—it had happened before—he cautiously walked back to her bedroom suite, and knocking on the door, waited another few moments before he opened it. He saw her right away, on the floor by the side of the bed. He ran to her calling her name, but she didn't respond. He didn't bother to wait, got out his cell phone and called 9-1-1. Kneeling next to her, he determined that she was breathing, and although her color was awful, her pulse was strong and regular. He carefully rolled her over on her side and covered her with a blanket. After he unlocked the front door for the squad, he went back and sat on the floor next to Pam, patting her back and telling her she would be okay, that she wasn't alone. The squad finally got to the house and gently picked Pam up off the floor for the ride on a stretcher. Once she was out of the house, Jeff started to cry. He and Pam had become dependent on each other and when she got sick, he felt like the rug had been pulled out from underneath him. She said much the same thing when he traveled to Spain with his mother in September.

"I'm so thrilled that you had the opportunity to get away, but I felt completely abandoned by you!" she'd laughed, but Jeff felt awful.

"I'll never leave again," he said. But they were just kidding each other. Pam's new boyfriend didn't fully understand the dynamic that drove the friendship until this latest hospital scare. Unlike Andy, who would use his policeman's authority to invade Pam's privacy while she was unconscious, Dave would listen to Jeff when he called him to notify him that Pam was ill.

"This is Pam's neighbor, Jeff Babcock. I wanted to let you know that she is in the hospital." Jeff let a second pass for Dave to ask questions and when there was shocked silence, he continued. "I tried calling her all morning and when she didn't answer, I came over to make sure she was okay. I found her unresponsive; I called for the squad. They just came to get her."

"I don't know what to say," Dave said. "What could be wrong with her? She was fine yesterday!"

"You know how she is, working out like a fiend and not eating enough to keep a bird alive. I bet it's something minor like that. She's had this before, where she gets depleted and it takes her down. She doesn't like anyone seeing her without makeup and a hairdo, so it's best if we both

Prayers for the Dying

stay away until the hospital calls me that she is awake. I'll call you as soon as I hear anything. Does that work for you?" Jeff asked.

"Okay, please do let me know right away. Thank you for calling me, Jeff." They hung up and Jeff went back into Pam's bedroom to her closet and retrieved the overnight bag that contained everything she needed for an emergency room visit. It turned out that she was simply suffering from exhaustion and after an EKG came back showing a normal heart, they discharged her. She was waiting in the lobby, embarrassed and contrite, when Jeff came to get her. Jeff was her rescuer.

He told her about his call to Dave and she resolved to phone him as soon as she got home.

"What would I do without you? Jeff, you are my best friend," she said. "I hope I can pay you back some day."

He patted her hand. "You pay me back every day just by being there for me. Thank you, Pam," he said. He dropped her off at the front door. She promised to call him later in the evening. She wanted to freshen up and get in touch with Dave. She was sure he was concerned and probably confused, as well.

"I was shocked to get the call from that guy," he said when Pam called him. "I've been worried all afternoon."

"That's why I'm getting in touch now, Dave. I knew you'd be concerned." She detected a tone in his voice and decided to ignore it; it could be her imagination.

"Why does Jeff have a key to your house, if I may ask?" Dave said.

Pam thought, *This guy is jealous of my gay friend?* However, she wasn't going to out Jeff, who was as private as she was. Not only that, but it didn't escape her that rather than asking about her health and well-being, Dave was concentrating on Jeff. *Oh shit, not another jerk.*

"He's my friend and neighbor, that's all, Dave. I trust him to be discreet, as he does me." She was praying that he would notice he hadn't said anything about her health before too long; if the conversation lingered on Jeff she would chalk it up to bad manners on Dave's part and call it a day. She couldn't be in another relationship that revolved around the man.

Dave was silent for several moments. "So how do you feel?" he asked.

"I'm better, thanks." She was biting her tongue and realized she was not going to ignore his bad behavior. "I was wondering when you were going to ask me."

"Well, since you're discharged already, there must not be anything wrong with you. False alarm!" he said, laughing.

Something about his cavalier attitude bothered Pam. It was one thing for the patient to laugh off an unnecessary trip to the ER, but quite another for an observer to do so. She was so relieved that she hadn't slept with him yet, and for a moment she never wanted to see him again. *Oh my God,* she thought. *I'm running through all the single men in town. First the cop, then the grocer. Who will be next? The hardware guy? My husband has only been dead for seven months. I'm going to end up with a reputation if I'm not careful. Would Dave tell his next girlfriend I have AIDS like that awful Andy did?* Pam's imagination went wild. She decided then to let him think that she was fine, that there was nothing wrong. She thought Dave wasn't going to be loyal to her. He was critical and jealous. She would be cagey about ending their relationship; let him think he was in control.

"Yes, false alarm! I probably would have come to if Jeff hadn't come by." A lie, but one that would serve.

"I'll bring dinner tonight," he said. "What are you hungry for?"

Pam had no desire to spend a quiet evening by the fire with Dave. But she had just said she felt fine; how would she get out of it? "The doctors said I need to rest. I might be fine and a false alarm as you said, but I was still unconscious for three hours. I better beg off tonight," she said with a hint of tiredness in her voice that was real.

"I'm sorry," Dave said. "Get some rest, then. We'll talk tomorrow?"

"Okay, tomorrow it is. Good-bye, Dave." She hung up without waiting for his reply.

19

By the time both of his children were in college, Jack was finding it more and more difficult to spend an entire weekend at the beach. He still loved Pam, but his "craziness," as his friends called it, was escalating. Ashton was getting worried about him, too. They were still close, but their relationship had taken on a platonic character as Jack aged and his testosterone level got lower and lower, their sexual acts limited to mutual masturbation.

"I'm worn out," he said. "Who'd have ever thought it? Me! Spent!"

Ashton was trying not to drop to the floor laughing. "Oh my God, now you're a drama queen, too! Honestly Jack, you should hear yourself. If you are worn out you should go home and stay there with your wife. From what I hear around town, she looks better now than she did ten years ago," Ashton said. "I don't understand what those other women are supposed to do for you. You have a beautiful wife waiting for you, and then you spend the evening with Maryanne."

"Don't talk about her. You don't know anything about it," Jack snapped defensively.

"That's my point! Why don't I know? It doesn't make any sense, Jack." Ashton wasn't going to let it go this time. He was tired of Jack's elusiveness. If Jack got angry and left, never to return, it would be the best thing that could happen for Ashton.

"What doesn't make any sense is for me to be with *you*," Jack said, hoping to leave a little sting behind. "I'm not gay. I'm a straight man, married with two children who are both in college. I have a lovely wife and a beautiful house on the ocean. And let's not forget, a gorgeous girlfriend waiting for me every night."

Ashton laughed out loud. "I hate to tell you my dear friend, but that blow job you just got? The one where you cried out my name and held onto my head like a basketball? You're gay! Oh Jesus Christ, you have really lost your mind." Once he stopped laughing he looked at Jack. Suddenly, it wasn't a laughing matter. Ashton saw the glassy look in Jack's eyes, the gaunt frame, stylish in its slenderness but the opposite of the healthy Jack, the vibrant Jack. He'd been watching his weight; the doctor said his blood pressure was high. But Ashton wondered if the doctor really said that—if he was really supposed to be watching his weight. Could Jack's HIV-positive status have converted? Did he now have AIDS? He walked to Jack's chair and bent over him, wrapping his arms around his old friend, his lifetime lover. He took Jack's chin in his hand and looked into his eyes. They told the story. Jack was dying. The whites of his eyes were slightly yellow, there was a vacancy in his stare that probably only Ashton could see. He knelt down next to Jack's chair and holding him, he started crying.

"How long have you known?" he whispered. "Why didn't you tell me?"

Jack reached up and stroked Ashton's back. "It had to happen eventually. What really irks me is that I had to start getting sick when Sandra came into my life. I think I love her, Ash. I think I want to be with her for the rest of my life, as short as that may be."

Ashton lifted his head up from Jack's shoulder. "Are you protecting her?" he asked. Jack could be careless about so much; Ashton hoped it didn't include keeping the woman he loved safe.

Jack wouldn't be drawn into the conversation; it was answer enough. He wasn't protecting Sandra, as he hadn't protected Pam or Maryanne or Dale or the other women he'd been with. He didn't care about them, because he didn't care about himself. "Don't cry, Ashton. I love you. You'll see; I'm not going anywhere. They say you can live a normal life with AIDS now."

"Yeah, but that's if you take the drugs for it, you fool! You should be taking everything they have to offer," Ashton said. "I take six pills a day."

Jack looked him, confused. "You take something for it? I didn't know," Jack said.

Ashton just shook his head. "We were together at the clinic, don't you remember? Oh, Jack." A fresh torrent of tears, but not for long. He wouldn't cry again for his beloved friend because the end was coming for their relationship. Ashton was tired of Jack disrupting the peace and rhythm of his life. He would no longer beg Jack to make time for him as he had in the past. Their morning coffee would be enough from now on. Ashton had made the vow to himself and it stuck. What troubled him was that Jack never asked for more. Was he being dragged into their relationship because Ashton demanded it? Pam would confirm it when she told Ashton after Jack's death that Jack hadn't really been there with her anymore. He'd responded, but never initiated. And he had a new young girlfriend who would later say that the sex was just so-so. Poor Jack was just tuckered out.

20

Nelda Fabian was doing the best she could to hide how annoyed she was at having her day disrupted. Pam called to report that Marie was ill; she'd been hospitalized over the weekend, and now her boyfriend had to go to work and wasn't comfortable leaving her alone.

"Mom, just go down there for a few hours a day until she up to taking care of herself. No one is asking you to move in with her," Pam said.

"How sick can she be that she needs a babysitter?" Nelda retorted with her usual compassion. "I finally have some time to myself and now I've got to start with Marie again."

"Mother, you've had time alone for the past thirty years. Marie needs someone to help her out and I can't do it. That leaves you. If you aren't able to, maybe you shouldn't be left alone, either," Pam said, hinting at the assisted living center two miles east.

Nelda huffed, "Well! You don't have to threaten me! I'll go! What's the address? I suppose I have to take the subway," she complained.

"Mother, when in God's name did you ever have to take the subway? Ben is right there at your beck and call. He'll drive you downtown." Pam was prepared to harp at her mother until she caved, and Nelda felt it. She noticed that her wimpy daughter was not going to back down. She had to admit it; the girl had gotten it together.

Nelda rode to Twenty-Third Street in a limousine. She sat in the back like a prim little bird and waited for Ben to get out and open her door, and then insisted that he help her up a flight of six stairs, even though in the mansion, she ran up and down flights of twenty steps without problem.

"Please wait until she answers the door," Nelda instructed Ben with her chin in the air. In less than a minute, the buzzer sounded and Ben opened the door for her. "Please come back for me in an hour."

Ben tipped his hat and turned his back to her to descend the steps, rolling his eyeballs. She could be impossible. He would call Pam to find out when to pick Nelda up.

Nelda expected Marie to be waiting at the door, so as she mounted the steps to the apartment, the tension built in her neck and shoulders. She set her jaw. *This child has been a pain from the beginning.* Nelda conveniently forgot the stress of having a mentally ill child while she was living at the mansion. She pretended to belong there, that the staff were her servants. She forgot about grandchildren and anorexia, dead husbands, and houses in Brooklyn. When she got to the top of the landing, the door was open a crack, so she pushed it open and went in.

The apparition sitting in the chair at the kitchen table wasn't anyone she knew. It was a skeleton with a ravaged face, scalp showing through bald patches of dirty hair, smoking a cigarette. She was sitting with one stick leg under her.

"Marie?" Nelda asked, unsure if she had walked into her death chamber or if this was the house of her daughter. The apparition blew cigarette smoke out in a stream and focused her eyes on her mother.

"That's me. So, mother! You made the trip down! Was it awful? Or did that limo driver take some of the effort from you?" Marie lowered her eyelids. "Did you come on your own? Or did Pam have to pay you to visit me?"

Nelda felt Marie's hostility. In times past, it would have angered her but this time she was frightened. She knew she'd been a bad mother, but since everyone had turned out okay, she thought maybe she'd gotten away with it. Maybe there wouldn't be any retribution. Now she wasn't so sure.

"Of course Pam didn't have to pay me! She told me you're sick and needed someone to come by and see you. If you are going to be mean to me, I'll leave," Nelda said, knowing that if she did, there would be hell to pay.

"Leave. It won't be any sweat off my ass. As you can see, I'm not in any position to make you stay." Marie took a last drag off the cigarette and smashed it out on a saucer. She got up from the chair slowly, Nelda gasping at the vision. *Was Marie on crystal meth?* Nelda watched enough TV to know what drugs did to people. Something was definitely not right.

Marie noticed her mother's shock. "Yeah, I look like hell, don't I?" She walked to the sink, holding onto chairs and the counter as she made her way slowly across the room.

Nelda finally came back to reality. This was her daughter! She'd make amends for neglecting her as a small child. There was obviously something very wrong with Marie. Nelda put her purse down on a kitchen chair and started taking her coat off. "Do you need water?" Nelda asked as Marie fumbled at the sink.

Once Marie had reached the sink she'd forgotten why she was there. It didn't look to Nelda like she knew how to turn the water on. Nelda walked around the table to the sink and stood next to her daughter. "Can I help you?" she asked gently. *Oh God, no.*

"I need something," Marie said, confused, trying to figure out what the faucets were for.

Nelda was confounded. Did Pam know her sister was this bad off? Nelda opened cupboards until she found a glass. "How about some water?" Nelda filled the glass part way and held it for Marie, not sure if she had the strength to hold it up to her mouth. *What in God's name has happened to my daughter?* She would call Pam as soon as she could. Gently putting an arm around Marie, Nelda prompted her to walk toward the couch. "Would you like to sit down?"

Marie followed her mother into the sitting area and slowly lowered herself onto the cushion. Nelda could see the bones of Marie's pelvis through the back of her sweatpants. Her heart started pounding. This was more than anorexia. "Here's an afghan," Nelda said, covering her. "Do you want the TV on?" But Marie had put her head back and closed her eyes. Nelda looked around the room for a telephone; there was one on a small dresser in the hallway entrance. She quietly walked into the back of the apartment, not noticing much about it except it seemed clean enough. She punched in the numbers to Pam.

Seeing it was Steve's number, Pam answered on the first ring.

"What the hell happened here?" Nelda whispered, the unaccustomed cursing evidence of her concern.

"I know, Mother. That's why you needed to be there. What condition is she in today?" Pam didn't want to divulge more than was necessary, unless Marie was in agreement.

"She couldn't even pour her own glass of water because she couldn't figure out the faucet. What's wrong with her?" The magnitude of what it could be was lurking in Nelda's mind, but she didn't know the cause. *Had Marie lost her mind?* she thought in her simplicity. Pam decided to stick to basic facts.

"She has some kind of brain infection, Mother. Steve brought here for the weekend, and half the time I'm not sure she knew where she was. She had a doctor's appointment this morning." Pam's concern was growing; the temptation to start worrying about what was going to happen was strong. They should really start making some kind of arrangements for Marie's care.

"Oh no, that sounds so awful. How did she get a brain infection? It doesn't make any sense. Why isn't she in the hospital?" Nelda often revealed her intellect at the worst possible time.

"The hows and whys are not important, Mother. Who knows? The doctor said she is too vulnerable to stay in the hospital because of resistant bacteria or something like that, so they're going to treat her at home. A visiting nurse is supposed to come by later this evening to start an

IV and give her some drugs." Nelda's anxiety was transferring to Pam. *What the hell are we going to do about Marie?*

"Mom, I'm hungry!" Marie yelled. She'd roused out of her somnolence long enough to feel pain in her stomach.

"Let me go; she's calling for food," Nelda told Pam. They said good-bye.

Pam hoped that in her stupor, Marie would reveal all to her mother and therefore take the burden of proof off Pam.

Nelda set about doing nurturing tasks for her youngest daughter, who would drift in and out of sleep for the rest of the afternoon. When Steve got home, Nelda cornered him without mercy. "What is going on?" she demanded. "My daughter can't even bathe herself."

Steve was backed up against a wall, literally. "Hi, my name is Steve. Who are you?"

Nelda visibly relaxed and gave a rare laugh. She stuck out her hand to shake his. "I'm Marie's mother, Nelda Fabian. I'm sorry. This is just such a shock. No one told me she'd been sick." She turned and went back into the sitting area to see if Marie was still sleeping, pulling the afghan up around boney shoulders. "I know from just the few hours I was here today that she can't stay home alone." Nelda turned to look at him. "I'd like to take her home with me, to the mansion. I'm sure Pam will agree. You are welcome to come, too, of course."

The offer was so welcome that Steve fought the urge to embrace Nelda, whose reputation for being a cold bitch preceded her visit. But the truth was that if Marie was so bad that Nelda was bathing her, her AIDS status needed to be revealed as well as the pregnancy. *This is turning out to be a huge cluster fuck. What the hell did I do to deserve this?*

⁂

Pam and Steve spoke briefly on the phone and agreed that Nelda needed to be told the truth if she was willing to care for her daughter. But who would do it? Pam didn't want to, but she didn't think it was fair to unload the task on Steve. In the end, they decided to get Marie to do it in one of her lucid moments, which occurred throughout the day. He walked out into the kitchen where Nelda was making tea. Marie was up, sitting at the table, looking better.

"My mom's here," she said to Steve, winking at him. "Surprise, surprise."

Nelda wasn't laughing. "What's that supposed to mean?" she asked. "I come when I'm needed."

Marie decided to cut her a break. "Yeah, you do most of the time. So how'd work go, Steve? Who's going to take my projects?" They chatted about business for a few minutes, Steve putting her mind at ease.

"I've got your back, honey. Don't worry about work." Nelda listened to the exchange and it brought tears to her eyes. It was obvious that Steve cared for her daughter.

"So I think we should tell your mom our news, Marie." Steve walked around to the back of her chair and hugged her.

Marie looked up at him, fear and a little confusion mixed together. "You do? Oh boy," she said.

Nelda was frozen in place. Steve placed his hand over Marie's sunken belly while Nelda looked on, stunned. She figured it out right away; Marie had to be pregnant. *Great!* Nelda thought. *Pregnant and a brain infection! How much worse could this get? One daughter with AIDS and now a pregnant imbecile.*

Marie looked up to speak to Nelda. But by the look on Nelda's face, a grimace almost, even a confused Marie got it that her mother was on to her. "Well, did you figure it out, Mom? I'm pregnant! Forty-five, fucked up, and pregnant. But I'm happy about it and want the baby, so don't start with your negative crap."

"I would *never* say anything negative about a baby on its way! If you had asked me when you were trying, I may have advised against it, but not after it's already there. You must have me confused with someone else." She stood at the sink folding a towel, observing her daughter.

Marie wasn't finished though. "Yeah, well it wasn't like we were trying, okay? I didn't *set out to get pregnant*, if that's what you're driving at." She looked up at Steve and smiled. "Stevie, I think now is as good a time as any to break the *other news*." Steve took a step toward her. He was not sure why but he had the impulse to clamp his hand across her mouth.

Nelda saw the gesture and felt his intention and she started to laugh. "Oh, my! I know exactly what you're feeling. You don't know how many times I have wanted to shove a sock down that throat just to shut her up!" What she had just revealed embarrassed her; she didn't intend to expose such an intimate and negative feeling to a complete stranger.

Marie frowned. "Thanks, Mom. Maybe that's why I grew up at Pam's house."

Prayers for the Dying

Fortunately, she stopped there. Steve was panic-stricken, wanting Nelda to take Marie with her. If AIDS or HIV or Jack, the child molester, were brought up, they'd never leave.

"I think it's more important to get you settled uptown. We can continue this conversation there, okay you two?" Steve urged Marie to get up. "Come on, you can't go out dressed like this." Nelda watched him but didn't offer to help. *There's more here than meets the eye*, she thought, suspicious. The couple disappeared back into their bedroom.

"Where are you taking me?" she asked.

"Your mother is going to nurse you back to health up in that mansion. The life of Riley!" he said cryptically.

Marie started pouting. "I don't want to go up there. I want to stay with you." she raised her arms up while he pulled her sweatshirt off.

"I was invited. But you can't stay here alone during the day," he explained. "Let's try it out tonight and if you really hate it, I'll come and get you after work tomorrow. That might be a plan. You can stay up there while I work." They pulled a few things together, a book she was reading and her makeup bag and a few clothes. He'd bring up more of her things later. They walked out to the kitchen together, Marie looking slightly better in clean clothes, but still in need of a major weight gain. Nelda couldn't believe that Marie's decrepit frame could maintain a pregnancy.

"I'll drive us up in Marie's car so we can leave it there, if that's okay. We only have street parking here," Steve said. "Should we call and announce our intentions?"

"Good idea," Nelda said. "Can I have the phone?" Steve retrieved the phone and Nelda called and spoke with Mildred. She would get a room ready for Marie.

Steve stashed everything in the trunk of Marie's car. Nelda and Marie sat in the back seat, silent. Steve looked at them in the rearview mirror; mother and daughter had the same facial structure and although Nelda wasn't a bad looking woman, compared to her daughter, she was gorgeous. Marie's illness was ravaging her appearance.

They arrived at the mansion and Nelda instructed Steve to drive through the gate to the private entrance at the back of the house; the door the help used. He wondered if she was being cagy because her daughter looked so bad. A uniformed man, probably their driver, was waiting, along with a younger woman in surgical scrubs. Nelda introduced them as Ben and Candy. Candy got Steve's attention and he hung back as Mildred and Nelda helped Marie into the house.

"Miss Pam called a few minutes ago. She told me about Marie having AIDS. I don't see any reason for the rest of the household to have that information, okay? I didn't know if you already mentioned it to Nelda or intended on doing so?" Candy asked.

Steve shook his head no. "If Marie wants to divulge it to her mother, she can do that in her own time. I wanted to get her settled first. Are you a nurse?" He was clearly confused. Who else worked here?

"No, I'm Mrs. Smith's personal care assistant, but I worked as a nurse's aide at Lenox Hill for years," she explained. "There's plenty of time for all revelations to be made."

He followed her into the house, looking around in amazement at the space. His entire apartment would fit in the kitchen alone. Mildred led the entourage through the expansive house and up a daunting staircase to a bedroom at the top. It was a generic guest room, but comfortable, and Nelda's room was across the hall so she would be available if necessary. Marie would have her own bathroom, with bulbous, old-fashioned fixtures and a giant stained-glass window above the tub. It was very church-like.

Marie looked around at the high ceilings and ornate moldings, the damask drapery, and satin bedcovers. "I feel like you guys are preparing for me to die," Marie said.

Bernice joined the group and they all murmured placations. Only Steve stayed silent. *Why am I leaving her here? Is it only because she needs care during the day? Or is it her last resting place before she dies?* His thoughts unnerved him and he stepped forward, grabbing her and hugging her. This was his Marie. "Oh God, no! Don't even say that! We want you to be safe and taken care of so you'll get better. When the baby comes, you want to be able to take care of him yourself, don't you?" He looked down at her, staring into her eyes. She looked so awful, emaciated, and haggard. He had to choke back the tears.

But Marie was slick. She might not let on that she knew what the MO was. She played dumb so that Steve could go home and get some rest before another day at work. As far as her mother was concerned, she planned to run her to death. Her mother would be the scapegoat for the years of abuse at the hand of Jack, and all the detritus he left behind.

21

Pam called the mansion after eight for an update from Candy. Marie was resting comfortably in her new room, calling out orders and requests so that Nelda hadn't stopped since they'd arrived. She'd eaten a substantial dinner and was watching TV and talking on the phone to Steve, who'd left a while ago, taking the subway back downtown. Breathing a sigh of relief, Pam felt like she could put Marie aside now and deal with her own issues for a while, the most pressing being Dave from Organic Bonanza. She paced, attempting to formulate a narrative to use when she called him. She made a cup of tea and took it into her bedroom, sitting on the chaise with the tea nearby and the phone in her hand. He hadn't called her since their discussion regarding Jeff Babcock. She punched in Dave's number and sat back waiting for him to answer.

"Hello. I wondered if you were going to call tonight," he said with just a hint of accusation.

"Yes, I'm sorry; I had a problem with my sister today. She's too ill to be left alone while her boyfriend goes to work, so I had to call my mother to go downtown. Once she got there, she determined that my sister needs her care around the clock. So I've basically been on the phone for the past four hours," she explained.

"How old's your sister?" Dave asked, confused.

"Forty-five," Pam answered, worried that any explanation she offered that didn't include AIDS or pregnancy would sound defensive. But she kept silent. It was bad enough that he knew about her physical condition without exposing her sister's, too.

"Why do you need to run interference for your forty-five-year-old sister?" he asked.

She was silent for a moment. Why indeed? "She's too ill to make wise decisions right now. It's just what our family does for each other," she said, thinking *maybe my needy family will be my graceful way out of this relationship.*

Dave snickered. "Hey!" he exclaimed, changing the subject. "I've got salesmen for holiday merchandise coming in all week so I'll be busy during most lunchtimes. If I can get away, I'll call you before I come, okay?" He'd never been unavailable during lunch before.

"No problem," she said. "I have to go into the city tomorrow and I don't know when I'll be back." She'd let him say good-bye. It was the least she could do.

It took him a minute to decide. Was this it, or was it just a break? She had to hand it to him. "Okay Pam, have a safe trip in. Talk to you later." And he hung up.

Was he leaving a door open? she wondered. *Do I care?* Pam took her tea to the den. It was dark, but the landscaping lights illuminated enough of the beach for Pam to see that although some of the snow was still on the ground, most had either melted or been blown away. She sat in her overstuffed, leather chair with one leg under her. She aimed the remote at the fireplace and a flame burst on, lighting up the dark, shedding a mysterious gloom over the room. Not thinking about anything in particular, Pam burst out laughing. For a moment she was unexplainably at peace. It didn't make any sense, with all the turmoil around her. But without warning, it occurred to her that she had forgiven herself. In a split second, she'd stopped rationalizing for Jack, stopped making excuses, and inexplicably decided to cut herself a break. She couldn't do anything to turn back the clock, and she had so much at stake. Since there would be opportunities for others to blame her; she needed to be strong for herself. The children would be home for Thanksgiving. She planned to make it a fun time like it was when they were kids. Their friends would come to the house like they used to. She'd have a big meal with all of their favorite Thanksgiving foods. The only thing missing would be Jack. Jack and Marie. She let her imagination run with the image of their faces. Jack and Marie, leaving to golf. Jack and Marie running on the beach. How many times did she see Marie running up to the house, to be caught by Jack? He'd swoop her up in his arms, twirling her around while she screamed and he laughed. Lisa would be standing off to the side, watching. Was she jealous of her aunt? Of the attention given her by Jack? What had they been doing out of sight of the beach? She remembered walking out to Lisa and encouraging her to join in the fun. "That's okay, Mother," Lisa would say. What was okay? That Jack was playing with Marie? Or that she was being neglected? When questioned, Lisa swore that she felt she and Brent had had the perfect childhood. Pam could remember telling her mother the same thing when Nelda was doing some rare introspection of her parenting during one of Marie's anorexic episodes.

"Mom, you were fine!" Pam insisted. "Everything was fine!" *It hadn't been. But what was the point of digging up a child's nebulous complaints to justify a parent's guilt? Now, were my children doing the same thing? Were they protecting me from my own failings?* Her stomach started growling. She'd missed dinner. Getting up to go into the kitchen, she thought of the weekend nights when she'd be in her kitchen alone, preparing dinner for the family. The four would come in from their activities and Pam would serve them while they continued talking and laughing, or arguing. Marie confided recently that the children hadn't contacted her since Jack died. She was astonished, thinking the three were inseparable. But Jack was the glue that held Marie to the family. Marie didn't really care about Lisa and Brent or she would have stayed in touch. It was so depressing. Earlier, Pam had made a vow not to dwell on Marie and Jack, but the truth was that she had to come to terms with these revelations as they came to her and not push them back down. Remembering Marie's current status, Pam laughed. A lot of good it would do to try to pin anything on her now. And then a wave of sadness came over her. Her poor sister. She'd really been neglected and abused. It was too late to make amends. All they could do was try to make her comfortable and compliant. She got a banana and another cup of tea. It would have to do. She was too lonely to bother eating dinner. And that elusive peace? It was out the door.

22

For a very brief time, Jack and Ashton tried living together. There was nothing suspicious about it; after all, they'd been childhood friends. Harold didn't want Jack to move out, but after college when he refused to pay for Jack's graduate program, there was nothing obligating Jack to stay home.

"I'm going to move in with Ashton, and while I'm out of the house, I expect you to keep your hands off Bill. I'll make good my former threats if I hear otherwise," Jack told him quietly. Harold wanted to bash Jack's head in, but he was afraid of him, and had been afraid since Jack held exposure of molestation over his head.

"It's all in your imagination, Jack," was Harold's standard reply. Harold was a man with intimidating size. But sitting in a leather armchair having to look up at Jack diminished his stature. He was certain it would take more than the words of a pencil-neck college kid to bring him down, but the fear of it was always in the back his mind. Sex had been a game to his own father and uncles, as it had been with the generations before. Incest was an accepted practice in his grandfather's homeland and he had brought it with him to America. Exposure now would mean financial ruin, social catastrophe.

"Whatever you say, Dad. Just don't let me hear that you have been bothering Billy," Jack warned. "I'm leaving now. Tell Mom I said good-bye." He left quietly, before Bernice came down.

Billy was running up the sidewalk when he saw Jack leaving. Jack was his protector, his savior. His absence could only mean one thing for Billy and that was brutality at the hands of his father. They embraced but quickly separated in case Harold was watching.

"You're really gonna do it?" Billy asked. "He'll kill me if you leave, Jack!" The boy started crying, backing up, away from the view of the house. When they were standing behind a brick post, Jack grabbed him and hugged him.

"You'll be okay. I told him to leave you alone. Keep your door locked and don't come when he calls. I wish I had done it. I didn't know any better. But you do. Threaten him, Billy. Tell him you'll tell!" Jack lowered his head and began to weep. Calling the police wasn't an option; who'd pay the bills if Harold was arrested? Jack knew he was being a coward. He would regret being passive for the rest of his life. He hugged his brother again. "I love you, Billy. I'll always take care of you." Those words would come back to haunt him later.

Jack walked away from the mansion and his brother toward Broadway. He'd take the subway to the Village where he and Ashton would have two weeks of playing house. Ashton couldn't stand Jack's carousing, however, and when he laid down the law, Jack left happily. "I didn't like you in the role of Mother, anyway," Jack told him.

"What the hell is that supposed to mean?" Ashton whined.

"I don't need dinners and laundry. I'll pay for that shit if I want it," Jack replied. "I need a playmate and a lover. When I walk in, I don't want to be reminded that I'm late or that I need to drink my orange juice or change my underwear." He went to their shared bedroom and began stuffing clothes into a suitcase. When he finished, he grabbed his jacket and walked over to Ashton, kissing him on the cheek. "I got an apartment Midtown, off Broadway and Thirty-Ninth Street."

"Jack, that's an awful neighborhood. What are you going to do? Turn tricks for extra cash?" Ashton sat down on the edge of the bed and starting crying.

"Oh great, here goes old waterworks. If there is anything that turns me off, it's you crying," Jack said. But he did go over to Ashton and hug him with one arm. "I'll call you later and you can come and help me decorate. We just can't live together." Jack secretly hated the Village anyway; it reminded him of college and youth and vulnerability. He was so done with being young. And sex with one person was boring. The alternative was to live alone and seek additional partners on the sly. Eventually, Jack wanted to get married and have a family. He wanted a sober wife and children who didn't feel threatened by their father, who could leave their bedroom doors unlocked and feel safe. That his ideal would be an isolated island in the center of a sea of depravity of his creation never ever entered his mind, even in the midst of his worst nightmares at the end of his life.

※

Jack dragged his suitcases out to the curb. A cab pulled up right away, hoping for a big fare out to the airport, but Jack was just going a few miles uptown. He was excited; it would be the first time he'd lived alone. He'd fantasized about what it would be like, how he'd be free to bring as many people there as he chose to, whenever he wanted. The first week would be filled with so much fun; he'd remember it as the best one of his life for many years. Old friends found their way to his door for weeks until the cops finally came, and seeing his old family name, gave him a warning to keep it down, or else. After the allure wore off and they found more intriguing places to party, Jack was free to start bringing new friends there. He experimented with new fetishes, too. Living alone gave him the freedom to live his life the way he wanted with no holds barred.

In contrast, it was at this time that he began the ritual of taking his mother out to lunch every Wednesday. Like all abused children, he made excuses for his mother's inability to protect him. He did love her, no matter what her omissions were. They never spoke of Harold, or Billy, or home. Their conversations were always about what was happening in town, politics, the arts, the latest *Times* editorial. As an adult, Jack developed a warm, loyal relationship with his mother. He slowly put aside the animosity he felt for his father, shoving the memories down, pretending they didn't matter. But in real time, they lurked; his father coming home from work, the sound of the limousine pulling into the driveway; his mother, sleeping off a drunken stupor, leaping up out of bed to shower and dress. The boys always being freshly showered at the dinner table because afterward, Harold's other appetites would come to life.

Jack's early heterosexual encounters revolved around flashbacks of his father's punishing abuse. Later, he would substitute other images; music, or beautiful women, or the ocean, the moment painful memories tried to dominate his thoughts. He learned that there was a special place where he could cultivate the more violent desires he was curious to explore. Ashton, actually, was the one who introduced him to the place where those antisocial behaviors would be accepted, encouraged, even developed further when he was unable to accommodate Jack.

"Look, I understand what you want from me, but it's not going to happen, my friend," Ashton said seriously. But his inner monologue was laughing. Jack liked the full regalia of sadomasochistic practice, including the leather chaps and dog collars. He'd already spent a small fortune on whips and chains and had a wall in his bedroom with Peg-Board and hooks where he arranged the props. The first time Jack dressed up for Ash, he had to put a pillow over his face to keep the neighbors from hearing his hysterical laughing. Jack was insulted and refused to speak to Ashton for days afterward, and never again about "leather."

For the "messiest" of his desires, he had tile installed on the floor and walls of a small office in the rear of the apartment. If things got out of hand, all he had to do was get a bucket of soapy water and a mop. He installed a weight-bearing hook in the ceiling and it became one of his most useful devices. When he was alone in the apartment, he used it to perform circus-type exercises, such as suspended summersaults and upside-down hanging, for relaxation. When he admitted to Ashton that he often used the hook by himself, an argument ensued.

"So what you're saying is that if a cop comes to my door and asks if I know you, it could be because you were found strangled to death in your golden showers room," Ashton complained.

"You're nuts! I'm not into any kind of autoerotic strangulation. No, I promise you I won't strangle myself," Jack said, thinking *it may be the only thing I'm not into*. It was why Jack didn't drink or take drugs. He liked being aware of every single moment.

His hole-in-the-wall off Broadway would be a hidden place of respite, remarkable only for the number of strangers who'd been there as the perverted partners of Jack Smith.

23

Historically, Thanksgiving at the beach meant two things; continuous food and card games until two in the morning. Dave still hadn't called Pam back and she didn't see him at Organic Bonanza. It was a mixed blessing; she missed his companionship, but was happy that she didn't need to worry about him judging her again. The altercation over Jeff Babcock had been an eye-opener. Not having him around meant she didn't need to worry about introducing him to her children. Brent came in Tuesday night and had arranged for a friend to pick him up in Newark and bring him home. Lisa flew in to Kennedy on Wednesday and Brent picked her up with a group of her friends. Until that week, Pam hadn't felt much joy since Jack had died. She was home, preparing for the children's arrival, changing their bedding, putting fresh flowers all over the place, stocking up on their favorite foods. It was almost like old times.

Not a big baker because Nelda and Marie usually took care of it, she began making pies the weekend before, going to a local stand and getting apples and the last of the tart cherries. Her mind was an empty vessel while she baked. She listened to the radio, or talked on the phone with Jeff Babcock or her sisters. Susan was staying in New Jersey for Thanksgiving, on call for her dental practice; and Sharon was going to her mother-in-law's. It didn't escape

Pam that neither sister invited her to share the day, even though they'd spent Thanksgiving at the beach house for more than twenty years. Nelda and Bernice were going to be at the mansion with Marie and Steve.

That no one thought to include her and her children six months after Jack died was simply a breach of etiquette. Or was it? Could it be that people came here to enjoy the house and didn't really care about her? Pam felt her blood pressure rising as she allowed these thoughts to dominate. Apple and paring knife in hand, she stopped peeling and resolved that she wasn't going to pump negativity into her fruit pies. Looking out over the ocean, she decided not allow anyone to have control over her opinion of herself.

Making Thanksgiving dinner for her children and their friends was enough. She was grateful not to have a huge crowd for the day—having to bite her tongue, or be nice to her mother and sister, or deal with her nieces and nephews. There were so many pluses about it; she found it shocking that she'd formerly enjoyed hosting the entire clan. She started peeling again. But it was hopeless. The memory of Jack and Marie sitting in the kitchen, kicking each other under the kitchen table popped into her head. At the time she thought it was nothing more than childish tormenting, Marie purposely trying to make Jack lose his composure. But now she wondered if they weren't doing more, playing footsy, or worse. Suddenly, Pam had a thought: She would ask Marie to come clean. She wanted to know more about Jack's betrayal. *Did he have any respect for me?* She thought of the old cliché, Curiosity killed the cat. Her hairdresser had a rebuttal: Satisfaction brought it back. The relationship between Pam and Marie was already on such tenuous ground that nothing more could hurt it. *Yes, I am going to ask for details.*

A big concern of Pam's was the dialogue about AIDS that was bound to occur while the children were home. She would answer any questions they had, but the latest ER visit would remain a secret. The doctors couldn't find any reason for her periods of unconsciousness, and didn't relate them to AIDS or any other condition. It would worry her children unnecessarily if they knew.

"It could simply be your body's response to stress. You said you've had a lot of it lately, correct? Pam, try to stay away from stress if you can," the last doctor told her.

She giggled to herself. Stay away from stress? Good luck.

As she was sliding a pie into the oven, the phone rang. It was Jeff Babcock.

"Well, are you alive?" he asked.

Pam laughed. "Oh yes, I'm baking pies! My children are home from school and running around with their friends," she said.

"I'm glad you're doing better. You sure know how to worry a guy," he said.

"Thank you for being there for me, Jeff. I hope it's the last time I need you. Are you getting ready for turkey day?" Pam asked, hoping to change the topic.

"Well, my plans just fell through. My sister-in-law called and my brother is sick. Flu, they think. Do you have extra room at your table?" Jeff asked.

It was uncharacteristic of him to be so forward. Pam thought for just a second before she answered him. Having a stranger there might be a good thing—a buffer to ensure against any intense conversation. "My friend! Please do come. I'm cooking about the same amount of food I did when we were expecting thirty people," Pam said.

"Great! Thank you so much. I was hopeful you would have room for me. Can I bring anything? I was taking vegetables to my brother's," Jeff said. "Roasted root veggies and sautéed mixed mushrooms."

"Vegetables would be fine. We have a few standards at our house that I'll make, as well." Since Jeff was a graduate of the Culinary Institute of America, she added, "Very non CIA...green bean casserole and spinach-and-artichoke casserole." She started laughing.

"Oh wow! With canned soup and canned French fried onions? I love that!" Jeff said.

"Okay, let me get back to my pies. I'll see you tomorrow at five sharp," Pam said. She hung up the phone and was just turning to go to her room to freshen up when the phone rang again. Thinking it was Jeff again she allowed her jocular mood to show through her voice, sing-songing, "Hello." But it was her mother.

"Someone's in a good mood today. Must be nice to have something to be happy about," Nelda growled.

"Yes, Mother! How nice to hear from you today. What can I do for you?" Pam said, turning back to the kitchen. She'd wash mixing bowls while her mother complained. "How's the patient today?"

"She's running me ragged, that's how she is. But Marie isn't why I'm calling. I noticed you didn't invite us to have dinner with you tomorrow," Nelda replied.

"I wanted to have dinner with my children here. I noticed you didn't invite us there, Mother. Since my husband just died six months ago and I've been ill, it would be the least you could have done," Pam said. She wasn't taking any crap from Nelda about Thanksgiving.

"Well!" Nelda exclaimed. "Having a little tragedy in your life doesn't give you the right to be disrespectful to your mother!"

Pam could hear Nelda begin to weep. *Oh crap, I don't want to make her cry.*

"We've spent every holiday with you since Genoa was alive! Daddy and I drove her out to Babylon the first year you lived there, and she died two weeks later. All she could talk about was what a wonderful time she had! Why's that have to stop? Why? If you are too tired to make dinner for us, for heaven's sake, ask for my help! I can't read your mind, Pamela." Nelda stopped to blow her nose, snorting loudly into the phone.

Pam pulled the phone away from her ear. Maybe she was being unreasonable. She'd only wanted to be alone with her kids to be free to talk. But now Jeff was coming. "I see your point. Well, of course, if it means that much to you, come." What would Steve and Marie do if Nelda came here? What about Bernice? *Oh, for God's sake.* "You might as well bring everyone else. Just let me know by tonight how many are coming so I can set the table."

Nelda agreed and said she'd call after dinner. Pam walked toward her bedroom to get out of her flour-covered athletic suit and the thought crossed her mind that she'd better warn the children about Marie's appearance. What she had hoped to avoid was about to be realized. Maybe she would let them think that Marie *was* a crystal meth addict.

24

Ashton and Jack slowly fell into a new routine that would take them to the end of Jack's life. During the week, they got together every morning for coffee before Jack traveled downtown to his office. Rarely, they would meet for sex; although they didn't call it that. Jack would call Ashton in the middle of the day and ask him if they could "reconnect." "I miss you," he'd say. Ashton never refused him. They would lie in bed together and hold each other, Jack often falling asleep for a few minutes in Ashton's arms. Even Jack's breathing concerned Ashton; was he the only one who noticed how sick the man was? After Jack's death, it was clear that no one else did notice. Jack continued meeting Maryanne at the diner, but he went up to her apartment less and less often. He still refused to talk about her to Ashton. He stopped seeing Dale and the others.

But Jack mentioned Sandra's name more and more often, always in terms of praise. *Sandra discovered discrepancies in lot lines of a building project that would save millions of dollars. Sandra wore a Camali knit dress that showed every curve on her body. Sandra agreed to spend the night with him.* They never went to his Madison Avenue flat, but always to a hotel. Sandra didn't want to go to her apartment, either. "If you dump me, I'll have your memories where I live," she'd explained. Jack thought she was brilliant; here was a woman who stood up for what she wanted and wouldn't compromise. Ashton thought that she sounded like a self-centered youngster who would get involved with a married man and not give his wife a thought. *Ha ha! What about me?* Ashton had been jealous of Pam. He'd never regretted taking time with Jack away from her. They were all amoral pigs.

◊

Sandra Benson put herself in neutral for the long weekend. Tom's family had traditions that were sacrosanct. He had brunch with his father and Gwen and dinner with his mother and sisters. Football was center stage. They got up early and had coffee together before leaving for Bayside. It was Tom's responsibility to stop at a local baker and get a pastry tray for brunch and a pie for dinner. Sandra didn't get it; it was clear from looking at both John and Gwen that nothing like one of the gooey caramel rolls Tom ordered would ever cross their lips.

A few days after their flea market expedition with John and Gwen, Tom had taken Sandra to meet his mother and sisters. His mother was adorable, but he sisters were real bitches. Faith and Emma had deluded themselves into thinking they preferred lonely, celibate lives that allowed nighttime cookie binges and ice cream pig-outs instead of relationships leading to independence from Mom. Tom's mother, Virginia, was the sweetest little Scottish woman. She had a thick accent in spite of having come to the states forty years before. She worshiped Tom, and her adoration included anyone he was going to bless with their presence. He didn't bring dates home. His sisters tried to get him to date their friends, and friends of friends. They even signed him up for online dating. But he wasn't interested. He was waiting for Sandra.

When they pulled up in front of the apartment, Sandra thought she saw a quick motion at the window. They were waiting for a glimpse. They didn't expect Sandra. Emma thought Tom would have a short, chubby girlfriend and Faith said she'd always pictured him with a small, athletic type, like a tomboy. Both of them held their stomachs in and tried to smile, but it was hopeless.

Sandra's presence would ruin Thanksgiving for both women. How could they put the feed bags on when Twiggy was in the house? After that initial visit, Emma begged Virginia to let Tom go to his father's for Thanksgiving dinner, but she was having none of it.

"No friggin' way! He's coming here where he belongs," she said. "What's wrong with you two?" She knew what it was; they were green with envy. "Don't let the green-eyed monster ruin your relationship with your brother."

Faith didn't argue because her mother was right. If she really cared, she'd enlist Sandra's help with weight loss and exercise. Didn't all skinny people love to give diet and workout advice? But Emma wasn't going there. She was incensed. Tom was just as shallow as the rest of the men she knew. Unless a woman was starving to death, she couldn't get a second look from a guy. Emma could barely make eye contact with her brother on that first visit and never addressed Sandra once. Thanksgiving would be a horrible day to be gotten through.

For Tom, Thanksgiving morning, at least, was relaxing and pleasant. Gwen served coffee and put the rolls

Tom brought out on a china serving platter. Surprisingly, she took one, put it in the microwave, smeared it with butter that promptly melted all over, and began to stuff it into her mouth. She ate two of the caramel rolls with coffee, and then went to the kitchen to begin putting out the brunch dishes. She had bagels from the bakery in their neighborhood, lox and cream cheese, smoked turkey, chicken livers, cheeses, a platter of bacon and sausage, and a huge frittata. Gwen could put it away. She piled her plate up with food while the others followed behind her.

"Eat up! There's fruit, cream puffs, and chocolate éclairs," she said. The fruit was presented in a hollowed-out watermelon. Where she found watermelon in Queens in November was a mystery. They took their plates to an enclosed porch that overlooked Little Neck Bay. The setting reminded Sandra of Pam, and sadness tried to ruin her day. She decided to fight it by stepping out of her comfort zone and initiating the conversation instead of making others draw her out, as usual. "So Gwen, what do you do for a living?" Sandra asked, assuming she still worked because she was so much younger than the retired John. Why would they be in Bayside if they could travel?

"I'm a nurse," she said. "Next year I am going to go part-time so we can start doing a little traveling. Do you travel much?"

"I think I can count the number of times I've been out of the city on one hand." They laughed. "Coming to Brooklyn is in that count."

"Sandra was born and raised in Manhattan, Gwen. Hell's Kitchen, right, honey?" Tom asked. Sandra nodded her head yes.

"Brooklyn must have been a tough change for you," Gwen said. But Sandra shook her head.

"No, everyone says that, but I love it. Williamsburg is completely unpretentious. I feel like I could be happy here permanently," Sandra explained. Tom reached an arm around her and hugged. "It's a fallacy, actually, that people from the city never want to leave it—something Woody Allen propagated in *Manhattan*. We might be *afraid* to leave. I just have never known anything else. It's not that I don't love the city, but I am not thrilled with what it's become. The familiar is being replaced by the generic. There was a burger joint in my old neighborhood and the rent was raised until he could no longer afford to pay. The usual story. Last week, a friend told me that a national sandwich chain is going in there. Yuck. A coffee chain took over the coffee shop I visited with my mother and sister every Saturday for ten years. It makes me sad. You won't know where you are when you get off the subway. It could be anyplace in the country." The clanking of cutlery on china increased as they ate.

"I have no desire to go anywhere. When you say we are going to travel, what do you have in mind?" John asked Gwen. The group laughed.

"I'll think of something you won't be able to resist," she said.

Sandra could see they were in love, devoted to each other. It would be pleasant being part of this family. After brunch, they talked for a while longer and then it was time to head back home before going to Tom's mother's house. When they got back to Tom's apartment, Sandra wished she could feign illness and stay home. But she did some quick deep breathing and the impulse to hide went away. She'd be okay. Just going with the flow was a new discipline for Sandra. She liked being in control but found that relinquishing some of it to Tom was easier than she thought. As long as the conversation wasn't threatening at his mother's house, she would be fine.

They were at Virginia's for less than fifteen minutes when the first comment was made that shifted Sandra's self-protection mechanism to the front line. They were sitting around a small, round table in the front of the apartment and Virginia was serving tea and hors d'oeuvres. Faith was talking a blue streak about a new computer system her employer had put in and Sandra tried to stay focused. Without meaning to, she let her eyes glaze over and she started daydreaming.

Emma picked up on it immediately. "Shut up for a minute, will you, Faith? You're boring Sandra," Emma said.

Tom looked over at her with a "you okay?" expression. She smiled back at him. "Not at all," Sandra said. "I don't know much about computers but I'm always willing to learn!" The comment rang false to her own ears, but she didn't think anyone else noticed.

"You'll have to put up with us catching up with Tommy when you come around. We never see him now," Faith said. Sandra kept her smile plastered across her face. *What the hell were they talking about? He spent every Saturday afternoon with them.*

"Get on with it, Faith. I'm going to fall asleep myself," Tom said jokingly. But Faith took it seriously.

Sandra thought, *Oh great, now the ally is pissed, too.*

"Forget it," she said, pushing herself away. The action made the small table move six inches. The vase of flowers teetered and everyone's tea cups sloshed. She stomped off toward the back of the apartment with enough gusto that the plates rattled. No one said anything for a moment, and then Virginia got up from her chair.

"I'll go retrieve Princess Faith," she said.

Sandra wondered if that behavior was Faith's norm. She picked up her tea and sipped. She could do anything for one afternoon. Tom patted her knee and smiled at her while they waited. Emma glared at Sandra, piling more food on her plate. They'd only been sitting there for twenty minutes and Sandra already felt like she could throw up, she'd eaten so much. There was still the huge meal to wade through.

Finally, Virginia returned alone. "Faith will be out shortly. Shall we move into the dining room?"

She led the way into a tiny, windowless room behind the kitchen. She'd fashioned heavy draperies across one wall. The other walls were covered with a gallery of old, framed prints, flea market finds mixed with family treasures. Sandra was of the minimalist decorating school, where form followed function, but she was finding the space more relaxing and cozy than confining, as she'd thought it might be. The furniture was oversized for the small space, with four large armchairs around the table. They'd brought in a kitchen chair for Sandra.

She was uncomfortable being served, but the room was too small for more than one person to be up at a time. Virginia dished the food up in the kitchen and brought plates to the table. She'd taken pity on Sandra, maybe because of her size. The plate she prepared for Sandra had child-sized portions of turkey, mashed potatoes, and stuffing, and a tablespoon of something green. Creamed spinach. She would make it last throughout the meal.

When Tom was done, he announced that he was going to the living room to check out the scores and thankfully, he motioned for Sandra to go with him. No one had directed any conversation or questions to her. They weren't interested and that was okay with Sandra. She remembered an experience with a high school date. The young man lived on the Upper West Side and had a maid serving the meal. His parents acted like they had never eaten a meal with anyone who wasn't a member of their church, let alone someone who lived in Hell's Kitchen.

"What did you say your father does again?" they asked, in disbelief that she could be telling the truth; her father was among the legal counsel for the ACLU. After the meal was over, she politely left the room and told her date to go fuck himself for throwing her to the wolves. She walked home, and on the way, resolved that she would never allow that sort of treatment again. Yet here she was— slipping into a state of not belonging or feeling inferior. The others were still eating. The smell of turkey was making Sandra sick, and she decided to step out of her comfort zone and risk making Tom angry.

"How long do we have to stay?" she whispered. He looked around and shrugged his shoulders. "How about half-time?" he asked.

She nodded her head yes. *Fifteen more minutes.* When the time finally arrived, she stayed calm and didn't rush to the door, although she was feeling more and more panicked the longer they stayed.

"Mom, we're heading out!" Tom yelled to Virginia. "I'll come by tomorrow for leftovers."

His mother walked out, a confused look on her face. "You're leaving already?" she asked. "What's going on?"

"I've got a little headache, Ma, nothing to worry about. I want to get home and lay on the couch."

Emma snickered.

"What's that supposed to mean?" Tom asked. Sandra pressed closer to the door.

"Emma, mind your business," Virginia said.

"No, I don't think I will. You cooked all day yesterday and I think its mean of him to come for dinner and stay for an hour and think that's enough," Emma stated, and then, the question they dreaded, "How long'd you stay at Dad's, Tommy?"

Faith came out of the bedroom and stood in the hallway, waiting. The struggle Virginia was having was clear. Tom stepped back into the living room. Sandra closed her eyes. He was going to get into it with his sister.

"We were there all morning. And you know what, Faith? No one treated my girlfriend like shit over there. No one whined and complained, or expected anything of us. They treated Sandra with respect at Dad's. Mother," he said addressing Virginia, "thank you for a delicious meal. You were a lovely hostess. But your daughters are bitches and I'm not subjecting my girlfriend to this again." He walked over to his mother and kissed her cheek. "Love you, Mom, thank you for dinner," he repeated. "I'll be by tomorrow." He glared at his sisters and turned back to the door where Sandra stood, embarrassed.

They were silent on the walk to his car. He unlocked the door and held it for her while she got in. She watched him walking around the front to his door. She felt a combination of relief and regret. She was hoping for the sense of family that she'd missed since her parents died. But she wasn't going to find it with Faith and Emma lurking around, no matter how long they hung out at Virginia's. She may have found what she was looking for at John and Gwen's, which would make things worse for Tom. He was already walking a fine line between the two parents.

"I blame myself. I felt comfortable at your dad's and they may have picked up on my discomfort at dinner," she said.

Tom shook his head. "I have played this game for years now, where I pretend my father doesn't exist so my mother won't be hurt. It's been long enough since my dad left; they should be over it by now. Maybe this is a good thing; I can start being myself again and stop allowing my sisters to walk all over me. You never have to go there again."

Sandra looked out the window so he wouldn't see her give the eyeball-roll of relief. Thank God. "I can't wait to get home. My stomach is never going to be the same," Sandra said. They'd weathered yet another storm and come out with new respect for each other.

25

After Jeff and Nelda called asking to come to dinner, the phone didn't stop ringing. Marie called; she wanted to make sure it was okay that Steve was bringing Nelda, Bernice, and herself. Then, surprisingly, Dave from Organic Bonanza called. He was fishing for an invitation and Pam just couldn't be so mean as to not invite him. The good thing was that he would bring whatever food from the deli she wanted. But she warned him that Jeff and her mother also had called, so the entire Manhattan crowd would be there. He could attend at his own risk. The mention of Jeff's name seemed to cement his determination not to be left out.

"I'll be there!" he exclaimed. So what was supposed to be an intimate family dinner with her children and their friends was slowly taking on the dynamic of a three-ring circus. The only preparation she gave the kids was a warning that Marie had been ill and looked awful, and that a man she'd been dating was going to come. They would figure out everything else.

Thursday morning, Pam woke up early. She lay in bed, the one she'd shared with Jack for so many years. It no longer felt lonely without him. She'd successfully removed all of what reminded her of him so the room was truly hers now. The first hour that the kids were home, she invited them into Jack's closet and instructed them to take what they wanted; the rest was going to Goodwill the following Monday. She was surprised at what they took. Although Brent was more slender than Jack, he took—with Pam's blessing—the Armani suits. They would go to the tailor to see if they could be taken in. Lisa took all of his college sweatshirts, threadbare rags that she remembered him wearing around the house while she was growing up. All of his silk ties, and there were hundreds of them, and his handkerchiefs went. The only things they left were his shoes (he wore size twelves and Brent wore thirteens) and his underwear, although both kids took some of his undershirts. They took armloads of Jack's things to their rooms. She told them to stash everything; she didn't want to go to into their rooms to clean after they returned to school and have to deal with it all. And then to Pam's surprise, they returned to help her box and bag and rest of the stuff for donation. With their help, the task was accomplished in less than an hour. Pam felt sad; before the disclosure to them of AIDS, she was sure the experience would have been bittersweet. But now, neither child seemed saddened at all. As a matter of fact, Jack's name was only mentioned in passing. He'd brought it on, Pam reminded herself. It was his doing.

  The comfort of her bed had taken care of her for months. She rarely had insomnia; the minute her head hit the pillow, she was out. She'd even taken to sleeping on what was formerly Jack's side of the bed because it was closer to the hallway. She'd moved her personal items to the bed stand. The impressive stack of books she was reading was piled on the floor. She'd never have done that when Jack was alive. Slowly, she was taking her favorite artwork from the rest of the house and mixing it with things she'd bought since he died. Her bedroom was reflecting more of her personality; it was less a sterile, showcase room. The children noticed right away.

"Wow Mom, your room looks great! It's so interesting!" Lisa said, looking around. "Where'd all this come from?" She touched the frame of photograph of the beach.

"Oh, just stuff I picked up here and there that means something to me," Pam said. There was never much evidence that Jack lived there and now it was lessened, but his presence was powerful with the children home. It was the place where he'd come each weekend to see his family. Lisa seemed to be on the same cosmic plane that Pam was at that moment, and she walked to her mother and embraced her. Pam could feel the slight shaking of her slender body as Lisa began to weep.

"He did love you Mom. I know he did. He told both Brent and I he loved you and that you were a wonderful wife."

Pam remained silent, wanting Lisa to feel that her words were important, although Pam didn't believe them. What her daughter said to her, repeating more lies from Jack, hurt intensely, the words ricocheting around inside her head. *He did love you. He told us you were a wonderful wife...*Pam put her arms around her daughter. Jack's daughter. How was her child's life going to change as his secrets were revealed? Pam remembered the carefree days of Lisa and Brent's childhood. Surely, Jack, in his ignorance, never planned on hurting them the way they were bound to be hurt.

She stretched as she lay in bed and debated trying to sleep a little longer; daylight hadn't peeked over the tops of the drapes yet. She rolled over, reaching for her glasses. The bedside clock said five-thirty. If she got up now she'd be exhausted by dinnertime. She curled up and pulled the covers under her chin. The hum of the furnace was a comforting sound that took her to a different time.

She'd awakened in the middle of the night with the sense that she was alone although it was the weekend, and Jack should be lying next to her in bed. She'd reached over and felt his side of the bed. He wasn't there. She'd gotten up, taking her robe from the chaise, and as she'd walked across the hallway to the kitchen, she saw lights on. Jack was standing in his underpants, bare-chested, leaning against the counter with a glass of juice in his hand. Pam was about ready to ask the inane, *Can't you sleep?* when a naked Marie started coming out of the children's wing.

"Oops!" she yelped. "I didn't know anyone else was up!" and Pam could hear her running back to her room and sound of her door closing. At the time, she and Jack had laughed.

"I guess we scared her!" he'd said. Pam shook her head and turned to go back to bed.

"Coming?" she'd asked her husband.

"Almost done," he'd said, lifting his glass to her. She'd never given the incident a second thought.

But now, years later, the impact of that night hit her fully. Her children had been asleep, or not, in the next rooms. It was obvious that Jack and Marie had been together. Pam closed her eyes and allowed her imagination to take over. She tried to remember every detail of that night, or her husband standing there, so totally out of character, in his underpants. She looked at his face, which had failed him because he was clearly surprised, but at the time, she just thought it was because he didn't except her. In her memory, she saw his smooth chest and tight abdomen, and the waist band of his underpants. Her eyes moved down to his crotch. Did he have an erection? She rolled over in bed. *God damned Jack. He always seemed to have an erection! You stupid jerk.* But that was meant for herself.

Several minutes later, Jack did come back to bed. He went into the bathroom and she could hear water running and teeth brushing. He came back in the dark and she could feel the mattress shift as he got into bed. Without hesitation, he crept over to her side of the bed and began to kiss her, sticking his tongue in her mouth. His breath was tangy with toothpaste and orange juice. She wanted him to climb on top of her, but as was their usual procedure, he started kissing her neck with his tongue, going down lower and lower and lower. *Jack was so unselfish,* she used to think. But this morning, the realization dawned that Jack probably was spent from screwing her sister all night and couldn't do it again. She laughed. "You stupid jerk!" she said out loud. And then she started to cry. *One last time*, she thought. *I'll cry one last time.*

❦

She fell back to sleep and the sun was up, shining through the cracks in the drapes when she woke up again. It was after eight. She got up and went to the hallway; silence. The children were still sleeping. She made a cup of coffee and took it back to her bedroom. Everything was under control. All she had to do today was put the turkey in the oven at about ten. She'd told people to come at four; in the old days they'd be arriving by noon, the children going down to the recreation room in the lower level to play pool and Ping-Pong, usually with a movie blaring away in the background. The men and some of the women would pile onto the ample leather sofas and chairs in the den to watch football on Jack's gigantic television. Before flat screen, they'd had projection TV that covered the area above the fireplace. Its size was ridiculous, but Jack had to have it. Pam would spend the entire day standing behind the island in the kitchen like a robot, making coffee, washing glasses, putting out trays of snacks. It didn't end. She ran up and down the stairs to retrieve glasses and make sure her kids were okay every thirty minutes or so and if she was up to her elbows, she'd get one of her sisters to go and do it.

"Check on the kids, will you Susan?" she'd ask. After their husbands died, Nelda would sit at the island, having helped with whatever Pam needed, and Bernice watched football with her sons. Nelda was indispensable; she remembered things like olives and napkins. You couldn't have Thanksgiving dinner without olive dishes on the table. When Harold was alive, he sat alone in the living room reading until the game started. Pam's dad, Frank, liked being with the kids or in the kitchen while Pam cooked.

As she puttered around her bedroom that morning thinking of family and friends, Pam realized that it wasn't the past she was yearning for; it was the desire to release it. All of this drama was making it impossible to move forward. Now with everyone coming here again, which was exactly what she'd hoped to avoid, it was inevitable that Jack's name would be mentioned. She took a deep breath. It was too late to change anything today; she'd succumbed to guilt. It was out of her control. She'd be strong the next time; if she wanted to be alone with the children, she only had to say no. *Wasn't that the way it worked?* Pam laughed out loud. It was never a question before now. She was exploring new territory.

26

Holidays were difficult for Ashton. When they were young, he and Jack spent them together, often running back and forth across the park between their respective houses. Once Pam came into the picture, they rarely saw each other. It wasn't too difficult if the holiday fell on the weekend because he was accustomed to being alone. Long weekends were terrors; three days apart were the absolute maximum for Ashton. He'd call Jack hourly, crying, until they could be together. Jack tried to fit Ashton in whenever he could; often inviting him to golf at his club on Long Island, but Ashton didn't like leaving the city. Since he didn't drive, it would mean hiring a car. And then when it was time to say good-bye, it was so depressing to leave Jack there that well, it just wasn't worth it.

After Jack died, Ashton dreaded the first major holiday even though it shouldn't have been any different at all. Ashton's mother and father were still alive, but they went to Palm Beach in October. He decided to contact Dale; she was just a few blocks away and although they hadn't gotten together in a while, they often talked about spending holidays together. He dialed her number but there was no answer on Monday or Tuesday. On Wednesday he decided to walk to her apartment. It had been snowing lightly all day, but it was warm enough that it wasn't sticking on the ground. He bundled up; the wind was biting, and he was glad for his woolen scarf and long wool overcoat.

He got to her apartment and pushed the button on the intercom. It was answered immediately with the sound of the door unlocking. He quickly glanced at her address; the apartment was on the second floor. He ran up the stairs to her door, which was open slightly. He tapped on it, and an older woman in a nurse's uniform pushed it farther.

"Oh! Sorry, I thought you were my replacement. Can I help you?" she asked.

"I'm here to see Dale," Ashton answered, frightened at the necessity for a nurse.

"She's not seeing anyone," the nurse answered.

"Could you tell her Ashton is here? Jack's friend? I think she'll want to see me," he said.

The nurse pointed to a chair in the hallway and reluctantly retreated to the back of the apartment after she saw that he was going to sit down and not follow her. Less than a minute passed and the nurse returned. "She'll see you," the nurse informed Ashton. "Follow me."

Ashton got up and walked to the rear of the apartment. He'd expected the faint medicinal smell—the nurse was a dead giveaway. She stood aside and motioned for him to go ahead of her. Dale was propped up in bed, a pink satin bed jacket with a matching ribbon in her hair. It was so Dale that Ashton took in a rush of air that caused him to snort involuntarily, and then out of his control, he started crying.

He went to her and she was laughing at him with her arms outstretched. "Oh no, Ashton! Not you! It's not as grim as it looks. I'm just having a rough day because I had a treatment yesterday and it always knocks the wind out of my sails." She held his chin in her hands and looked into his eyes. Her breath was minty; he saw the tin next to the tissue box on her bedside table. She patted the side of the bed for him to sit down.

"What's wrong with you?" he muttered, almost afraid to ask.

"It's cancer. But I have to die eventually and evidently this is not as bad as it could be. I'm responding to treatment or something like that. I'm just glad it was discovered after Jack died. He didn't do well with illness and all that malarkey," she said.

"Well, I was calling all week to see if you want to spend tomorrow together. I think Jack would have liked that," Ashton said.

She reached for his hand and squeezed it, resting her head back on the pillow. Nodding her head yes, she said, "Let's. I probably won't be up for a big turkey dinner, but we can spend the day together, absolutely." She closed her eyes, intending just to rest for a minute, but when she opened them, Ashton was gone. There was a note on her table that said, "See you tomorrow! Love, Ashton."

27

Steve Marks woke up, later than he planned, to ringing of the telephone. He knew who it would be before he reached for it.

"Jesus, don't tell me you're still in bed," Marie said. "I've got to get out of here. Should I tell them I'm leaving and get Ben to bring me home?"

"No! Stay there. I'll get myself together and come right up. What do you want to wear?" He hoped Thanksgiving dinner in Babylon didn't mean Sunday best. He wanted to wear sneakers and jeans.

"I'm wearing sweats," she said. "Look, if we leave by noon we won't get there until two. She won't mind that we're early, I don't think. I could be wrong. I heard my mother talking to her yesterday and she was begging admittance for us."

Steve wished they could stay home; Marie uptown and he in his apartment, alone with a bottle of scotch. "Okay, well, do you mind if I take the time to have some breakfast?" *Or is she expecting me to rush up there to get her fed and dressed?*

"No, go ahead and eat. That bitch Candy will be in here in a few minutes raggin' on me to get up and get showered. I really hate her."

"She's just trying to help you," Steve said, glad he wasn't in the caretaker role.

"Don't take her side! Hurry up and get me out of here or I am going to leave and take the subway," she threatened.

Steve snickered. She didn't have the strength to sit on the toilet by herself let alone walk to the subway. But there was no arguing with her. "Okay, get up and get a shower like she says and I'll be there in half an hour," he promised. He didn't relish driving for two hours with two old ladies bitching at him in the backseat. He wouldn't be able to smoke, either. *Oh shit, why'd I ever chase after her?*

◊

Pam spent the morning getting the turkey stuffed and into the oven. When her children finally got up, the three of them went out for a late breakfast. They had a great time telling their mother all the wonderful things they did at school that parents are never supposed to find out about. Several times, Pam laughed so hard she had tears coursing down her face. The hostess gave them a "look" saved for unruly customers. The worst involved a long story about alcohol consumption; passing out in the back of a strange, unlocked car; and waking up to find the president of the college scared to death that his wife would find out there was a half-naked girl sleeping in his backseat. He drove the young woman to a McDonald's parking lot, pulled around behind the Dumpsters, gave her a shirt he'd dug out of his dirty laundry bag, a fist full of money, and begged her to get lost.

"Oh my!" Pam exclaimed. "She could've said he got her drunk, or worse! Lock your cars, people!"

"What time's everyone coming?" Brent asked, yawning.

"Not till four," Pam replied. "Look you two, there are few things I should probably explain. Marie is ill and looks awful, and she is pregnant." She paused to let the full effect sink in.

"Great! That's just great. She is about as ready to raise a kid as Brent, here, is," Lisa said.

Brent laughed out loud. "How'd I get involved? Jeeze!" he said. "You're right, though, she can't even fend for herself."

Pam let the kids have their say before she went any further. She was slightly surprised; they'd never voiced negativity about Marie before, and now she wondered if they'd always had such contemptuous feelings toward her.

"She is very frail," Pam added, curious that they hadn't inquired about who the father was. "Her boyfriend is a very nice older man. You'll meet him this afternoon."

"Who is he? I can just imagine," Lisa said with a sneer.

Wow, Pam thought, *where's this coming from?* "Someone she met at work. He's really devoted to her, you'll see," Pam said, trying to smooth things over. Brent wasn't saying much, but Pam could see the wheels turning.

"She makes me sick," Lisa replied. "She acted like Dad was her *amore* and as soon as he dies, she screws some old man and gets pregnant."

Speechless, Pam wondered if it was smart to have caved in to her mother's demands for an invitation to the beach. If she called them now, made an excuse, they'd have time to find something else to do for dinner.

"What do you think, Brent? Are you as angry as I am?"

"I really don't give a shit," Brent answered.

"Okay, you two, what's going on?" Pam asked, almost certain she already knew, but so appalled that she couldn't bear saying the words out loud. Her children knew about Marie and Jack.

"Mom, trust me, you don't want to know," Brent said. "Lisa, shut up."

Pam didn't want to give away too much, just in case what she was thinking and what they were thinking were two different things. "Look, I am all about honesty right now. We can't have secrets and move forward. At least I can't," she added. "I need truth, and I want to give it, too."

Brent was staring at her intensely.

"We don't want to cause trouble," Lisa said, and Brent agreed.

"There's no trouble," Pam said. "Only freedom. You both have to know that I have had some struggles lately." It was her first reference to AIDS since they'd gotten home.

"We don't want to hurt you, either," Brent said.

"I won't say that there is nothing more that can hurt me," Pam explained. She'd been so worried about protecting their image of their father and now it looked like they may have been on to him long before she learned the truth. "But one of you better spill the beans!"

Lisa rolled her eyeballs.

"Poor Mom, you are such a nerd," Lisa said.

Pam laughed. Nerd was a nice word for what she was.

Lisa looked at Brent. He frowned in agreement. Lisa continued. "Marie was after Dad all the time, from when we were little until right before I left for school." Lisa stopped and looked at her mother to see what the effect was.

Pam was trying to look expressionless, but it was a losing battle. Why did she fail to see something that her "little" children saw? Pam didn't know what the next question should be. Only one came to mind. "What did you see?" Pam asked. Her heart was pounding in her chest.

"She was always on him, always dragging him off somewhere. I hated it! I told him finally. He said he would tell her to stop. But she continued whispering to him, and I know she had him in her room," Lisa said.

"Lisa, for Christ's sake," Brent hissed.

"It's okay," Pam told him. "But I think we should leave. I want to continue this where we can express ourselves freely without a waitress coming by."

They agreed and Brent signaled for the check. The diner was on a lagoon. There were benches placed in a protected cove where they could see the water and hear the gulls.

Pam was struggling with whether to make Marie the fall guy, or to be honest and tell them that Jack abused her when the children were toddlers. She wished there was a psychiatrist's office they could run to. But she was on her own, and her gut was telling her to stop making excuses, stop hiding, and start telling the truth. She'd let the kids lead the way and if there was a chance where clarity was needed, she would provide it. She felt awful about having put them in this situation because of her failure to observe.

"Did you see Daddy in Marie's room?" Pam asked, hoping Lisa would pick up where she left off.

Lisa was looking out at the water, where the lagoon widened and mingled with the water from the ocean. Even in the freezing weather, there were diehard fishermen on the causeway, throwing their lines in.

"I did," Brent said. "It was so frequent it was normal to see Dad come out of Marie's room in the middle of the night."

Pam gasped. She grabbed her son's hand. "I'm so sorry, Brent. This is my fault. I mean, not that Daddy did it, or that Marie allowed it, but that I didn't protect you both from the knowledge of it. That's not right, either. I didn't protect you from the *exposure* to it. I must have been in denial or, as Marie liked to say, had my head stuck in the sand. I just feel terrible and it is too late to do anything about it." There was an uncomfortable silence.

"So what you are saying is that you *didn't* know," Lisa said. It was a statement. She had turned to look at her mother, and Pam couldn't decipher the look Lisa was giving her. Was she disgusted with Pam, or pitying her? "Or did you? For God's sake, Mother! Do you have any idea how this affected me?" Lisa asked, but she didn't wait for Pam to reply. "I have felt like crap about myself because my father preferred my aunt to me, and now it would seem that you are confirming that he was fucking her. Am I right, Mother?" Her eyes were piercing, flashing anger as they stared right into Pam. "I even wondered for a while what an appropriate relationship with my father would encompass. How sick!" she sputtered. "I mean, my God! I've been defending him and saying that there was no way he could be responsible for your AIDS when all along, you knew!"

Pam grabbed Lisa's arm. "I didn't know! I swear to you. I only found out after Jack died. You have to believe me. When I say I had my head stuck in the sand, it refers to all knowledge of him. I had no idea. I couldn't protect you because I didn't know. I was too stupid to know, maybe that's correct. But I truly did not know!"

Brent chimed in and directed his statement at his sister. "Lisa, I think you have to listen to what she is saying. You didn't know about it, correct Mom?" Brent asked her gently.

Pam shook her head no. "In retrospect, I realize that it seems unlikely, but truly, I believed we had the perfect, charmed life. You children never said anything to me or even let on that there was a problem. Never! You never had a nightmare or bad behavior, never had a call from a teacher at school, or gave me one moment of worry. How would I have known?" Pam explained. And then softly, "Why didn't you come to me?"

"I didn't want to hurt you," Brent said.

Pam was confused. Were they attacking her or not? She remembered the time at the beach when Jack was twirling Marie in the air and Lisa stood away from them, brooding. She reminded Lisa of it.

"When I saw what was happening, that Jack was paying attention to Marie, and you were standing there looking left out, I intervened immediately. Whenever I saw anything that didn't seem right, I challenged you guys, and Daddy. But if you were afraid to tell me, what could I do? I had no idea you were holding back!" There was another period of silence during which the family looked out to sea.

Lisa stood up and stretched with her arms up over her head. "We should've had this discussion last spring. I'm pissed!" Lisa turned to look at Pam. "I guess it's pointless for me to ask why you didn't say anything when you found out the truth. I'm almost afraid to ask how you found out."

Brent started laughing. "Jesus Christ! Isn't it clear why she didn't say anything? Boy, you are younger than I thought," he said.

"What does that mean?" Lisa asked. "Mom should've asked us right away if we had any suspicions."

"Hindsight and all that," Brent said.

Pam was feeling worse by the minute. "All I could think of was protecting you two," she explained. "Should I tell you how I found out?" She was looking for a way to make them understand, but was the truth too awful to unload on them?

Lisa nodded. She wanted to know; curiosity was devouring her.

"Your father had a young girlfriend, Sandra, the one he left his business to in the will. She got to the hospital before I did to identify the body. They'd called her first." Pam felt defiant, as bad as at that was. Her own children had pushed her to this. "She saw his body before I did; we passed as I was on my in. I knew right away."

Lisa burst into tears. "Oh my God, how sad, Mom! But how'd Marie figure into this?"

Pam realized she hadn't answered that question yet. "Marie was jealous of Sandra. It was as simple as that. She made sure the two of us knew that she also had a relationship with your father. It was a case of one-up-man-ship." For the time being, she decided to leave out the child-abuse accusation and Sandra's pregnancy. Suddenly exhausted, Pam made the split-second decision that Thanksgiving dinner was not taking place in Babylon this year after all. "Let's get home, shall we? I need to call our guests and tell them the family meal is off. Why I allowed myself to be talked into it in the first place is a mystery." She stood up and starting walking toward the car. If her wonderful children chose to stay there in the wind and cold, that was up to them. But she heard them approach the car as she unlocked the doors and got in to drive. The silence permeated the car and when they returned to the beach, it spread to the house as well.

28

By the time Steve Marks arrived at the mansion to drive the women to Babylon, dinner was canceled. Marie was furious, cursing her sister for being selfish and thoughtless. Nelda was dying of curiosity about the reason; it must have been a real doozy for Pam Smith to cancel a celebratory meal. Jeff Babcock was sad that his friend was upset enough to have made the call. Dave was disappointed and curious, but little else. Bernice forgot it was Thanksgiving within five minutes of being told they were staying home.

"Well, I want to go back to your apartment," Marie insisted. "You have four days off. Why should I stay up here in hell if you're home?"

Steve vacillated between joy that he didn't have to go for a two-hour car ride to a place where he couldn't smoke and terror that he'd have to take Marie home. *Why did I ever get involved with her?* She made the effort to get dressed and was pulling things together that she cared about; her purse and phone and a book she was reading. "Look Steve, I'm leaving. If you don't want me at your place, I'm going back to my own apartment." Unsteady on her feet but determined, Marie was going to leave if it meant taking a subway downtown. "I can do it blindfolded."

Steve's shoulders slumped in such resignation that Marie started laughing.

"Okay, let's go. I guess I have myself to blame for this," he said.

"Stop. It's not that bad!" she said.

"What are you going to do for dinner?" Nelda asked. She already had a small ham baking and was thinking about what other accompaniments there were in the mansion larder.

"I'm about ready to puke as it is. All you can think of doing is force-feeding me. I want to go home!"

Steve tapped her arm, nodding toward the front door. With all the energy she could muster, Marie went for the stairs. She was getting out of there.

※

When Ashton got back to his apartment, the first thing he did was arrange for Thanksgiving dinner to be delivered to Dale's apartment from Balducci's. They'd had a wonderful visit and he didn't think about being lonely for Jack. The next morning he spent a little extra time on his appearance. On the way over to her place, he picked up a bouquet of pink roses. There was pink all over her apartment, and she had a rose on her bed jacket.

He got to her apartment promptly at two; the food was going to be delivered at two-thirty. As he skipped up the stairs to the front door, a taxi pulled up in front of Dale's building and a man about Ashton's age got out. Ashton pushed the button on the intercom but there was no answer. Maybe the nurse was off for the holiday and it was taking Dale a while to get to the buzzer. The man saw Ashton pushing the button.

Prayers for the Dying

"Dale's my aunt," he said, smiling. "Are you here to see her?"

Ashton turned to him and offered a hand. "Yes, yes! Dale is an old friend; she was my math professor in college!" Ashton started laughing at the ludicrousness of it. "We are having dinner together today."

The man pulled out a key. "Come in," he said. They walked up the stairs together with Ashton following. "I hate to have to be the one to tell you this," he said as they got to her door. He put the key in and turned the handle, standing aside so Ashton could go through first. Ash looked around the apartment; it was a physical sensation that she wasn't there. He didn't even have to go into her bedroom to check. "She died last night. About midnight. The nurse said she was expecting a friend today but no one knew your name. I'm sorry."

Ashton couldn't help himself. She was his last link. With Dale gone, there was no one left. He started to cry. Ugly, hiccupping sobs that grown men hate to admit having. He plunked down in a chair and put his face in his hands. The man stood aside and allowed him this one dignity and didn't interrupt him. It seemed like an eternity, but probably only lasted for a minute or two, and he was spent. He dug in his pocket and pulled out a perfectly ironed handkerchief to wipe his eyes and nose. "May I use the bathroom?"

The man nodded and pointed to the back of the apartment. Ashton went in and shut the door. He let the water run until it was warm and with his overcoat and scarf still on, he washed his hands and face. There was a towel folded on a shelf above the toilet and he hoped it was clean. After he dried himself off, he took a length of toilet paper and blew his nose. So that was that. He wanted to get out of there, but it was too late to call Balducci's. What to do? He walked out and the man was still standing in the same place, waiting.

"Are you okay?" he asked.

Ashton nodded his head.

The man stuck his hand out. "I'm Dale's nephew, Ted." The two men shook hands again.

"I ordered dinner to be delivered in half an hour," Ashton said. "It's too late to cancel it."

"Do you want to wait?" Ted asked. "I have to start looking through her papers today, so you're not inconveniencing me if you want to wait. I didn't usually have Thanksgiving dinner with her. We were the last two holdouts in the city." Ted smiled.

Ashton was having a hard time getting a read on the man, but he was almost certain that Ted was gay. *Homophobic Dale having a gay nephew that she had meals with?*

"I don't want to put you out. You must be upset," Ashton said. "Yesterday she didn't seem that bad to me. I mean, I knew she was ill because of the nurse and having chemo, but otherwise, she seemed okay. We had lunch just two months ago and she never let on."

"She didn't want us to know how advanced the cancer was. As a matter of fact, she didn't even tell my mother, who's her older sister, until right after Labor Day. My folks live in Florida and, of course, they were frantic and called me. Aunt Dale and I tried to get together for dinner at least once a month." Ted looked around the apartment. "Look, it doesn't seem too strange; would you stay and have dinner here after all? I was going to go up to Franco's by Seventy-Ninth and eat there alone." Ted waited for Ashton's answer with expectation written all over his face.

Although a romantic entanglement was the last thing on his mind, Ashton didn't want to be alone today, and they had the bond of Dale to see them through. If there was nothing else to talk about, she would serve.

Dinner arrived promptly at two-thirty. The men pulled a small table and chairs out of the dining room and placed them in front of the bay window that overlooked the park. It was too nice a day to sit in the dark, windowless dining room. They took the containers of food out and prepared their plates to take to the table. Ashton thought of Jack, eating directly out of a Chinese food box. They sat across from each other and began to eat, making small talk.

"So what do you do for a living?" Ashton asked.

"I'm a real estate broker," Ted said. Ashton's heart did a little skip. "How about you?"

"I own a design business. I do all the real estate staging here on the East Side." Ashton took a sip of wine, trying to gauge what this news meant to Ted. "I'm surprised our paths never crossed. New York is such a small town."

"It does seem like that sometimes! Actually, I sell primarily industrial space in the Financial District," Ted said. "I live down there, too."

"So you are one of the few!" They laughed at the same time. "I didn't know anyone was brave enough to," Ashton said.

"It's actually nice. There is a real sense of community, believe it or not. The weekends aren't dead, as you would expect. I like it!" Ted said, asking, "Where do you live?"

"A few blocks from here," Ashton answered. "I was raised up here and loved it. My parents moved to Florida a few years ago and I miss them, but I would die in the summer. The heat, I mean. Yes, I will probably stay here for the rest of my life." Ashton laughed again. How much longer did he have? He still felt like a young man. "I'm a perpetual youth."

"Ha ha, me too!" Ted exclaimed. "My mother warned me that I was starting to look like Pat Boone. I wear sunscreen all the time now."

The men bantered back and forth for two hours. Ashton forgot where he was, enjoying the company of Ted, who seemed like a gentle, intelligent, decent human being, if one can make those deductions from an afternoon visit. Whatever he was, Ashton was determined that he would get to know him better.

"Are you in a relationship?" he finally asked. Ted was preparing to get up and make coffee, and the question stopped him in his tracks. Ashton was suddenly concerned that he'd misread the man and he would turn out to be straight after all. He could feel the heat spreading through his neck and face, probably bringing a red flush with it.

"No, not for a long time." Ted sat back down. "I don't have the energy." The men started laughing, Ashton shaking his head in exasperation.

"Me either. But I hope you and I can get to know each other. I'm comfortable talking with you. It seems like we have a lot in common. What do you think?" Ashton realized he was entering uncharted territory. He hadn't approached another man who wasn't in his circle of friends for years. Jack's death had freed him from restrictions he'd set for himself. It would be so much nicer to be with someone who *didn't* know Jack. Ted stared at him for what seemed like a long time, but finally he smiled.

"That might be nice. I am, for lack of a better word, jaded. I'm always with someone younger, someone who needs me. It might be nice to be with someone my own age who works for a living," Ted admitted. His words flooded Ashton with well-being. Finally, to be an adult. He would have remained a child with Jack, and now here was his chance to feel like a grownup.

They moved around the apartment, cleaning up their dinner mess, and then Ashton helped Ted find his aunt's safe and files. They locked the apartment up and Ash stayed, talking to him, until a cab came. They'd exchanged business cards, and hopefully, something would come of it. Ashton walked home with his scarf up over his mouth, but it couldn't hide the smile that went all the way to his eyes. A sad day had turned around for both men. Dale would've been happy.

29

Pam and her children drove home from the restaurant in silence. Everyone went to their own rooms; she could hear them close their doors and that made her sad. She waited for a few minutes and then walked back out to the kitchen. The smell of turkey permeated the house. It was nauseating. She took the phone back to her bedroom and made the calls canceling the dinner, starting with her mother-in-law; they had the farthest to drive. Nelda was angry, but for once, she kept her mouth shut. There would be plenty of time for disclosure later. The only one she was honest with was Jeff, and he felt horrible for her. She promised they would talk on Monday after the kids left for school.

The atmosphere in the house was worse than if someone had died. The discovery of years of deceit might never be recovered from. Pam knew she was to blame because of stupidity, but she had to find a way to not grovel. She also understood that she may be losing the love and respect of her children, the only two beings in the world that she really loved. She had to take responsibility, and she had to own up to her wrongdoing. It wouldn't work to feign ignorance. Her kids wouldn't accept it. Because of it, she had a glimmer of hope. Her kids were not going to tolerate rationalizing. They were going to confront where they had been wronged and try to overcome it. If she became the whipping boy, it was okay. Her skin was thick after Jack's shenanigans, and she would do anything for her kids, after all. The shocking thing was that she didn't expect it would be her children with whom she would exercise her new-found strength. Their relationship would probably suffer devastating consequences.

There was silence from the children's wing. At four, she took the turkey out of the oven. Going through the motions as she had taught herself to do over the months, she prepared the rest of the traditional dishes her family enjoyed. They would be light on veggies and hors d oeuvres; offerings Jeff and Dave were going to bring. But she always served too much food anyway, and turkey with stuffing, mashed potatoes, and cranberry sauce might be enough to lure them out of their bedrooms. She carefully set the table for them, one of the many useless tasks she had performed on their behalf over the years. The knowledge of the absolute frivolity of her life kept slapping her in the face as she moved around her kitchen and dining room, trying to justify her existence. It took so much energy to keep moving with these thoughts tormenting her that she almost gave in and went to her room for a nap. But she wanted to do everything she could to try to make a normal Thanksgiving for them, so she pressed on, knowing it was as much for her as it was for them. She dressed up as she would have if the entire family was still coming, taking extra time with her hair and makeup. When everything was perfect—table, meal, mother—she went to their doors and gently knocked.

"Dinner's ready. I hope you're hungry!" It was the same thing she'd said to them since they were small.

They'd be in the den or in the basement recreation room with their friends, and Pam would call to them, "I hope you have a big appetite!" She remembered Brent beaming with pride as he and his friends ran up the steps to join the family around the big pine table. It would be brimming with food, and there was another long harvest table alongside the wall that led to the veranda, and it would be loaded as well. She'd adorned the table with artwork from their grade school art projects: a papier-mâché pumpkin that Brent made in third grade, a construction-paper turkey with a full, colorful tail that Lisa made in first grade. There was a mobile of dried Indian corn that their father had made as a child and that Bernice had parted with. Kernels were missing where a mouse had gotten into Pam's storage box once, looking for a meal.

Brent opened his bedroom door and smiled at Pam. "Okay, mom, I'm coming," he said. He was talking on the phone with his girlfriend who was going to visit, but Brent had cancelled. Lisa was slower to open her door; it looked like she'd fallen asleep. She stepped out of her room and reached for her mother.

"Sorry mom, that was shitty of me. I must be getting my period," she explained.

Brent laughed and said, "Ugh."

Pam carefully exhaled a sigh of relief that would go undetected. Maybe she would get out of this without too much ugliness after all. "I'm glad we are alone."

"Me too," Lisa said.

Pam's children surrounded her as they walked out into the kitchen. Brent saw the table first. "Oh boy, I love this table," he said. He looked at Pam and smiled. "I have always loved the Thanksgiving table you make for us."

Lisa groaned. "That is so gross! You sound like a decorator, Brent. You better watch it."

Their banter was comforting. Brent took the place at the head of the table to carve the turkey, not that it was something that Jack ever did, but he was happy to help out and carving was the only thing he knew he could do. Lisa didn't have to do anything to help; always the princess. Pam was almost afraid to relax, there were more revelations to be made but maybe they didn't have to be made today after all. She'd allow the day to unfold as it was supposed to, with no plan.

Serving dinner ended up being a good thing after all; she was glad she hadn't abandoned it. Jack's name didn't come up once, which was unusual because they liked reminiscing about him. But with the new information, how could they be sure if their memories of him were real? She would have to find a way to get them to remember what was good; they'd said in the past that their childhood was charmed, and most of it was. They helped her clean up afterward. Brent was going to his girlfriend's house in White Plains and Lisa was headed to a local dive bar for a battle of the bands. Pam thought about calling Jeff and inviting him to come over to avoid being alone with her thoughts. *Will this ever end? Thank you again, Jack! I hate you.*

30

Pam spent Thursday night in solitude, after all. The kids weren't expected until late. She got into her pajamas early and, looking forward to a night of peace, got her favorite book, a cup of tea, and retreated to her bedroom. She fell asleep sometime after midnight and woke up about two, thinking she heard a key in the front door. A slow smile crept across her face as she heard the rustle of someone undressing, then creeping to bed, and pulling the covers back to get in next to her. She felt his body moving to the middle of the bed, and she rolled over to meet him half way, as was their habit. He reached around her shoulders and pulled Pam to his chest. She could smell the fresh air on him, on his cold skin and in his hair, from driving with his windows down. His lips went to her mouth without skipping a beat and they began to kiss like a perfectly synchronized dance, two people who had kissed like this for all of their adult lives. His tongue separated her lips and skimmed their surfaces tenderly. She felt his hands on the skin of her back, his lips move down along her chin and to her neck and ear. His free hand intertwined with hers, his fingers strong but gentle. She felt his love for her, could feel his caring and desire as his hand released hers and circled her waist, pulling her to him. *I love you, Pam. I've always loved you.*

A loud crash, a sound that penetrated her brain yet did not exist in reality, woke her with a start, her heart pounding in fright. Sitting up abruptly, she looked next to her at the empty bed, and to the chair where his clothes should be illuminated in the moonlight, but it was empty, too. It had been a dream. Jack was dead. Was it a spiritual apparition, wanting her to receive a message from him? Or her wishful thinking? Desire to make her life meaningful and not a charade? She could almost feel the dampness where his tongue had been on her mouth. She could smell that acrid smell of the car and the wind. Without meaning to, and not wanting to feel it, she started crying. It was so sad! Everyone's life was ruined because Jack was a deviant. She wasn't even able to grieve in peace. The positive thing was that in the morning, she knew she'd feel better. The sporadic night visitations often left her feeling empty, but it was just for the night. She didn't want it to end because she felt as though he was trying to help her keep an eye on what had been positive and good about their life together. *It wasn't all horrible, was it?* She reached over and turned the bedside light on. It was almost three. She got up and put her robe on. She'd make a cup of herbal tea and check to see if the kids were home. She went out to the mudroom and saw that the alarm was on. The last person in always set the alarm. The phantom hadn't tripped it. Carefully opening their bedroom doors, she saw they were in bed, safe and sound. A few more nights and they would be gone. Could she play make-believe until they left? Pretend everything was the same? Or would they demand the truth? Make her do penance for being a shitty mother? Making tea in her kitchen was a familiar task. She took it to the den but didn't turn the lights on. Once her eyes adjusted to the darkness, she could see the landscape lighting through the big window, the dune grass that lined the path to the beach, and the moonlight on the dark sea. She could hear the waves as they broke on the beach, but gentle tonight, not the crashing hits they made earlier in the week. A method to promote sanity, thinking about these little vignettes in the minutia of life made her grateful. She had so much to be thankful for. She was strong enough to take responsibility and her love for her kids was big enough no matter how they responded to her.

Daylight brought reality. Pam had fallen asleep on the leather davenport in the den and woke up to find a fully dressed, grim-faced Lisa standing over her. Without greeting her, she simply said, "I'm going back to Oahu, Mom. A friend is picking me up in ten minutes for the airport."

Pam sat up, staring at Lisa, the resolve she'd felt in the dark of night crumbling. She fought the urge to beg her child to stay home, to work things out, to listen to reason. But what was reason? It was all emptiness, lies, and excuses. There was nothing more to be said. Pam reached out to take Lisa's hand.

"Okay, honey," she said. "Do you want a cup of coffee first?"

She could almost see Lisa's shoulders sag. "That would be nice," she admitted.

Pam went to stand up and Lisa put her hand under her arm to give her a boost. They both started laughing. It was a moment between a mother and daughter. Everything might be okay, but not right now. They walked into the kitchen and Lisa slid onto the counter stool while Pam fixed coffee for them. The last moments would be spent peacefully. Nothing would be resolved, but a time-honored tradition of morning coffee would smooth over the pain for a while. They weren't going bring up any painful topics, so Pam enjoyed the pleasure of being in her daughter's company. Checking tears that welled up repeatedly, they were able to talk of immediate needs, money for books, health insurance cards, safe topics until the lights of the getaway car swept over the house.

Lisa slid off the stool and put her cup down. She went to Pam and embraced her warmly, but didn't say anything else, or make promises of forgiveness or give pat answers. Pam walked with her to the front door, and when Lisa walked out toward the car, Pam had to fight the urge to run after her, to beg her to stay home. Lisa didn't wave good-bye or even look at the house. If she was crying, it wasn't evident. Pam imagined she was speaking of relief to her friend. The sadness flowed over her as she closed and locked the door. Never in a million years did she ever think this sort of thing would happen to her. It was the worst—worse than Jack, worse than Marie, worse than her own guilt over sins of omission. The devastation of having a child angry with her made her physically ill. Only the presence of Brent kept her on her feet. Surely, if he came out with a similar story, she would kill herself; no, nothing that dramatic, but she would take to her bed. Staying upright would be too painful.

Fortunately, Brent wasn't leaving yet. He was quiet; he was the more serious one. "Lisa told me she was leaving early, and I tried to talk her out of it, but you know how stubborn she is," he said. They wouldn't spend the weekend talking about Lisa. Brent talked to Pam about leaving UCLA and transferring to a school closer to home, but Pam, trying to be unselfish, told him to stay in California until he graduated in June and then if he wanted to come home to look for a job, he was welcome. She felt it was best for him; maybe not for her, but for him. She didn't mention Lane, Smith and Romney because Sandra hadn't called again or sent a proposal as she had said she would, so maybe she'd changed her mind. Young people were getting on Pam's nerves.

Although Brent stayed in New York, he didn't stay in Babylon. He spent Friday morning at home and then went to his girlfriend's house in White Plains Friday afternoon, and didn't come home until early Sunday morning. It was young love. In the past, the girlfriend would've come to the beach for the weekend. Pam was feeling somewhat the pariah. She didn't have girlfriends to bounce ideas off of, but women's magazines often had articles in which mothers complained about feeling left out of their children's lives. Widows especially felt abandoned by their kids. Pam wasn't going there. And as much as she had tried to avoid it, she felt the old survival tools chipping away. Soon, she would be numb. Soon, even her own children wouldn't have the power to hurt her.

31

Sandra and Tom played house for the weekend. Finally, on Sunday morning, the time was right for Sandra to bring up her dilemma about the business. She was going to offer a proposal to Tom, and his answer would determine a lot of what the future might bring for them as a couple. She laid out their short history of what she felt she had changed for him, both those things in her control, like her relationship with Pam which Tom felt threatened by, and those out of her control, like the loss of baby Ellin.

"I appreciate how wonderful you were when I lost her. I never would have survived that experience without you," she said. "But we have to talk out this business issue. I know it bothers you, but then I got the mixed message when you told Gwen, with pride, that I ran a business. What is it? Do you resent it? Or do you like the idea of it?"

Tom looked baffled. "Honest to God, I have no friggin' idea what you are talking about."

"It's not my imagination that you get an attitude when I come home and share what's going on at work. It's all I do, Tom. I don't have any hobbies, and even if I wanted to, I wouldn't have the time."

"Look, if that's true, just ignore me. It doesn't mean anything," he said.

"No! I will not ignore you. We need to deal with it right now," Sandra exclaimed. "If you are treating me in a way that makes me feel bad, and it revolves around something that is integral to my life, it needs to change. I'm making you aware of it so you can do something about it, because if you feel that negative about me owning the business, I'll sell it. I've already talked to my attorney about it."

Tom got up and started pacing. She didn't say anymore to him. The ball was in his court, so to speak. Finally, he stopped and turned to look at her.

"Maybe I *am* reacting because it was 'his' business. But that's no reason for you to give it up unless you want to. I worry because you are stressed. Usually when you come home and tell me what your day was like, it's full of crap; people yelling, things going wrong, your partner being a prick. If I get an attitude, maybe that's why. I don't expect you to sell the damn thing, please believe me," Tom pleaded. "Besides, didn't I just apologize to you on Thursday for being jealous?"

Sandra saw where the problem might lie; he was trying to help her fix her work issues, just like a man would. It was nothing more than the battle of the sexes, after all.

"Wow, this is intense," she said with a laugh. "I think this is called 'working your problems out.' I promise to start buffering the negative with some positive. Do you think that will help?"

"Yes, and I promise to try to support you instead of being sarcastic," he said. They hugged and continued on their day. It seemed so easy and so perfect.

Steve and Marie got back to his apartment by early afternoon, having stopped off at a deli first. They would have corned beef on rye with pickles and chips for Thanksgiving dinner. Marie was getting around without trouble, and taking care of herself, rather than asking Steve to wait on her. She wanted to prove to him that she'd be alright alone next week when he went back to work. She wanted him to see that she did not require Nelda's care or a trip uptown. She wanted to work, too.

The nurse came on Friday morning and hung an IV bag of dirty brown fluid. It was attached to some kind of pump that regulated the speed that it infused. It was powerful stuff, the woman said. Cardio toxic if it went in too fast. And Marie was such a frail little thing that it was even more important to make sure it was done absolutely properly. Marie allowed the nurse to pamper her a little; Steve saw and chuckled. Whatever anyone else could do was less that he had to do.

"While the nurse is here, I think I'll step out for a minute," he said, grabbing his coat and not wasting any time. Marie looked at him with a sneer.

"Tell her I said 'hi'," she said.

Steve laughed. "Yeah, right! I'm such a prize," he said. He bent over to kiss her and Marie put her hand up to his cheek. She loved him as much as she was capable of loving another human being. He patted her belly. "Bye, baby."

He walked quickly to a dive bar around the block from his place. It was full for morning, regulars yelling, "Hey Steve," and waving at him. He perched on a stool and ordered a beer with a chaser.

"Where you been?" the bartender asked. "Missed seeing you around," she said with a wink.

"I'm gonna be a daddy, and my lady was having some problems," Steve answered, beaming with pride.

"No way! Hey everyone, Stevie here's gonna be a dad!" she yelled. The whole place cheered for him. He responded with a fist in the air and smiles.

"Yeah, I'm finally going to be a father." *How the hell did that happen?* Steve said to himself.

※

Dave, manager of Organic Bonanza, was acting the stock boy Friday morning. They were wiped out of everything remotely "holiday meal" due to Thanksgiving, and as difficult as it was to understand, women would begin shopping for Christmas that weekend. They were featuring organic, locally grown and ground wheat and dairy products from cows just north of there. His brother took care of the details of ordering and vendors, while Dave acted as the liaison between the customer and the store. Whatever his loyal customers wanted that fit the profile of the store, they would get.

They were open on Thanksgiving, so whatever went wrong at Pam's was okay in the long run. He was busy until six and would have been late anyway. He drove by her house after work and it was as dark as a tomb, with only what he assumed to be her daughter's car parked in the driveway instead of the garage, where it usually lived. When she first called to cancel her dinner invitation, Dave wasn't sure if she was trying to just get rid of him so she could entertain Jeff Babcock or if there was a family crisis. It was clear he didn't know her at all. As he stacked and arranged Christmas cookie ingredients, it occurred to him that he was about to allow a woman he thought he cared about to slip through his fingers.

He put down his pricing gun and pulled his apron up over his head.

"I'll be gone for about an hour," he yelled to the store manager. Pulling on his coat, he ran out to his truck and took off for Pam's. Nothing much had changed when he got to her house. The car was still in the driveway, and it didn't look like anyone was home. He pulled in behind the car and ran up to the door. He knocked lightly, and could hear Pam's light step on the slate in the entry foyer. She opened the door and looked surprised.

"Oh Dave! Hi," she said, stepping aside so he could pass through. It was an amazing day; the fast-moving clouds hadn't reached land, so although it was bright and sunny in her front yard, it was dark and foreboding over the water. The contrast was both unsettling and beautiful.

He reached for her and hugged her. She felt a bit unyielding in his arms.

"How are you?" he said, kissing the top of her head. She relaxed a little. "I guessed something pretty dramatic was taking place for you to cancel after all the money you spent on dinner."

She laughed out loud. But she wanted to get something else out of the way first. "I'm still uncomfortable about the way you responded to Jeff Babcock helping me out this week. It made me wonder if I can trust you. There was a lot of drama here yesterday, and now I'm not so sure that I can share this aspect of my life with you."

Dave was taken aback, but she had a point.

"Sorry, I guess I was jealous of Jeff," he admitted.

"Well, get over it. He's not a threat to you. It's impossible. And furthermore, if you really knew me, you would understand that I don't let *anyone* see me without my makeup on. No one. My husband didn't, my kids don't, my mother doesn't. So I really have to relinquish control to allow anyone access to my house. I'm not a well woman; you know that. So I have to have someone who can get into my house with a key if I am ill. And it's not going to be you! Maybe in a year, but not now," Pam said. "I think we have a decision to make. You can either accept it or not. If you can't, there's no point in spending one more second together."

He had never heard so many words from her at one time. He tried to imagine what it would be like if he'd never been involved with her. He would have to get used to loneliness all over again. She was definitely a trophy; he'd never had that before. She was straight forward and easy to talk to. She was wealthy and wouldn't be a drain on him financially. She didn't expect much from him but privacy and space. He was nuts if he didn't at least try to give her what she wanted, which would appear to be nothing much at all.

"I accept it! I'm sorry I was jealous of Jeff. It's not easy having someone you care about have a close friend of the opposite sex, but I will try to get used to it," Dave said.

Pam didn't tell him that Jeff was gay because it wasn't her place to out him in the community. He could let Dave know when it suited him. As he spoke, Pam was losing hope that she would ever feel the same about him. Jealousy was so small-minded that she didn't know how to deal with it. But as was her way, she offered him lunch, keeping it simple. There would be plenty of time to deal with the difficult issues.

"Are you turkey'd out? I have a twenty-pounder that no one ate much of. It ended up being just me and my kids," she said.

Dave shook his head no. "Turkey sounds nice. I made a steak for my dinner, steak that I ate all by myself, alone with my dogs," he said.

Pam laughed out loud as she went into the kitchen and started pulling things out of the refrigerator. "You didn't call me until Wednesday night for an invite. What you would you have eaten if I'd said no to you?" Pam teased.

"Steak. I don't cook anything else," he admitted. "It's too easy to grab something from the deli." They made plates of food and heated them in the microwave. Pam made fresh coffee. They took their lunches to the den, setting plates on TV trays in front of the window like they always did. The clouds continued rolling in from the south, black clouds that looked frightening enough without the prospect of snow.

"We might get snow again this weekend," Pam said. She was trying to decide whether to mention that Lisa had left for Hawaii already. No. It would mean too much explanation and she really didn't want to hear his opinion. "I'm afraid the winter is coming whether we want it to or not. They say this one will be a doozy because last year was so mild." She was talking about the weather? They ate in silence, Pam glad for it. It was a mystery that her feelings for Dave had changed so radically. Why did he have to have expectations that she was unable to meet? It just baffled her. Of course, he was comfortable again, but she was on edge; she didn't trust him now. She got up to clear their plates and told her first lie in memory. "I have an appointment this afternoon. I need to leave here in a few minutes."

He reluctantly followed her out to the kitchen. "Okay, I'll get back to work. Call me later?" he asked.

She nodded as they walked to the door. She let him kiss her on the cheek. *The poor man walked into a mess here,* she thought. *Maybe I should give him a break.* Pam didn't know if she was being unreasonable or not. Maybe some time alone would help her once Brent left. When did reason become so difficult?

"Bye for now," Pam said, hugging him. She watched as he walked down the path to his car, waving as he got in. When he was out of sight, she closed and locked her door. The food was still out from lunch. Anything left after dinner that night was going in the garbage. She cleaned up and went back to the den. Was she wasting Dave's time because it was still too early after Jack's death to try to be in a relationship? He'd rescued her from his disrespectful employees, but that didn't really mean she owed him a future, did it? Her immaturity in matters of dating slapped her in the face. Maybe she was the one whose expectations were too high. *Dummy, that's why you shouldn't date so soon after your husband dies.* Thinking about Dave was preferable to thinking about her daughter, however. That hurt. So Pam had a choice. She could get back into bed and pull the covers over her head, or go to the gym. The gym won.

32

Sandra Benson had to check on her apartment that weekend. On Sunday, Tom's mother invited him to come over to eat leftovers one last time, which presented a perfect opportunity for her to go uptown. She bundled up against the wind and started walking toward the train into Manhattan. The bright blue sky had high white clouds blowing quickly to the north. The smell of the subway, its dank pungent aroma, and the screeching of the train coming into the station brought back a rush of memories. She'd taken the train alone since she was ten years old. It was part of life. The ride uptown wasn't unpleasant or sad, as she thought it might be. When she stepped off the train and started walking to the next station, there was a tang of wood smoke in the air. Someone had a fire in his fireplace. Her neighborhood was different on Sunday. More locals out; fewer tourists. For some reason, she remembered a story that Pam had told her about living here early in her marriage, a melancholy story about loneliness and heartbreak. *Asking another human being to fill the gaps in our lives really isn't fair*, she thought. She'd sort of asked that of Tom without either of them knowing it. She had no one but him.

Speed walking up Broadway, she saw her old haunts, her drug store and grocery, the Korean store she liked, and they seemed unfamiliar and unimportant. In a few, short weeks, she'd forgotten about her old life. When she came to her street, nothing familiar about it brought any positive feelings. Maybe she would let the place go after all. She'd been reluctant to give her landlord notice, just in case things didn't work out with Tom.

The key was giving her a hard time, but she finally got the front door to her building opened. The familiar smell of the hallway made her smile. Her door was at the end of a hall so dark she could barely see the keyhole. When she opened the door, the light-filled space hit her right away. It really was a great apartment. There were a few stray pieces of mail that someone had slipped under her door; probably delivered to the wrong mailbox. She'd look through it later. She took her layers off, throwing them down on the couch. Everything looked fine. She went into the bedroom and a little scene in the corner took her breath away. It was the baby's crib. She couldn't deal with it at first, but today it seemed okay. She was feeling strong and removed from it. The crib was beautiful; she'd splurged on it. It would work out fine for any babies she and Tom would have together, unless he felt weird about using it. She took the folding screen and put it out of the way. The crib was full of baby clothes and folded baby linens. She'd need a container of some type to store them. She ran down to the lower level. There was a big plastic box that held a few stray Christmas decorations from her childhood that needed to be tossed. She hadn't had the strength to do it before, but it wasn't a problem now.

All of the baby things fit in the plastic box. She hauled it back downstairs. The mattress was easy to move, too. But the crib might need taking apart and she didn't feel like doing that now. Later she would talk to Tom about it, enlist his help. All traces of preparation for Ellin were gone. She hadn't had much time to buy more, or it could have been a problem. She went around checking windows and doors, flushed the toilets, and made sure there wasn't anything left in the refrigerator. There was rarely anything in it when she lived there. It was time to leave. *It's still my apartment*, she thought. Nothing needed to be done about it until after the first of the year. She'd make up her mind by then. As she prepared to leave, her phone rang. It startled her. She reluctantly answered it; it was her sister, the same one she hadn't talked to for almost a year.

"Oh my God! I was beginning to think we'd need to get a private investigator to find you!" Sylvia shouted. "Where have you been?"

Why'd I answer the phone? "Why didn't you call my cell phone?" Sandra asked.

"I lost mine and all the numbers that went with it! I'd never written your number down. It just went from phone to phone, you know how it is. But where have you been? We came to your apartment, I wrote letters." Sylvia seemed sincerely worried. Sandra didn't know what to say.

"I can't go into it now, but suffice it to say I have had a rough year. I'll give you the brief version, and please don't lecture me afterward if you ever want to speak to me again, okay?" Sandra asked.

Her sister laughed. "I promise. I'm sorry. Tell me what happened."

"I had a serious boyfriend and he died. Right after he died I found out I was pregnant. The man's brother tried to kidnap me and the cop who helped me asked me for a date. I lost the baby a few weeks ago. The cop and I are living together already. End of story. I happened to be here today just to check on everything and I was almost out the door when the phone rang." Sandra took a deep breath. She knew there were a lot of holes in her story, but that was the version she was relegating to her sister. She heard a sniff. *Sylvia crying? No way.*

"Oh how sad, Sandra. I'm so sorry for your loss, and that I wasn't there for you," she said.

"It was a little girl, and she had red hair like Mom. I named her Ellin," Sandra said. "It's been a really rough time."

"Well, I am truly sorry about little Ellin." She sniffed again. "I guess it must be pretty serious with the policeman. What's his name?" Sylvia asked.

Sandra couldn't believe she hadn't launched into detailed accounts of how wonderful her own life and kids and husband were. "Tom. Tom Adams. He's a detective. Anyway, get a pen and paper and let me give you some numbers. I live in Brooklyn now and have to head back home soon," she said. She gave her sister her cell number and Tom's address.

"Me, Jersey and you, Brooklyn. Dad wouldn't have understood," Sylvia said.

Sandra started laughing. It was good to talk to her. There were some things only a close relative would understand.

"I hope we can stay in touch. I'd like to meet your young man," Sylvia said. "Also, your nieces have asked after you."

"How are Lauren and Stephanie?" Sandra asked. "I haven't seen them since the folks died." The absurdity of it, that she lived less than an hour from her sister and hadn't seen her nieces in over two years, hit Sandra. In a rare display of humility, Sylvia apologized for abandoning her younger sister.

"Are you okay? I mean, are you hanging in there? How's work?" Sylvia asked.

"I'm a partner," Sandra replied with a shit-eating grin on her face.

"A partner! Wow, good for you. You're so young, too. Boy, Dad would be proud," Sylvia said, an intense validation for Sandra, even though secretly she knew she hadn't earned the partnership. Jack had trusted her with it and that's all that mattered.

"Thank you for calling, Sylvia, but I really need to get back to Brooklyn. Tell everyone I said hi, okay? And I'm sorry I worried you."

"Good-bye, Sandra, it was great talking again," Sylvia said, and she hung up the phone.

Sandra felt light-hearted after the call. She walked around her apartment and made sure the lights were off, scooped up her mail—which ended up being letters from her sister pleading for forgiveness for unknown slights, all with the incorrect apartment number—and after rechecking the lock on her door, she left the building. She walked down Broadway toward the subway entrance and remembered a time not so long ago that she made the same walk with Jack. The events of the day were vivid in her mind's eye. They'd spent a rare night together, and he had to get to Babylon the next day to help Pam prepare for the big

Memorial Day party they hosted. She was wearing a white sundress, and as they walked along that Saturday morning, Jack had his arm draped across her shoulder and he kept running his fingers under the spaghetti strap over her left shoulder. Back and forth he went with his fingers until she told him to stop; it was teasing her!

"Are you purposely trying to arouse me before you leave for home? I'll be alone all weekend and you won't be there to take care of me," she said. Now, the flush spread through her chest and face as she thought of the way she flirted with him, a fifty-five-year-old man, twice her age, and as she later found out, ready to drop dead of a heart attack. Jack had stammered when she said it, not used to her talking provocatively to him.

"Ah, what are you saying, my dear? I could always delay my return trip," Jack said, smiling at her with his devilish look. They'd reached the subway entrance though, and she had a lot to do, too.

"No, you better get home," she said. "I'll see you Tuesday at work."

He embraced her passionately in broad daylight, and with their arms around each other, they kissed like lovers. They released each other and Jack started down the staircase into the subway tunnel. Then he seemed to have a change of heart. He turned and started back up the stairs. "Are you sure you don't want me to stay?" Jack said, laughing.

Sandra felt guilty about teasing him. "No. Well, yes, but you have to go. I love you!" Sandra exclaimed.

"I love you, too," Jack said. And he turned and went down the stairs, disappearing into the subway tunnel.

It was that exchange between Jack and Sandra that Marie had observed from the other side of Broadway. She'd followed them to the subway, and then turned and followed Sandra back home. Learning it later was unsettling. Sandra had to remember that Marie couldn't hear what they were saying. She could only draw her conclusion from seeing them together, and she did see that kiss. It was a good one, and their last.

She reached the same subway entrance and ran down the steps. She could hear the train coming, headed to Fulton Street. Jack was dead. The apartment was there for a few more months, and hopefully by then, by the time her lease was up, she'd know for sure if she and Tom were going to make it. In the meantime, she'd try to take one day at a time. She had her "post-miscarriage" appointment with her ob/gyn doctor Monday. It would be the last time she would be formerly reminded of her loss. She'd told her sister, and everyone else of importance knew. Bernice was so nuts now that she didn't bother telling her, it wouldn't have made any difference. She didn't appear to remember that Sandra had been pregnant in her lucid moments, either. The pregnancy hadn't made as much difference to her as Sandra thought it would.

Baby Ellin. Sandra thought about her purposely, to remember what she looked like, to remember the hope she gave Sandra after Jack died. How could such a little life change so much around her?

A couple of years before, right out of college, an acquaintance got married and pregnant in quick succession. At a few months, she lost the baby. Sandra ran into her in Duane Reads and the girl looked like hell, pale skin, ratty hair, sweatpants and a T-shirt in public. She grabbed Sandra's arm and dragged her to an empty aisle in the store.

"I lost the baby," she said, and began to weep. Sandra was appalled; what did she expect her to do?

"Oh, I'm sorry," was all she could squeeze out. And then, what she now knew was cruel: "You weren't very far along, were you?" The young woman let go of Sandra's arm and lowered her eyes. The pain should've been obvious, but it was not to stupid Sandra, who'd lived the charmed life. "I've got to go," she'd said, and left the store.

Sandra now felt shamed, wishing she could call the girl and apologize. She'd say, "I am so sorry. I didn't understand." Even if the baby was a week old, and you wanted it, its loss would be difficult. She had to forgive herself for being callous; how was she to know?

The train rocked back and forth as it sped through the tunnel. She was looking forward to getting back to Tom's apartment. She smiled when she thought of the gossip he might have to share. She hoped his sisters had something exciting to say. She couldn't wait to tell him about Sylvia. They would have to make a trip to Bergen County, New Jersey, to see Sylvia and her family. Sandra could not see her in Brooklyn, no matter how hard she tried! Although Hell's Kitchen, where they grew up, was a trendy neighborhood now, it was a no-man's land when they were young. But it was Manhattan. *Face it, you're a snob,* Sandra thought. And then she smiled. *So what? I might live in Brooklyn now, but I was born and raised in Manhattan.*

A strange feeling flooded over her as she walked along Fourteenth Street to the Williamsburg train. *What are you doing, Sandra? You're running away. You can't run.* But she pushed it down, down, down. She couldn't make any decisions yet. They weren't hers to make.

※

Ashton spent the weekend at his computer, getting "caught up"; a misnomer in his industry if there ever was one. The jobs came along, you did them in real time, and when they were over you had exactly the same amount of time to tear them down and get to the next job. It was a revolving door of furniture, art, and rooms. He didn't have to look for the work anymore; it came to him in droves. He was grateful to Jack for much of his success. Every meeting Jack attended, every job he did, Ashton's cards were always passed out. Jack never carried his own business cards. When asked about it, he said, "Why? Everyone already knows me." Without Jack's referrals, he might still be scraping along.

Sunday morning, he took a break from work to read the paper. He saw Dale's obituary; her viewing and funeral would be at a funeral home in the neighborhood on Tuesday. He entered it in his calendar with an alarm reminder. He wanted to pay his respects, but more than that, he wanted to see Ted again. There was a nice symmetry about meeting a man who was related to Dale. Jack would have approved.

※

Early Saturday morning, Lisa Smith's plane landed on Oahu. She struggled getting her bag out of the overhead compartment, ignoring the offers of help from young men on each side of her. She wasn't able to hear them because she had her ear plugs in with house music blasting away, muffling her inner dialogue. It was the only way she could survive the flight after treating her gentle mother like shit. Yet she couldn't bring herself to get out her cell phone and call to apologize. Every time she came to the realization that she needed to do it quickly, something would hold her back. She had ten hours of flight time with a six-hour layover in LA to rationalize why she should be mad at her mother. Every reason she was able to come up with had a counter reason in her mother's favor, but she still couldn't make the call.

She dragged her carry-on behind her through the airport, marching with determination to the baggage claim area. Her mother was at fault. She allowed what should have been a perfectly lovely Thanksgiving Day to be destroyed. Well, that wasn't exactly true. Pam had taken the protective cover off so the truth about their life could seep out. Lisa lived a dichotomy; she was a consummate spoiled brat who had a brain full of skeletons from her father's closet. She grew up looking the other way. She had built a successful wall around the creepy shit she had seen. The wall needed to come down now, but she was afraid. How can you pretend your life was one way when it was just the opposite? And that was when reality hit her. *It must be inherited*, she thought. She'd accomplished exactly what she was accusing her mother of doing. Like an overfilled balloon poked with a pin, Lisa exploded in the middle of Honolulu International Airport. Pam would be called with an apology before the end of the day.

After her antibiotic treatment Friday morning, Marie went downhill steadily until she was confined to bed. Steve called her doctor, who said the drugs were powerful enough to knock a strong person down. Keep an eye on her and if she spiked a temperature, call him back. Steve tried to get her to eat, but she refused, only taking a little water when he threatened her with a trip to the ER. When she refused the suggestion of a bedpan, Steve carried her to the bathroom. Since he had to go back to work on Monday, there wasn't going to be an argument about her going back uptown to Columbus Avenue. Sunday night he called Nelda and told her to expect a much worse Marie. Nelda had to take care of her because there was no one else.

33

Sandra had a doctor's appointment in Manhattan late Monday morning. When Tom left, she kissed him good-bye and had the apartment to herself for a few hours. When she went to the refrigerator to get milk for her tea, she saw the multitude of plastic containers of food, leftovers from his mother's house. It made her sick, actually. They'd been in there for three days. She hoped he wasn't planning to force her to eat any of it.

His visit to Virginia's house while Sandra was uptown at her old apartment was uneventful, the behavior of his sisters forgotten. No one had apologized to him for the way they treated Sandra, or if they had, he didn't tell her. She imagined Sylvia treating Tom the way his sisters had treated her. She'd never speak to her again. Knowing she was nit-picking, Sandra reeled her thoughts in. She couldn't expect Tom to behave the same way she would. It wasn't realistic.

At ten she left the apartment and started to walk to the train. She tried to keep her head clear of thoughts of the baby; it would be enough that this visit would focus on the experience. Tom had offered to go with her, but she wanted to be alone. It wasn't his baby so there was really no reason for him to be put through the appointment.

She arrived at the doctor's office with time to spare. Sitting down in the waiting room, she picked up a magazine and as she was absently thumbing through it, she realized it was one she'd already read there. An old *Parents* magazine. She threw it back on the pile. Pregnant women sat around her reading old magazines, killing time. The receptionist came to the door and called her name. Sandra got up and followed her to an exam room, where she was told to take her clothes off and put on a paper gown. She did as she was told and got up on the table to wait. Her doctor came in with Sandra's chart in her hand, refreshing her memory. She shook Sandra's hand, which Sandra thought was a nice touch. They made small talk about Sandra's general health while the doctor read a report in her chart.

"The baby did test positive for HIV," she said. "We don't know why, since you were compliant about taking your drugs."

Sandra didn't hear the last part. She was falling down a rabbit hole with the echo following her. *The baby tested positive for HIV.* "I have to advise against another pregnancy, Miss Benson. Of course, it is your decision to make. But your own blood values are much lower than they should be, too. The pregnancy was hard on your body." She examined Sandra and said she was fine; she could have intercourse again since it was past six weeks. *Oops, didn't remember that one,* Sandra thought. The doctor shook Sandra's hand again and left the room. Like a robot, Sandra got dressed. She wadded up the paper gown and threw it on the table. She left the room, walking down the hall in a daze, not stopping at the receptionist window on her way out. She wouldn't be returning to this office.

She walked to the bus stop and got on a cross-town bus to go back to her apartment. She wasn't going to work today, and she certainly wasn't going back to Tom's, with his black vinyl chairs and chrome dining set, mother's leftovers in the fridge. *Advise against another pregnancy* echoed through her head, along with, *I want kids. I want a lot of them.* She would find a reason to reject Tom first, so he couldn't reject her. Maybe it would be enough that she wanted to get into flannel pajamas and get into her own bed. Unplug the phone, turn her cell off, close the blinds, and sleep. He'd find a reason to get pissed off at her for doing those things. She got to Eighty-Second Street and her pace picked up. She couldn't wait to get inside. The key was hard to turn again, but she got in. She locked her door and put up the chain. From the hallway she could see out the kitchen window at the empty birdfeeders rocking in the wind. Throwing her purse down, she ran down to the lower level and opened the plastic container of bird seed. She got a scoop of it and went out to the side yard to fill the birdfeeders. Immediately, a black-capped chickadee swooped down and took a seed, looking at her with reproach.

"I'm sorry!" she said to the bird. "Tell your friends to come back, please. It won't happen again."

34

Brent went back to school Sunday, leaving his mother in a state of depression. Pam lay in bed Monday morning as the sun started to peek over the tops of the drapes in her bedroom and she wondered why she should get up. What was the point? But after five minutes of self-pity, she pulled herself together and got up for her day. She took her usual extra care with her appearance and noticed that she truly was beginning to look like an "older" person. Well, plastic surgery wasn't an option. She hated the hospital too much and it would mean more people knowing about her AIDS status.

She was drinking her second cup of coffee when the phone rang. It was Lane, Smith and Romney.

"Mrs. Smith, its Jennifer," Jack's secretary said. "I hope this isn't too early."

"Not at all, Jennifer! How are you?" Pam said. She'd always liked the young woman, but wondered if her name was among the list of his conquered. She shook her head to clear the thought.

"I'm okay. We really miss your husband around here," she confided in a whisper. "It's so boring."

Pam laughed. "Yes, he knew how to liven up a place, that's for sure."

"Anyway, a registered letter came here for Jack late yesterday. It isn't a business matter; it looks like it's regarding a piece of rental property he has uptown. Do you want me to fax it to you?"

Pam was confused for a minute. "Is it a storage locker?" she asked.

"No, it looks like either an apartment or retail space off Broadway in the Times Square District. It may be something he was subletting for a client," she explained. "I've checked and there isn't a key, so maybe he left something there at home."

Pam thanked her and before they hung up, she could hear the fax machine in the den whirring. She walked in to get the paper, and sure enough it was a rental agreement renewal. *Oh hell*, she thought. She went back into the kitchen to finish her coffee with the rental agreement on the counter in front of her. She read through it and saw a date that took her breath away: 1992. Pam looked at the water and tried to piece time together. What was she doing thirty years ago? She slid off the stool and went into the mudroom to get the keys for which she couldn't find locks. On his Lexus fob was a gold key with Master Lock stamped on it. She never could figure out what it was for. In September, she'd finally made it to his club to clean out his locker and there was a small plastic box like those used by seamstresses to hold notions, and in the box was another set of keys. Reaching for those as well, she suddenly recognized what could be a safety deposit box key. She'd already cleared out one box they held jointly in Babylon, but this one had a different number on it. Deciding to throw caution to the wind and forget about her pride, she called Jennifer back.

"Jennifer, do you know if Jack used a particular bank in New York for work?" She realized it sounded secretive but that's all she was going to give up.

"Well, let me think a minute," she said. "I can't think of any that he used, but we use Bank of New York for the office. You could try that." They hung up.

Pam didn't want to go into Manhattan, but it might be what she needed to avoid sitting around thinking about how she'd destroyed her children's lives. The phone was still resting against the palm of Pam's hand when it rung again. This time it was Lisa.

"Mom! Mom, I am so sorry," she yelled. Pam held the phone from her ear.

"Lisa, are you okay?" Pam asked, ridiculous because it was clear she wasn't okay, but she just wanted to make sure she hadn't been in an accident or anything. "Are you in Honolulu?"

"Yes, yes, I'm here, I'm fine. Mom! I'm so sorry about leaving like I did. No matter what happened, I shouldn't be cruel. Do you forgive me?" Lisa asked.

Pam could hear her sniffing and blubbering. "Of course I do. But do you forgive me? We can't go back to pretending we had something that didn't exist," Pam said.

There was a brief pause. "Did dad give you AIDS?" Lisa finally asked the big question.

"Yes," Pam answered. "And to Marie, and Sandra, and many other women, I'm afraid. As a matter of fact, I've become friends with the people at the New York AIDS Surveillance Task Force." Pam could hear Lisa crying. "Lisa, if you can possibly manage it, don't make this about you. Your father was the one with the problems, not you. I didn't protect my children from information they didn't need to have."

"Oh Mom, I'm so sorry! I know you loved Dad! And he told us he loved you, many times. He must have been fucking sick. There is no other explanation," Lisa said.

Pam was glad she had reached that conclusion already. But she was getting tired and had a trip into the city ahead of her today. "You are so smart, Lisa. You'll figure this out. I can't really help you now; unfortunately, it's your issue to deal with. I have to go into the city today so I better hang up now, but we'll talk later, okay? Everything will be okay, I promise you." They spent a few more minutes confirming their love for each other and finally hung up. Talking to Lisa was almost always exhausting.

While she was getting dressed in her "goin' to town" garb, Pam decided to stop at the mansion to see her mother and sister and mother-in-law while she was in town since her day was already ruined. She was gathering up a bottle of water and putting some cut-up fruit into a baggie to take when the phone rang again. She looked at the caller ID and saw Sandra's apartment number and answered it right away. *What was she doing there during a work day?*

"Hi, I am surprised to see this number," Pam said.

Without wasting time with small talk, Sandra launched right in. "I know we haven't had much contact, but boy, do I need your friendship right now. I would love to see you today if I could. I can get on a train and be there by noon if you just say I can," Sandra said.

Pam paused for just a second; there was no reason on earth that she couldn't see Sandra unless Tom the Tyrant didn't want her to.

"I'm coming into town today. It is for a very strange reason; evidently Jack had a rental property in Times Square and the lease is up for renewal." Pam explained.

"Yes," Sandra said. "I just dropped in, but am thinking I might stay. Can I see you while you're here?"

"Do you want to go on an adventure with me? I don't know why, but I feel like this might be one experience I shouldn't have alone, and frankly there is no one else who could go with me," Pam confessed.

"Of course I'll go with you, but what about Marie?" Sandra asked.

"Marie's not well. That's a whole other story. How about I come to your apartment, in say, about two hours? I'm just getting ready to leave now. Traffic shouldn't be too bad," Pam said.

"I'm truly sorry about Marie," Sandra said.

"Yes, well, I'll tell you about it when I get there. Two hours then?" Pam repeated as she grabbed her keys. They confirmed it and said good-bye. Pam hung the phone up and went through the mudroom to the garage, feeling eager to see Sandra now, her one human contact that wasn't a needy relative or a guy with a possible agenda.

ೞ

Sandra's cell rang and it was Tom. He must have tried her office number first and discovered she wasn't there; her cell got horrible reception in the office so he rarely called her on it during the day.

"Where are you?" he said when she answered. She explained about the upsetting news from the doctor, although not specifically what the news was, and her need to be in her own space for a while.

He didn't get it. "I don't understand why you didn't call me right away. If you're upset about something, you should let me have a shot at supporting you," he said.

"I wasn't thinking about anything but the news," she said.

"Okay, what was so bad that you couldn't go to work?" he challenged.

"Well, I found out the baby tested positive for HIV. It's not why she died, but it's not good news. I'm also sicker than I was, which sucks," she explained.

"Do you have AIDS?" Tom asked quietly.

"No, not yet. But there's more. The doctor strongly advised me against getting pregnant again. She said it could have devastating results." *There, let him stew in that for a moment*, she thought.

"Oh boy, that's awful," he said. And there was a brief pause. "I'm so sorry Sandra. I see now why you wanted to be alone," Tom said. There was a longer silence.

"Pam just called. Evidently Marie is ill, so she is coming into the city to see her and asked to see me, as well," Sandra said. She would give more information to him as he asked for it.

"My radio just went off. I'll talk to you later, okay?" The phone went dead. Sandra started to laugh. Either his timing was perfect, or the guy was really a prick. She ended the call and went to her bedroom to change out of her work clothes into jeans. It should be an interesting day after all.

Nelda walked up the stairs to the second floor of the mansion for the sixth time that day. She was going to talk to her daughter about getting the elevator repaired the next time she called. She rested at the top of the stairs, more to prepare to enter Marie's room than to recover from the mount. Marie was propped up in bed, eating Cheez-Its out of the box, and watching Maury Povich.

"Honest to God, can't you find anything else to watch rather than that horrible man?" Nelda criticized.

"Mother, leave me alone. I vaguely remember you watching *Divorce Court* while you ironed dad's uniforms. What message did that send?" Marie asked.

Nelda laughed. "Okay, okay, you made your point. At least turn it down, will you? Your sister is coming, by the way. You should get washed up."

"Pam's coming? Yippee!!" she exclaimed sarcastically. "Why do I need to change my routine for Pam?" She nestled down further in the bed. Nelda would have to use a crow bar to get her out and into the shower.

"You're starting to smell. If you don't care for Steve, at least have mercy on me," Nelda said as she pulled the covers back. Waif was a word meant for Marie. She was almost invisible lying in bed, a skeleton with breasts. "Come on, your royal highness, you're getting up now or I will get Ben to pick you up for me. You don't want him seeing you naked, do you?"

"Yes, actually, get him in here. I need some excitement," Marie said. But she listened to Nelda and moved her legs over to the side of the bed. She reached up for her mother's shoulders to pull up on. Nelda helped her walk into the bathroom, overwhelmed with momentary sadness. Marie might be a bitch, but she was still her daughter. What did this mean? Was she dying? The tough questions hadn't been answered yet. As she helped Marie take off her pajamas, she saw the first evidence of a pregnancy; a low lump between her hip bones. Nelda couldn't help herself; she placed her hand over the rise on her daughter's body.

"Little baby, little baby," she said. "I'm your grandmother."

Marie giggled. "Yes you are, poor kid," Marie teased. Nelda shook her head in exasperation.

Pam got to Sandra's right before lunch. She'd see her family later, after the trip to Times Square. When they saw each other, it was like they'd talked to each other every day. Sandra told Pam the news from the doctor, and while she shed tears, Pam held her and consoled her. She told Pam about Tom's mother and sisters, and father and Gwen, and Pam told Sandra about her new friend, Dave, and the disastrous Thanksgiving Day. She saved the news about Marie for last; her pregnancy and her brain infection. Sandra felt a pang of regret that she wasn't able to like Marie enough to be happy for her about the baby; it was selfish and Sandra knew it. But she wasn't jealous. The poor woman had too many problems to be jealous of. What she did feel was sadness for the baby to be born into those circumstances, with an ill, crazy mother and an old father. *Yuck.*

"Do you want to drive down to Times Square with me?" Pam asked. "You're not obligated at all, trust me. I have no idea what I will find once I get there. I may not even be able to get in." She dangled keys in front of Sandra.

"Look, just for the record, he never took me there," Sandra confessed. "I don't want you to get any wrong ideas."

"It's too late for that!" Pam exclaimed, laughing. "Let's go see if Jack can surprise us anymore." They walked out to Pam's car together, continuing the conversation about Tom and his family. Pam wasn't clear yet if Sandra was considering leaving Tom's apartment or not.

"You could always keep dating Tom and give it some time. If he decides that he has to have kids, then you can say good-bye to him," Pam said. "Now I am sounding like a mother. Sorry."

"No, that was good advice. Why do I think it has to be all or nothing? He might dump me, which would be so much easier. Painful, but easy," Sandra said. As they drove south on Broadway, both women thought of Jack. Finally, they arrived at the right neighborhood and Sandra started looking for the address. Expecting a high-rise, Pam was shocked when they pulled up in front of a four-story, ramshackle, red brick building in a blighted neighborhood. There were a few hints of rehabilitation, but it looked like Jack's *pied-à-terre* had seen better days.

"Fuck," said Sandra.

"Yes," answered Pam, opening her car door to get out for a closer look. She reached into her handbag to pull out the rental agreement and the address matched. "Let's go see what there is to see," Pam said. They walked up the steps and looked at the mailboxes.

"J. Lane," Pam read. "He obviously was using old man Lane's name, unless this was his place, which I highly doubt." There was no intercom, so she turned the handle on the door and it opened freely. "Let's go!" The apartment number was a back unit on the second floor. They walked up the dusty staircase, someone's TV blasting away. Far in back of the building, they found the door to the apartment, and Pam tried the key. It worked, turning easily, and she pushed the door opened. The apartment was dark and smelled closed in; if it was Jack's, no one had been there for seven months. Pam tried the lights and they worked. Who'd been paying the Edison bill? They walked through the bare galley kitchen, but did notice what appeared to be a used coffee cup in the sink and trash in a small can by the bathroom. The living room was empty expect for a single chair by a lone window. They walked close together down a dark hallway, stopping at a closed door. Pam looked at Sandra. "I guess I have to open it," she whispered. The room was pitch black. She reached around to the wall and felt for a switch. Sandra gasped when she was able to see the room, but to Pam it looked like a big shower stall and nothing more. It was covered in subway tile, and had a large, heavy duty hook in the ceiling with some kind of halter attached to it. There was a cot of sorts with a rubbery-looking sheet stretched across it.

"Oh my Jesus Lord," Sandra said. Pam started to walk into the room but Sandra grabbed her arm and pulled her back. "Don't go in there!" she commanded.

Pam looked confused. "Why? What is this?"

Sandra flipped the switch off and pulled her friend out of the way so she could close the door.

"If this was Jack's place, he was a sick fuck. Sicker than I thought. Let's get out of here," Sandra said.

"Why? What is that room for?" Pam repeated. "I want to at least see the rest of the place." They walked back to the rear of the apartment where there was another room that may have been intended to be a bedroom. Two king-sized mattresses all but covered the floor and Peg-Board panels on the walls were dotted with hooks from which all kinds of leather and chain paraphernalia were hanging. Pam started to understand when she saw the whips and chains.

"I don't think I want to see the bathroom," Sandra said, but Pam ignored her and opened another door leading to the unknown.

"Ugh," she said. "You're right. Let's go."

"Do we want to take the chance of someone seeing this crap and associating Jack with it?" Sandra asked.

"Ha! I don't care! Do you?" Pam was clearly upset, not thinking correctly. "What is it for?" she asked yet again.

"Let me think about this for a minute," Sandra said. "Pam, you don't want your kids to find out about this. Even truthfulness has its limits."

Pam looked at her sharply and started laughing. "Who said that?" she asked.

"No one. I did. I mean you can admit things to your kids that will ultimately affect their life, like you being sick, but his fetishes won't make any difference to them. I have to tell you, this shocks me. It's like the homosexual thing. I had to idea! None. He never suggested anything that even hinted at this sort of interest," Sandra confided.

Pam looked back to the rear of the apartment. "What the hell is that tiled room used for, and I know you know, so don't lie to me," she said.

Sandra shook her head. "It's one of those things that you know exists because you hear of such things, but to really see it...well, I am still shocked," she said.

"Tell me!" Pam insisted, getting up into Sandra's face. She was like a wild woman. "What was he up to?"

"You know what all those leather things are in there, the junk hanging on the wall, right?" Sandra asked. She was embarrassed to even say their names.

"I think so. S and M stuff. Whips and dogs collars." *Jack! You lunatic!* "But what was the tile room? Did he hang people there and whip them? I hope he didn't kill anyone," she whispered.

"Okay Pam, listen to me, because I don't even want to have to say this once let alone repeat it. People pee on each other in a room like that, pee or worse. Do you get it? It's an aberration is what it is. Gross! I am so disgusted that I ever got involved with a pig like that! Oh God!" Sandra screamed and completely broke down in front of Pam.

Pam embraced her, supporting her so she wouldn't fall over. It was a shock to both of them; he wasn't normal, at least not to the women and their delicate sensibilities. That was true. Sandra thought in her moment of anguish, *He wasn't just an infidel who got AIDS from one of his conquests; he was a pervert who spent money having a special room installed in a derelict apartment so he could pee on someone, or worse, have people pee on him.*

"Let's get out of here, okay?" Pam demanded.

But Sandra was thinking about Pam's children again, and worse, the company that he helped found. This sort of garbage could ruin a business.

"We need to bag this shit up and get it in the trash somehow. Not until then can you relinquish the apartment. Who's been paying the rent, anyway?" Sandra asked, knowing that Pam didn't know. *Maybe his lawyer?* They were standing in the living room arguing about what they should do next when they heard a key in the door. They froze while someone turned the key and door opened. A pretty blonde woman, not expecting to see anyone standing there, screamed bloody murder.

"Who are you?" the woman screamed. "What do you want?"

Pam went to her and grabbed her arm; so like Pam, Sandra thought, remembering the first time they met in the hospital corridor. "Miss, please don't yell. I'm Pam Smith and this is Sandra Benson. This is evidently my late husband's apartment. Can you tell me who you are?"

The young woman looked from Pam to Sandra and with her hands up to her face, started crying.

"I have a client coming here in ten minutes. You have to leave. I've been paying the rent on this place since Jack died." She dug through her bag and gave Pam a business card. "Call me tonight after ten. But please, please get out. You have to leave, I beg you!" She hustled the women out to the hallway and slammed and locked the door. Sandra led the way, running down the steps with Pam following, both of them on the verge of hysteria. They got into Pam's car and she started it, grinding the starter after the engine caught, and took off, laying a little rubber in the street.

"Oh my God! That wasn't Jack's stuff in there after all, it was the woman's!" Pam yelled. And then she started to laugh like a crazy woman. "Yeah, right! But that's my story and I'm stickin' to it," she said. "What the hell am I supposed to do now?"

"Let's go see your sister and get that over with, okay? If I stop now, I'll never get started again," Sandra said.

"You want to go to the mansion to see those crazy women after that fiasco? No fucking way!" Pam yelled. Traffic was getting heavy with lunch being over and she didn't want to get stuck near the park, so she pulled over. She looked straight ahead for a while. Every so often she'd shake her head.

"I swear to you, I had no idea. None. He never, ever suggested the slightest bit of perversion. He was almost boring, he was so conventional. I mean, I was a virgin on our wedding night because Jack wouldn't sleep with me! How in God's name would I ever, *ever* know he was into anything so totally repulsive? There was a man at our wedding; he stood up for Jack, an Ashton Hageman. Did you meet him?" Pam asked.

Sandra shook her head no. "Well, he came to see me a few months ago, admitted he and Jack had been lovers since grade school. He told me Jack always wanted to get married because he wanted a 'normal life' after the horrible childhood he'd had. Those were the words the man used. Normal. Now I find out my husband may have been peeing on other people." She let out a burst of laughter. "There can be nothing more that will hurt me or surprise me now. I didn't tell you about my children." Pam looked at Sandra at this juncture. Was she unloading unfairly on this young woman? Or were they friends again? "So are we going to be friends now? Because I am about to tell something that is probably the most hurtful about all of this."

Sandra nodded yes, unable to speak for fear she would weep again, and she'd had enough of that. "My kids knew about Jack and Marie and never told me because they were afraid it would hurt me too much. Lisa said she knew from the time she was 'little' that Marie was after her father, and that Jack spent nights with Marie in her room. My little kids knew it but I didn't. You can stay as detached as is humanly possible if you want, and I proved it. My life is the evidence."

They sat in silence for ten minutes or more. There was a woman in a rundown Times Square apartment who, at that moment, was performing sexual acts for money. It occurred to Pam that she would be called a prostitute. She referred to Jack by name. Was she Jack's hooker? Pam snickered out loud unintentionally.

"That woman was a hooker," Pam said. Jack was using a hooker. *Oh my God.* She started the car up again. "Let's go to my mother-in-law's and get it over with, like you said." They drove the rest of the way uptown in silence.

"I'm not going back to Tom's. We can date, like you said. But I want to be alone for a while. I have to process this new information. Can you take me to Brooklyn first, to get my stuff from Tom's apartment?" Sandra said. She turned to look at Pam. "I'm sorry I hurt you, my friend."

Pam smiled at her in return. She'd take it under consideration. She'd missed Sandra, missed having a girlfriend to hash things out with. Now that an apology had been issued, what was keeping Pam from accepting it? It was all she had expected.

35

Ashton took extra care with his appearance for Dale's funeral. He got a haircut and a manicure on Monday, was careful not to cut himself shaving, and chose his favorite Mark Jacobs suit. His shirt was such a pale blue that it appeared blindingly white with a dark gray tie. He stopped to get his shoes shined on the way; he was going to walk to the funeral home. When he got there, Ted's parents were greeting people. They'd flown in from Florida. It was an open casket; Dale wore a Chanel suit; pink with black trim, her favorite. Ted was standing off to the side talking to a beautiful brunette woman in her late thirties or early forties. But when he saw Ashton, he left her and rushed over to him and embraced him with a hug.

"Oh, I am *so* glad you came. Sorry I didn't get to call you all weekend; my parents got here Thursday night and are staying at my place; Dale's was too difficult for them to navigate. Her aura just permeates it."

Ashton hadn't heard the word "aura" since 1970, but it did make him smile. Dale's place *was* filled with her aura. "How long will they be in town? I imagine there will be a lot of legal stuff to do. What are you going to do about her apartment?" Ashton asked.

"I'm not sure yet. There are a few more family members who I am sure will be circling the grave like vultures.

I'll point them out to you at the funeral. You are coming to it, aren't you?"

Ashton nodded yes. It was the least he could do for Jack, but to Ted he just said, "Of course I'll be there. I loved Dale."

"Come over and have a seat up front. You can be with the family," Ted said. Ashton felt it in his chest; Ted was as interested in him as he was in Ted. He didn't think he would have the energy to be in a relationship again at age fifty-six. But Ted calmed him. He was the antithesis of Jack.

The viewing lasted for two hours and during that time, the room filled with a few of Dale's family and friends and many of her students. She brought an interesting mix of people together in her death. Ashton remembered Jack saying that she was a loner most of her life. This turnout of people belied that. *Maybe Jack needed to believe he was her only contact and source of excitement to justify his own existence. Jack the benevolent. Jack the savior.* Jack also said that Dale was a homophobe, but how could that be true? Her favorite nephew was gay. Ashton had spent several lovely afternoons with her since Jack's death. Had Jack lied so Ashton would keep his distance? *Hmmmmm...*

Usually a careful, law-abiding driver, Pam drove like a woman possessed after dropping Sandra off at her apartment. It was close to nine by the time she got home. She'd taken Sandra to Brooklyn to get her things from Tom's apartment before he got home from work. After they unloaded the car, they drove the few blocks to Columbus Avenue. Both women were shocked by Marie's appearance. She didn't look anything like herself. Pam hated that expression, but there was no other way to describe what had happened to her sister. She was demented, and she looked demented as well. Nelda said she was "with it" most of the time, but had periods when she didn't seem to know where she was. It was clear she needed round-the-clock supervision. Pam didn't know if Nelda was hinting for Pam to help out with her care, but she knew for certain that it wasn't happening. Pam had taken care of Marie since she was a child with disastrous results. It was definitely Nelda's turn. Marie wasn't rude to Sandra, but she wasn't warm and fuzzy, either.

"I didn't think I would ever see you again!" Marie greeted Sandra. Only the three of them knew the real meaning of those words, and had a chuckle. Sandra was taken aback by Marie's appearance and oddly felt rare compassion for her.

"Sorry, Marie. I've been a little busy myself these past few months."

That seemed to pull Marie back to earth. She leaned forward in her chair and reached for Sandra's hand. "I'm so sorry. Of course, you've had a lot on your plate. Forgive me for being flip," Marie said. "So, what are you two up to today? What made you come into town, Pam?"

"I had some business to attend to regarding you-know-who," she said.

Marie frowned. "Will he ever go away?"

Pam walked to the door to make sure no one was outside listening. She carefully closed it. "His influence is diminishing for me; we found evidence that he was into kinky stuff with some shady characters," Pam said softly. She'd kept private the many visits she had from Jack's lovers, but it wasn't fair to let Marie go on thinking his behavior was isolated to just her and Sandra.

Marie looked at her with eyebrows raised. "What was it? I mean, he was always trying to get me to do some sick shit. Sorry, Pam." Marie was clearly embarrassed.

"Like what? I'm really interested, Marie. I promise I won't get angry with you. I have to have the truth about everything. I can't get on with my life, can't date anyone. It's impossible to even have a normal relationship with my children. Why'd I have to find all this out now? Twenty years ago I could have still protected you from him," Pam said.

Marie didn't answer her. What could she say? The gruesome details of her relationship with Jack were best kept under wraps. She was afraid that if she put the acts into words, she would never recover from it, mentally. The physical wounds were clear for all to see.

"It won't do any good to rehash all that garbage now," Marie said. "Let it go, Pam. If you found out something that might make it easier to let go of Jack, go for it. But dwelling on anything I did with him won't help you. And it might hurt me to have to speak it. I am so ready to bury Jack in the deepest part of the ocean."

Marie's wisdom had some validity. Pam stood up and kissed her on the cheek. "I hope you'll feel better soon. I better get going before it gets too late," she said. "Do you think we can get out of here without having to say goodbye?"

"She'll be hurt if you sneak out and then I'll get the brunt of it," Marie said, laughing. "Say good-bye to the old lady, too. She's really out of it."

Pam couldn't stand seeing Bernice and didn't care if Marie took some heat because she sneaked out of the house. "They'll both get over it," Pam said. "Come on, Sandra, let's get out of here." They said good-bye and quietly left the bedroom, tiptoeing down the staircase and out the door without discovery. Pam didn't care if her mother never spoke to her again. She was in self-preservation mode, and until she felt stronger, she wasn't going to worry about her family.

There was just a sliver of moon, but it was so clear that the stars provided some light on the beach in Babylon. Pam put the car away and went around locking the front of the house, but tonight she was going to bundle up and do some serious beach sitting. Hopefully, the solitude and the sound of the waves would help her come to some conclusions. She had an hour before she could call the young woman she encountered in the Times Square apartment. *Call me after ten*, she'd said.

Looking out over the water, she decided she would simply let the woman talk. She wanted her to have the apartment if she wanted it; it appeared that she was utilizing the devices in there, but the lease needed to go into her name. Pam considered that the woman might try to blackmail her to keep quiet. But wouldn't she have come forward sooner? Pam gathered up her beach chair and the blanket she'd taken out and walked back up the pathway to the house. The holiday weekend had wiped away any trace of peace she'd garnered. A cup of tea and a snack was in order since she'd skipped dinner unintentionally; had she eaten at all today? The clock ticked the minutes and finally it was just after ten. Pam dug the card out of her purse. Blythe Smith. *Smith?* Confidential. And the phone number. Pam snickered. Confidential? She dialed the number and after it rang at least eight times, Pam was ready to hang up when it was answered. An out of breath Blythe.

"Hello? Mrs. Smith? Sorry, I left my phone in another room," she said, catching her breath. "Thank you for calling me. I knew the lease would be up soon and didn't know what to do. If you will allow it, I would like to keep the apartment."

"Okay, that was my question. Do you want to go through the landlord? I'll have to let him know Jack is deceased," Pam said.

"Yes, I guess there is no way around it," Blythe said. Pam was fighting the urge to ask questions. Did she need to know anything about this woman? What purpose would it serve?

"How'd you find out about the apartment?" Blythe asked.

"The landlord sent a renewal form for the lease to Jack's former office," Pam answered.

"Were you surprised? I mean, did you have any idea?" Blythe was pumping Pam for information and that was okay.

"I was completely surprised by the apartment, but I knew Jack had another life. I didn't know about you," Pam admitted.

"No, I guess you wouldn't have known about me. You are so calm, I guess I'm a little taken aback by it," Blythe said.

"I've had surprises since the day he died, Blythe. It's old hat now," Pam said. "Not that it hasn't hurt me beyond anything I could have imagined."

"Well, I don't want to add to it. My life is ruined because of Jack, but somehow I have to keep going. All I know is what you saw in that apartment. That's Jack's doing. I have a bachelor's degree in education from Stony Brook. I had a teaching job in Smithtown but I met Jack in July before school started. That was it for me. I have spent the last seventeen years bartending and waiting for Jack to come into the bar. That was my life. All the junk you saw hanging from the Peg-Boards? It was Jack's legacy to me. At least I can support myself now," Blythe said. Pam remembered the pathetic Maryanne who had asked for money. Why didn't Blythe?

"Where do you live?" Pam asked, sure that it wasn't that awful apartment.

"Near Jack's other place, near Madison. Another dump, but not quite as bad as the one you saw. I bartend at the same place where I met Jack. I have to do this other work to supplement my income," Blythe said, like it was commonplace to take money for whipping people.

Pam was silent. Blythe was blaming Jack for ruining her life. She had a college degree, and before she was even able to start a job utilizing it, she was sucked in by Jack. What was it about these women that allowed someone like Jack to overpower them? He was able to make rational, thinking people let down their guard and adopt behaviors that previously they wouldn't have even considered. This woman made a choice to waste her life waiting for Jack. She may have thought there would be something in it for her—he was obviously wealthy. Or he may have lied to her and told her a future together was a possibility. Something. It made Pam sick. Pam wanted to ask her why she let it happen but she knew that might make her defensive. Blythe didn't seem to have anything to lose by going public. *Look everyone! Look at what the great Jack Smith did to me!* Pam didn't want to provoke her, realizing there was an element of fear. She was still protecting Jack.

"I'm sorry, Blythe. I'll do what I can to transfer the apartment into your name. I hope that will help," she said, eager to end the conversation.

"Yes, well thank you. Sorry I frightened you when I came into the apartment today," Blythe said.

"That's okay. Good-bye," Pam said, and hung up. Irrationally, she washed her hands, scrubbing to remove anything that might have come through the phone. Relieved that she didn't encourage Blythe to take a walk down memory lane, Pam was still uneasy about her encounter with her. Who else was going to crawl out from under the woodwork? The morning dream about Jack popped into her head and made her gorge rise. It was clearly wishful thinking. *I love you so much.* She marched into her bedroom and began tearing her bed apart. Even the illusion of him being in her bed was disgusting. Gasping, the thought came to her, *no wonder I have AIDS.* As she stuffed the tainted sheets in the washing machine, she was overcome with the longing to have peace. Was it even possible after all that had transpired?

She made up the bed in fresh sheets, pulling them tightly and smoothing the wrinkles out. Maybe she would resume her quest for perfection. Now that Jack was gone, it might actually be possible.

36

Christmas arrived in Babylon with no fanfare. Pam didn't hire the handyman to hang lights outside of the house on Black Friday as she had in years past. Marie and Jack didn't pop popcorn in the fireplace, with the resulting shriek of the smoke alarm and burnt kernels flying all over the den. Lisa and Brent came home, but it was melancholy; Pam hadn't bothered with a real tree or decorations. They made due with a small fake one, already decorated, that she bought at the CVS. No one talked about AIDS, or Jack's behavior, or bad parenting. They overate, played cards until dawn, laughed, drank too much wine. It was probably the first adult Christmas they'd had. Lisa even bought gifts for the others, a first. Jeff Babcock joined them a few evenings, and Dave came on Christmas Eve with the complete Seven Fishes dinner.

They didn't see Nelda or Bernice or Marie. Susan and Sharon drove into the city at separate times with their families to see their mother and Marie, but no invitation had been extended from the beach. Pam wasn't up to entertaining.

Sandra Benson got a huge tree and invited Tom and his father and Gwen; her sister, Sylvia, and brother-in-law; and anyone else who wanted to come for dinner. Virginia, Faith, and Emma were invited but declined; they really did have other things to do. Tom said the idea that they'd even responded to something his father was invited to was a positive sign.

Nelda cooked dinner for the Columbus Avenue crowd, set the table in the dining room, and used all the heavy silver and beautiful china. Bernice was thrilled. Marie and Steve were impressed, too.

On New Year's Eve, Jeff Babcock brought his new friend to meet Pam. Brent's girlfriend came down from White Plains to meet the family, and Lisa had several old friends in. Dave came by with the food again; this time a lavish buffet.

Pam had the fire lit every night. They sat by the window and looked out over the ocean, reminiscing about old times but keeping it light and pleasant. There was an unspoken rule that nothing sad would be talked about. The presence of the guests helped the conversations stay benign. Pam almost felt like it was old times, but something inevitably would happen to remind her otherwise. She'd get a call from her mother complaining about Marie, or have to take a call from the management company that was handling Jack's Madison Avenue apartment. That everything was back to normal was just an illusion. She started counting the days, and then the minutes, until her beloved children went back to their own lives and she could exhale.

On January 2, she got up at daybreak. Taking a cup of coffee into the den, she gazed out the window as the sun began to peek over the horizon. Once the kids got off on their respective flights in the afternoon, she could start examining what needed to be done to make her life work again. The old way obviously had to be abandoned. What she was going through was not so different from the process many other women her age faced. Husbands died, kids grew up and left home. Women without careers had a chance at a second life. That her husband was a liar didn't change anything. It didn't reflect on her; they weren't her secrets or sins to be deal with. If she allowed it, she could let it ruin what was left of her life. Her pride was almost nonexistent. For a few weeks that fall, she'd stooped to an all-time low, purposely intimidating the clerks at Organic Bonanza who'd been rude and Andy's new girlfriend, whom she'd met at the gym. But it was the rubber band effect, going from one extreme to another. Fortunately, she'd come to her senses. She ran into Linda Potts and grabbed her, apologizing and admitting it was a horrible lie; she had nothing to excuse herself but bad behavior and embarrassment. Linda hugged her and thanked her, but said it wasn't necessary; she had dumped Andy, deciding he wasn't to be trusted after all.

"With my history," Linda said, "any man who would betray a confidence like that isn't worth the time of day."

Everything Pam had read about grief, especially the grief of a widow, advised against making any life-changing decisions until a year had passed. Pam played with the idea of spending the winter in the city but once Marie took up residence on Columbus Avenue, she nixed that idea completely. Now, the idea drifted through her mind to leave Long Island, to try something new, far, far away from New York City. It was just a tiny thought, but she hoped to dwell on it and see if it went anywhere. She had no earthly idea what she would do with her time besides primping and working out.

37

Do you, Ashton Hageman, take Theodore Broderick to be thy lawfully wedded husband? In joy and in sorrow? In plenty and in want? To have and to hold? Until death do you part?

Ashton slipped the silver band onto Ted's left ring finger, and then said, "I do!"

They grabbed hands and started laughing, and with the blessing of Father Allen, turned to the audience and the entire congregation yelled, *"Hurray!"*

The next six hours went by in a blur. Ash remembered Jack and Pam's wedding, how Jack said later that they didn't even know what the menu was they were so busy. Ashton made sure he stayed by Ted, to support him, to show him that he was really there with him. Ted put a tremendous amount of effort into planning each detail of the ceremony and reception. His mother was in her glory, making sure every last promise the caterer had made was carried out. Later, they were informed that it was a fabulous wedding!

They went to France for their honeymoon, taking hiking trips through the most picturesque countryside Ashton could've imagined. When they were planning the trip, he thought they'd go to Fire Island, but Ted wanted to take him out of the country. Knowing Ashton had rarely left Manhattan, Ted was hopeful he would love it so much that he'd want to keep going. He was correct.

Theirs was a whirlwind romance, but they were so meant for each other. All of their friends exclaimed, "We should have figured out a way to get you two to meet years ago!" But Ashton knew that was ludicrous. The timing for the two of them was perfect. Almost a year ago, Jack was still alive. Ashton never would have gotten married if Jack hadn't died.

※

New Yorkers commented that it was the worst winter they'd seen in many years. Over ninety inches of snow fell between January and the middle of March. But by April Fool's Day, the snow was gone and the weather was fabulous. Pam was in the middle of a big garden cleanup on a Saturday in mid April, Dave helping her, when the phone rang. She ran into the house through the veranda and seeing it was Nelda, answered it right away.

"We called the squad the morning. They took her to Columbia. I just thought you should know," Nelda said. Marie had been going downhill steadily since Christmas, so Pam shouldn't have been surprised. But she was. She felt sick to her stomach. Dave came in to see if everything was okay and she covered the receiver with hand, mouthing *Marie.* He mouthed back *Oh God*.

"Do you want me to come?" Pam asked.

"Not yet. Steve just called and they are admitting her to the ICU. She's in respiratory distress, so they have to put the breathing tube in. The baby is okay so far." And then Nelda did something rarely seen or heard of: she broke down and started to cry. "It's the worst thing I thought I would ever see," she said. "My baby daughter."

Pam felt terrible for her mother. She'd gone to see her sister at least once a week, but after the last visit on Easter, she didn't go back. Marie didn't know who Pam was, and she looked so terrible, Pam thought they should admit her then. Steve and Nelda wanted her to stay home because the longer they could keep her out of the hospital, away from MERSA and other horrible bugs, the longer they might maintain her pregnancy, and the baby had become an icon for them. It was no longer about Marie, who for all intents and purposes was dying, but it was for the baby, who miraculously was doing well.

Marie was skin and bones. A nurse came in every eight hours to make sure her intravenous fluids were running and to mix the liquid meals she was getting. She had a feeding tube that went directly into her stomach and Nelda had become adept at hanging the bags of liquid nourishment that would keep her alive a little longer. The nurses marveled that Marie's skin was so sound on her back; it was due to Nelda's constant vigilance in keeping her daughter clean and dry and turning her from side to side hourly or more often. She wasn't going to get a bedsore on Nelda's watch.

Every night when Steve came in from work, they got Marie out of bed, but not just up to sit in a chair. He picked her up like a baby and sat with her in his lap in Bernice's old rocking chair, rocking her until it was time for him to go back home and get some sleep. Marie had taken to sucking on her thumb again like she did when she was two years old, and although she had almost sucked her nail off, they let her do it because it seemed to offer some relief for her suffering. They had no way of knowing if she was in horrible pain or not, except for occasional screaming. She would manage to sit up in bed, as weak and frail as she had become, and just start screaming. No other sound was heard from her after the end of March.

The years of anorexia and bulimia had taken their toll on her teeth; her gums had receded so far back that it wasn't unusual for Nelda to find a tooth on her pillow. Her hair was almost completely gone. She looked like a toothless, bald, little old man. That Friday for some reason, Steve decided he had to stay with her through the night. He came in and puttered around her room, straightening what Nelda had already straightened. He fussed with the covers on the bed and pretended like he knew what he was doing with the IV lines, and then when he'd done enough, he gave up and plunked down at the edge of the bed and bent over to hold her. He started to cry. She often opened her eyes, usually staring vacantly, but when Steve was there that night, she had a knowing look about her. They sensed she knew that he was devastated and it might bring her some peace to be embraced by him.

Throughout the night he noticed she was struggling to breathe and finally, early in the morning, they called the doctor, who agreed she needed to go to the emergency room. Nelda fussed with her while they were waiting for the ambulance; she put a lovely nightgown on her and combed the few strands of hair she had, securing them with a ribbon. Steve sat by her side, waiting. He knew it was critical, but still had that tiny bit of hope that something would happen and she would pull out of it. That all of the damage that had been done to her body would miraculously disappear. He kept his hand on her belly, really just a small melon hanging there, and he could feel their little baby rolling around inside in spite of her sad situation. It was a her; they'd determined it shortly after the holidays. Marie was thrilled. Her only verbalizations toward the end of consciousness were, "It's a girl."

When they got to the hospital, Dr. Garpow met them and told them what they feared: she was near death. Her obstetrician thought the baby needed a few more weeks for her lung development to be optimal, so with the family's consent, he wanted to intubate her—put a breathing tube down her into her lungs and let a machine breathe for her. They agreed without question that it was the best thing, stifling their fears, those words *near death*.

Nelda would later call Pam and tell her, "Marie is near death. They are going to try to keep her alive for a few more days for the baby's sake." It was surreal. Was she really saying her daughter was near death? How could it be? At night as she sat with Steve next to Marie's bed, listening to the ventilator pumping oxygen into her daughter's lungs, regrets flooded over her. She remembered finding out she was pregnant with Marie. She thought it was the change starting early. Her period didn't come and it was a joy. *Thank God I'm done with that mess.* And then she started to show. Frank's mother was furious with her. How could she even think about having another? Genoa was indispensable and she knew it; Nelda wouldn't have survived motherhood without her mother-in-law. Now there would be a fourth baby. Frank was delighted; he loved being a father. But he wasn't home all day, didn't see his wife unable to cope with the stress of watching four children.

When Pam got married, they practically packed Marie's bags so she could stay with her. Pam never batted an eyelash. She loved having her there! Why was Nelda so guilt-filled? Because she knew there was something wrong and never addressed it. Her daughter was anorexic. She had trouble in school. She was a behavior problem. And then a few months ago in the middle of one of her screaming night terrors, Nelda discovered the truth. Marie fell back on her pillow and started mumbling about Jack. She loved Jack. They'd been in love all of her life. She used words Nelda had never heard a female use before, words Marie used to describe the *way* she loved Jack.

Nelda was going to lash out at Pam the next time she visited, but then Nelda saw her oldest daughter, saw how thin and pale she was, and thought that possibly AIDS was taking its toll on her as well. She bit her tongue. And that night, when Steve saw Nelda without gloves on, wiping up blood where Marie had scratched her face, he told Nelda that Marie had AIDS, too, and that cinched it in her mind. All the pieces fell into place. Both of her daughters must have gotten AIDS from the same man. From Jack. It made Nelda ill. She went through all of the stages of grief in one day, so angry she could have killed someone, and finally that night, she resolved that it was what it was. There was nothing she could do about any of it but make restitution for being an awful parent by caring for Marie now to the best of her ability. She became her servant in those last months.

One day shortly before Marie stopped talking, Nelda was fussing with the bedside table, trying to neaten things up, and Marie grabbed her wrist with surprising strength.

"Mom, stop that for a minute, you're making me nuts," she mumbled. Nelda forced herself to stop fidgeting and looked at Marie.

"What?"

Marie gave a rare laugh. "I love you, Mom," she said.

Nelda relaxed, her shoulders sagging, and she bent over to kiss her daughter on the cheek. "I love you too, Marie. I'm sorry for everything," she said.

"Me, too, Mom. I'm sorry, too. Now we both sound like Pam," Marie said. They laughed, and then the effort made Marie close her eyes. She could barely speak without becoming exhausted. Before she fell asleep, though, she had one more thing to say. "Mom, help Steve with the baby, okay?"

Nelda was taking the trash can out of the room to empty, and she stopped in the doorway. She walked back to Marie's bedside. "Are you sure you want me to help? I would think you'd want Pam," Nelda said, sincere.

"Pam has enough on her plate. I want you to help him. Tell me you will so I can take a nap. I'm tired, goddamnit!"

Nelda said she would and consoled her, staying at her side until she could tell that Marie was sleeping. Nelda felt better about life from then on, until the nights in the ICU. Then, all of the boogeymen came out full force. Sitting with Steve was difficult enough. He had two modes: sleeping with his head thrown back, snoring for all he was worth; or sitting next to Marie's bed with his head on the sheets, sobbing his heart out.

"Steve!" she said one night. "Go get in the other bed. Your snoring is giving me a headache." He got up and did as he was told, climbing into the empty bed next to Marie's. The nurses were wonderful. Someone from labor and delivery would come in every hour to check the fetal monitor and Marie's vital signs. *How long could she go on like this?*

"It won't be much longer," a nurse finally told them one night. The doctors seemed afraid their words would be too harsh to hear, but Nelda needed the truth. "She's deteriorating further. We need to deliver the baby before the blood supply to her placenta starts to diminish."

They were doing tests to determine its blood flow, first daily, then more frequently. Finally, it was time. They would take her to the Operating Room that afternoon to deliver the baby. And although no one said it, after she was born, they would take Marie off life support with Nelda's permission. Nelda called Pam, Sharon, and Susan, who arrived in time to say good-bye to Marie. The doctor said it was possible that the dramatic drop in fluid volume after the delivery might make death come naturally.

The family was waiting for the team to come to get Marie. There was nothing left to say to each other. Pam was drained emotionally and physically; it was obvious to Nelda that this might be all it took to push her over the edge, too. She couldn't lose two daughters. At four p.m., they came to get her. Marie's entire bed with all the monitors and pumps would go rather than moving her onto a stretcher. Nelda fully expected to be told to step out of the room while they prepared her, but they didn't, instead telling her what a great job she had done taking care of Marie, her hair adorned with ribbons still. As the bed was pushed out of the room, a nurse asked the sisters and Steve and Nelda to accompany them to the OR. The nurses and family crowded onto an elevator together, and the harsh light, after the dim room lights, showed the damage the days had done to Marie. It was clear she was dying.

Steve was invited to don surgical scrubs and come into the delivery room, but he declined. Instead, he turned to Nelda. "I wish you would go," he said. "I feel like she was more relaxed when you were around. I can't stand the sight of blood, anyway."

So Nelda went into the dressing room and changed into the smallest scrubs they had, still too large for her, and a bouffant cap to cover her hair. When she came out of the room, Pam had to choke back the tears. There was her mother, high heels and nylons under her scrubs, the too long pants rolled up, her makeup on like she was attending a party. Nelda was all business, though. The nurse gave her a mask to put on and led the way into the room where Marie was laid out, her arms stretched out at her sides, entirely covered with blue paper drapes. Just her belly was exposed through a big square cut out so they could get at the baby. Nelda was directed to stand off to the side, next to the heated table where the baby would come. In a normal C-section, the loved one would stand at the head of the table to offer support, but it wasn't really needed in this case. If Marie should crash and die, it would be better if Nelda were occupied with the baby.

The whole process didn't take as long as they thought, and before she knew it, a tiny baby girl, one who looked exactly like her mother did at birth, was whisked to the heated table and looked over by a team of pediatric doctors and nurses. Nelda was encouraged to join them; after what she had been through, nothing needed to be hidden from her. But as it turned out, little baby girl Marks was perfect, if slightly underweight. The doctor left to give Steve a report, while Nelda planted herself like glue at the baby's side. She was being given a second chance and no one was going to take it away from her.

38

On the first Friday in June, Dave from Organic Bonanza pulled into Pam's driveway with a load of mulch in the back of his pickup truck. She was kneeling down in the flower beds directly in front of the house, planting a flat of marigolds that Dave had started from seed.

"That was fast," she said as she walked toward him, brushing dirt off her gloved hands. He hopped out of the cab of the truck and walked around the back to meet her.

"Is this the right stuff? There was another type that looked like shredded tires. I didn't think you wanted it so dark," he said.

"No! This is perfect." She stepped up on her tiptoes and kissed him on the cheek, the kiss of a friend to another. "Thank you." He put his arm around her shoulders as they walked to the garage to get the tarp onto which they would shovel the mulch. "Can you believe this day?" she asked, looking up at the blue, cloudless sky. The crash of the waves on the beach behind the house could be heard clearly through the din of sea gulls swooping in the air.

"Who'd believe we had snow three weeks ago? It's almost hot in the sun," Dave said. They stood together and looked up at the sky. The kitchen window was open and they could hear baby Miranda crying and Nelda singing to her while she fixed her bottle.

"Oh, I've only got one shovel," Pam complained. They looked over the perfectly aligned garden tools. "And only one with a square bottom. Darn."

"Come on, let's go back to the garden center. I want to get a weeping cherry for my side yard and they're on sale this week," Dave said. Pam hid her delight. It was the one wish she had: that she could walk through a garden center with a man like other, regular couples did. It was a small thing, and probably not enough to sustain her forever, but for today, she'd take it as a step toward normalcy.

∽∾

Steve Marks was hurrying around the office trying to tie up loose ends. His secretary, who was supposed to have completed a file for him to send to a client, had gotten bogged down with another researcher's work. He cursed under his breath.

"What's your hurry, Stevie boy, got a hot date?" a coworker said.

"Yes, actually, I do. I'm meeting a girl at the beach tonight and I have been waiting all week to see her," he said with a smile. He stuffed everything into his briefcase and locked his office as he headed out. If he was fast, he'd miss the worst traffic going into Long Island on a Friday afternoon.

"Give Miranda a kiss for me," another colleague said.

Steve smiled and yelled, "Okay."

"He likes them young," the co-worker said, and there was laughter. Steve ran to his car, got it unlocked and loaded up, and headed toward the Fifth-Ninth Street Bridge in record time. He focused on getting out of the city before he'd allow himself to start thinking. He avoided thinking at all costs, but it was safe to do so when he was driving to the beach. One hour and twenty minutes of time, once a week, was all he rationed for thinking.

This was the fourth time he'd made the trip. As often happens, things had changed dramatically in a short period of time. It seemed like once Miranda was born, and poor Marie died, everyone had been thrown into a storm of change. The first thing that happened was that Candy quit working for Bernice. That afternoon, Bernice fell down the entire flight of stairs in the mansion, and didn't break a thing. But it was a heads-up: she couldn't stay there without care. Nelda was occupied with the baby and it would be too much for her to be responsible for Bernice, too. So Pam made the tough decision without hesitation. Bernice was going into Eagle's Nest Assisted Living.

Steve snickered to himself. Eagle's Nest was a fancy hotel where old ladies of means lived out their golden years in complete comfort. He hated to guess what it was costing Pam to put her there, when any number of places would have been just as nice without the Park Avenue address. But it was none of his business. He couldn't ask for a nicer, more helpful family and he wasn't going to criticize them.

※

The coup de grace came two weeks after Bernice moved out. The mansion sold after just six months on the market. A big developer from Japan bought it with the intent of tearing it down. The community was up in arms, but Pam refused to cave in to their demands and sold it with the knowledge that the new owners had working plans that already had been accepted by the city. When Dave asked Pam if she was sad that the mansion was no longer in the family, her response was, "Good riddance." She thought of the evil that took place there, and the evil that it spawned. It was a house of horrors. Steve didn't know most of the story, and Pam wanted to protect he and Nelda from it.

She and Dave were flying to Los Angeles for Brent's graduation from UCLA. He'd taken a job in San Diego, due to start in July, so there wasn't time for him to come home. He had to get an apartment and move out of his current place. Pam knew the likelihood of Brent ever living in New York again was slim, and she was ready to make the trips to California that her son needed to her make. Lisa was coming in from Oahu. When they spoke on the phone last, Lisa was more upbeat than Pam could remember having seen her in months.

"What's going on?" she asked her daughter. Lisa laughed into the phone.

"Boy, you haven't lost it, have you Mother! You can still read me like a book," she teased. Pam was getting nervous, starting to pace and laughing into the phone at the same time.

"What's going on?" she repeated. "Stop stalling, you're scaring me." But she was still smiling. Her daughter had something positive going on, it was clear.

"Well," she hesitated. "Well, I've met somebody! And it's serious, Mom. I think you are really going to like him. He's from New Jersey and we are going to fly back east together after Brent's ceremony. He's coming to graduation, by the way," Lisa said. Pam's heart quickened. She saw Lisa married and living in New Jersey. Pam was suddenly questioning what her reluctance to leave Long Island had been. She'd go to New Jersey or California as often as her children needed her.

Everything was falling into place. The grad students who were renting Bill and Anne's house in Greenwich Village finished school and were moving out. Bill was spending the next five years in Rikers for trying to kidnap Sandra, as well as his assault on Nelda. Anne divorced him and took their boys to live with her mother. They'd defaulted on their mortgage and now the house belonged to Pam. Pam thought that if Steve agreed, it would be a perfect family home. Nelda could have a room there so she could continue helping out with baby Miranda if she wanted to.

Pam had drilled her unmercifully. "Mother, the last thing that little baby needs is a reluctant caregiver, and if you are doing this out of some kind of guilt, it won't be good for her."

"I'm enjoying it," Nelda said. "Besides, Marie asked me to do it. Those were the last words she said to me that I could understand."

"Well, Marie is dead. And speaking of last things, the last thing you need to do is take care of a newborn at the age of seventy-five because your daughter, who didn't know what she was saying at the end, asked you to do it," Pam said.

"Pam, I promise you, I want to do it. We have so many secrets and lies in our family; I know I want it different for Miranda. I want her to have a different life than

I had and I really want her to have a different life than her mother had," Nelda confessed

"Don't you want some freedom now?" she asked sarcastically. Pam remembered that just a few short months ago, Nelda complained about having to help Marie out; now she was willing to raise her baby.

"Yeah, yeah, don't remind me of that, okay? What do I need freedom for? My kids don't want me hanging around and now that Bernice has lost her mind, she's only good for a few hours a day. Besides, Steve is a good man, he likes to drink and play cards, all the important stuff. It'll be fun," Nelda confessed.

"Well, don't say I didn't warn you. I'd make sure Steve got another sitter in line in case you get tired. It's not a good idea to let him think he can depend on you 100 percent. I don't care how much you want to take care of Miranda," Pam said.

"So, Miss Know-it-all, am I moving into that brownstone of your brother-in-law's? That is what I heard, is it now?"

"I offered it to Steve. He can pay me what he's paying for his current rental. It's in a family neighborhood, almost the same distance to his job, and perfect for two adults and a child. I'll have Marie's furniture moved over there if he wants it. I'm here to serve," Pam said, snickering under her breath.

Nelda looked at her sharply. *Is my daughter being a smart-ass?*

As Steve merged onto the Long Island Expressway, he started to think about the baby. She was so perfect, and her HIV status was negative. It was the best news. The doctors were amazed, but they assured Steve that a negative test in a baby was negative. She wouldn't come down with it later. After she was born, they closed Marie's abdominal wound and rather than sending her to recovery and putting those nurses through the trauma of taking care of a brain-dead patient, Marie was sent back up to her ICU room. The nurses in the unit had taken care of her since day one and wanted to support the family. The doctors gave them an hour with the new baby and then came in to talk to them about taking Marie off life support.

"You have been so wonderful to her," Dr. Garpow said to Nelda and Steve, "and your care accomplished the goal of having an almost full-term baby. But now we need to set the focus back on Marie. She is tired. She's clinically ready to go. The ventilator is keeping her alive," he said, and then softly, "it will be a kindness to take the tube out. I don't think she'll last long."

Steve had his head bowed and his arm around Nelda. Susan, Sharon, and Pam were standing around them, offering support, but no opinions. Even Nelda was keeping quiet and deferring to Steve. Secretly, she felt strongly about taking the tube out, but didn't want to burden Steve with it if he felt differently.

"Take it out," Steve said, as he began to weep. "But I'd like to be with her if I could."

"You can all stay here with Marie," Dr. Garpow said before he left to write the order, *Discontinue life support.*

39

Sandra Benson got home early Friday. Tom was going to swing by to pick her up so she didn't have to take the train back to Brooklyn. She decided to spend the weekend in Williamsburg at Tom's apartment but had to go to her apartment first to pack a bag.

"Why don't you leave some stuff here?" he asked. "Then if you feel like coming over for the weekend, you don't have to make that trip all the way uptown."

"I know I should, but I have a hang-up. I like all my stuff together," she confessed.

Tom laughed at her. "I think I might have a loony girlfriend. But only in the best way possible." They agreed that he'd pick her up on his way downtown; he had to be up in the Bronx in the late afternoon anyway.

She was waiting for him with her suitcase packed, standing on the sidewalk. She had confirmed her decision to move back in with Tom soon, to go to Brooklyn permanently, but was waiting to ask him first, in case he didn't want her there. The time they'd spent living apart was fine, but she was ready to resume co-habitation. She missed him, and came to the realization that she was being silly, trying to prove a point that didn't need to be made. They could work out their myriad problems together. Besides, she wanted to be in his bed permanently.

As he drove down the street in the patrol car, his heart quickened as it always did when he saw her, especially after a week-long absence. She smiled as he pulled up and pushed the door open for her.

"Hi," she said. "Thank you so much." She gave him a quick peck on the cheek and reached for her seatbelt.

"My pleasure. Before I forget, there's something for you in the backseat. If you want to, get it before I take off and you can leave your belt off for a second." He was smiling that smile that just made her crazy. She twisted in her seat and reached through the open window to the backseat. There was big Macy's bag on the backseat and nothing else.

"The bag?" she asked. He nodded yes just as his radio went off. His presence was required downtown.

"Yes, pull it up front. Get your belt on, my dear," he instructed. "We have to go for a ride." He sped off from the curb once her belt was on safely. "I'll drop you off at the coffee shop under the bridge, okay? It might be nothing, but it might be somethin' and I don't want you around if it is." The adrenaline was pumping once he got the cruiser going, and she was hoping that he was going to put his lights on, too, but he said, no, that wasn't necessary, yet. "Peek in the bag," he said. He was clearly excited by his surprise, but distracted by having to go to a call.

She dug through layers of tissue paper until she found what was at the bottom of the bag, a sea-green Tiffany box.

"Oh no, oh no," she said loudly. "Oh no! What'd you do, Tommy, what'd you do?" She pressed her hand against her chest. Her heart was beating like a wild drum, like it was trying to find its way out of her ribcage. "What'd you do?"

He laughed at her. "Knucklehead, open it up! Sheesh!" He stepped on it when there was clear space on the road, and when traffic blocked his way, he let the siren go for a second and put the lights on for less than a second. Drivers pulled over as far as they could to let him through, and then, seeing the woman in the front seat with him, wondered what was up. She slowly took the white ribbon off the box; this was going right into her treasure box. With shaking hands, she lifted the top of the box off. There was a smaller box, a maroon leather box, within the box. She took that out while Tom wove in and out of traffic. She set the bottom of the box down on her lap; that was going to be saved as well. Hands still shaking, she pried open the leather lid and there it was. An engagement ring that couldn't have been bought on a cop's salary. It was sacrifice, or debt, or trust fund. *It would have done Jack Smith proud*. And then, shocked that she had thought of such a thing, Sandra laughed and screamed a soft, cop car scream.

"Oh, Tom Adams!" she yelled again. He looked at her, smirking.

"Is it okay? I mean, do you like it?" he asked sheepishly.

"Like it! I love it! This is the last thing I expected today! The last! And it's exactly what I would have picked out for myself!" She looked down at the ring again. "I am going to wait for you to put it on me, okay?"

He turned and smiled at her. "Okay, if it'll make you happy."

She took the box and closed the lid and with her hands wrapped around it, held it up to the center of her chest. She closed her eyes while Tom was occupied with traffic and sirens and lights. With her lips moving ever so slightly, she whispered, *Thank you, God. Thank you.*

Made in the USA
Charleston, SC
13 August 2012